RAGE begets MURDER

MARSHALL STEIN

POST MORTEM PRESS

CINCINNATI

For my beloved wife Helene.

Prologue

"Miz Naomi, I wouldn't go in there right now," Liz warned me. Her thin body was shaking.

"That Mister Chumsky is as mean as any Georgia cracker."

"What's going on?"

"Your daddy and some others are in there with Mister Greene, talkin' about movin' his radio show to TV. I brought in coffee, and Mister Chumsky said I was spying and that I should be fired."

I walked into my parents' dining room. Seated at the table were Daddy, Morris Chumsky, two men I did not know, and Eddie Greene. Eddie was my husband's cousin and hosted a radio show that played colored and rock-a-billy music, Fats Domino, and Jerry Lee Lewis. It was very popular with teenagers. Eddie's show was owned by the Karps. Maybe the fat man was Jay Karp. Daddy had money in it. He kept saying it was the best investment he ever made.

Morris had his back to me and did not hear me on the thick carpeting. He was facing Eddie. "It's one thing to play the records, but something else to see the kids dancing to it. White kids at that. Philly's got a big Catholic population. There's already grumbling from some of the priests."

"The way we'll set it up will work," Eddie said.

"Hi, Daddy."

"Hi, Princess. What are you doing here?"

"I was driving over to see Rachel and thought I'd drop in while I was nearby."

"Well, we're having a business meeting right now." Daddy ran his tongue across his bottom lip. He was nervous.

"Is there a problem with Liz?" I asked.

Morris swiveled around in his chair. "I told you to fire the *schvartza*. The sooner the better. I want her out of here now."

"Maybe you should be the one to leave, sir," I told Morris. "And please stop using that word. Liz has been with us for a long time."

The skin drew tight on Morris's face. He stood up. Daddy jumped between us and led me into the kitchen, closing the swinging door behind us.

He whispered, "You have no idea what you're doing. Morris can be very dangerous."

"Then why is he your friend? Why are you in business with him?"

Daddy asked if Mother was home. I told him she was out shopping.

"Take Liz and leave. Now! I've got to get back and apologize to Morris." Daddy was pale and sweaty.

"Why?" I demanded.

He grabbed me by the arm and pushed me toward the door leading outside.

"Liz, come with me," I told her. "You have a new job. In my home."

When I turned around I saw Daddy from the rear in the now open space leading to the dining room. He took out his handkerchief and wiped his face. Then he disappeared, and I heard him say, "Morris, I'm sorry. I love Naomi, but she's really a child. A thirty-eight-year-old child."

Liz and I marched out of the kitchen and down the driveway to my car.

Chapter One
Sophia

Sophia was thinking that every Sunday was Judgment Day at Uncle Julie's. He sat at the head of the table, Aunt Tina to his right, Sophia's mother, Rose, to his left. Julie wore short-sleeve shirts showing off his thick forearms. A scar ran down the ridge of his nose. What was different about him were his eyes: gray like puddle water. Sophia had never seen another Italian with eyes that color.

Julie pointed a finger at Sophia and said, "Rose, did you know Sophia's leaving school before her last class?" He made the question into an accusation that Rose had failed as a mother.

Rose wrung her hands. "Sophia, is this true?"

Sophia stood up. "Mom, it's not like that. The end of the day is study hall. Uncle Julie makes it sound like I'm cutting classes."

Uncle Julie, anger boiling in his voice, said, "When I went to school study hall was for homework, not for leaving to get into *Varsity Dance*."

Rose asked, "What's *Varsity Dance*?"

Sophia's cousins laughed. Her hands clenched into fists.

Julie barked at Rose but stared at Sophia. "It's that damned TV show where kids dance to Negro music. I found Sophia dancing with a colored boy."

Rose stood up, stretched her arms out and said, "Oh Sophia, tell me this is not so."

"Mom, stop it." Sophia turned to Julie. "What's wrong with you? You've got her crying. You always make her cry. Why don't you tell the rest of the story?"

Rose sat down. "Don't talk to your uncle that way! He just feels, you know, without a father . . . Well, he's got to step in."

Sophia looked at her mother and Julie. "He beat the colored kid so bad they took him to a hospital. Is that what you want me to have in a father?"

Julie's face was red; spit flew out of his mouth. "It's not my fault. I warned Eddie Greene what would happen if he allowed coloreds on the show. He promised me they wouldn't dance with white kids. If he can't control it, I will!"

Sophia screamed, "You're a creep!"

Julie pushed himself up, back bent forward, head leaning toward Sophia, like a gorilla at the zoo. He lifted one arm and cocked a fist. Rose jumped between them, tears filling her eyes.

"Don't. Dear God, Julie, don't. She can't help it. I try the best I can. Please, please—" Rose had her hands on top of Julie's fist, and her body was shaking. If Sophia had a knife she would have slit his throat.

Julie took deep breaths as the blood left his face. Unlocking his fist, he put an arm around Rose and said, "It's none of our faults. It's that bastard Eddie Greene! Having both whites and coloreds together, dancing to that music. Call me a creep! I don't try to hide who I am— Julie Rabelli and proud of it! Eddie Greene? He was born Eddie Greenberg. Like no one knows he's a Jew? Leopard can't change his spots!"

Sophia looked at Julie with his embrace of Rose and knew she was outside the circle. If he had his way, she would be a stranger's child left with her mother. Sophia had heard there are birds that do that, leave their babies in another nest, fly away and never look back. She took a step toward her mother. Julie's arm pulled Rose closer to him. Sophia was dizzy. The rug felt like it had moved her away; Rose grew smaller. Sophia turned and ran out of the house.

On the street she was surprised how bright it was. Sophia looked back to see if her mother had come out to find her. The doorway was empty. It was two blocks to Sophia's house. In Little Italy, family was always near. If Julie had had his way, Rose would live next door. Sophia looked at the houses as she walked. Two-story homes, side by side, one after another. Worn white steps led up to brick walls. The day was warm. October always had a week like this, before it gave in to the cold. People called it Indian summer. Sophia wondered what the Indians had to do with it. If she asked one of the nuns they'd shoot back, why was she daydreaming about the weather when she should have her nose in her schoolbooks? *To hell with them,* she thought.

Young kids were out on the steps. Excused from the dinner table while the women cleared and washed the dishes, the older men sat and talked, some smoking cigars—the women opened the windows. Now and then a woman in her twenties would come out to check on the kids and report back that Sophia Rabelli was going down the street. By the time Sophia walked into the house, the neighborhood would know Julie and Sophia had been screaming at each other about *Varsity Dance.*

She passed Vinnie slow-pitching a hollow rubber ball cut in half to his eight-year-old. The kid hit it. Sophia watched the pink ball cross the sun. It bounced in her palm and she closed her fingers around it. It felt good. Sophia wished she were eight again instead of sixteen.

Vinnie said, "Toss it here."

Sophia shook her head from side to side and cocked one hip. Vinnie stared at her. She puckered her lips to watch him redden, and then he shuffled to her. "What's with you, Sophia?"

"What's with the rocket in your pocket?"

He grabbed the ball out of her hand, turned and quickly walked away.

Sophia felt bad. Vinnie was one of the neighborhood men who didn't have hungry eyes. By the time she had turned thirteen, Sophia was developed. Not as much as now, but enough. Julie had always been angry with her, but it got worse when she turned thirteen. She had heard it in his voice. She did not know how it had sounded to anyone else, but to Sophia it had been the screech of trolley wheels on the tracks, that scream of metal on metal. She had to get away from it, run and run until the pounding in her chest had washed away the rage she heard in Julie.

Reaching her house, she turned toward the door and stopped. If Sophia went in, the walls would close in on her. She needed to see Eddie. She felt it all over her body—the weight of everyone smothering her. Julie, her mother, the nuns, the neighbors. When Sophia was with Eddie she was in control. She could breathe.

Since Sophia was twelve she had known who Eddie Greene was—the guy on the radio playing the music that was so colored she had felt the heat inside her. And the words, the words the grown-ups didn't hear, and when they finally caught on the words made them nuts, or maybe just scared. There was Little Richard. God—she could not believe Eddie had gotten away with playing "Long Tall Sally." When they finally realized what he was singing, the politicians and priests had gone bullshit. One of them, a councilman from Little Italy, had passed something banning "Long Tall Sally" from the radio. Sophia had been amazed that someone over thirty knew what "ballin'" was.

Then everyone had started tuning in to hear what else Eddie had slipped by. He told Sophia that was when the money guys had asked him to do a dance show on TV. They had been nervous. Eddie said they didn't know which way to jump. They knew they'd hit the jackpot with rock 'n' roll—what Eddie called the jungle rhythm. But they didn't want to get shut down. Eddie had figured it out for them. Have the show broadcast with girls from parochial schools—the long skirts, knee high socks and buttoned up white blouses would tone down the colored music.

A flyer had been handed out a block from Saint Agnes. About a dozen girls had gone. Eddie spotted Sophia right off, told the guys to give her plenty of camera time. Sophia had known he was coming on to her. She also knew he needed her.

Overnight they were stars. The guys from Saint Bernard's knew them by name. Popular singers were on the show. Fats Domino had told Sophia she was a "fine little white chicken." Her cousin Angie had heard that story and told Julie. The next day Julie had screamed at Eddie, who had promised that no Negro singers would talk to white girls again.

Sophia had to see Eddie now, even if it was Sunday. She walked up the stoop, took out a key, and let herself in. In a half hour Rose would be there, standing next to Sophia, trying to get her head next to the earpiece to hear who it was. Sophia would circle away, and Rose would move with her like they were dancing. If it were Teresa or one of Sophia's other friends, she would start to laugh and Rose would too, and then Rose would walk away. Sophia liked her mother then. But if it were Eddie, Sophia would push her away, hard, and finally slam the phone down before she lost it completely.

"Hello, Eddie Greene's," the woman said.

Sophia's thumbnail dug into her finger. "Let me talk to him. Tell him it's Sophia."

After a pause, she heard Eddie say he'd take it. "Hi, Sophia." His voice was smooth, like he always had a woman answer when she called.

"Screw you. Who's with you? You in the bedroom?" Sophia snarled.

Eddie's voice was still calm, in control. "Whoa, slow down. Her name is Linda. She works for me at a place in Jersey."

"What place? What're you talking about?" Sophia said, nervous that there was something big she did not know about Eddie's life.

"Sophia, I don't want to talk about this on the phone. Can you get out?"

Sophia thought, *Still Mr. Cool.* "How? I don't have a car—or a license." Sophia shook her head from side to side, saying to herself that Linda must be distracting him.

"I know, I know. Let me think for a second . . . Call a cab. I'll pay him when you get here." Sophia knew that Eddie needed to call the shots. It was who he thought he was.

"If a cab pulls up here, it'll be back to Mom and Uncle Julie in no time flat. He's so crazy he'd have the cops pull the cab over before I got there."

Eddie spoke faster, like he was sweating. "You're right. Last thing I need is your uncle. Look, today may be a problem. We'll talk tomorrow after the show. I have something I think you'll be interested in. A little night work. You get dressed up, just like someone in the magazine ads."

Sophia said, "Let me guess. 'I dreamed I was a hooker in my Maidenform bra.'" Sophia hoped that would get his mind off Linda and back on her.

Eddie yelled, "Will you shut up? You're nuts, you know that. I can't be involved with anyone crazy. And I sure as hell won't have a telephone conversation with someone crazy."

Sophia put some soothing into her voice. "Okay, okay. Don't hang up. Having a woman answer your phone gets me going."

Eddie's voice was low, trying to hide what he was saying from Linda. "I told you, it's only business."

Sophia purred, "Eddie, I see us on your bed. You're on your back . . ."

"Shut up. I'm hanging up the phone now. Don't call back. I'll see you tomorrow."

She heard the excitement in his voice. At first Sophia felt she had won. Then she realized Eddie might be so hot from her egging him on he would be dying to get into Linda's pants.

Twenty minutes later Rose walked in. Sophia knew that Rose needed to get on with her life. Sophia understood that Dad had been her mother's great love. Fourteen years since he'd died. To the family he was a war hero. But by 1957, Rose needed to give up the past. Rose worked at making herself unattractive: bony thin, straggly hair, shapeless dresses. She needed her grieving to be over and move along with a life of her own. She could start by telling Julie to back off. He could order around whoever he wanted to on the vice squad, but not Rose and Sophia.

"Sophia, it's so dark in here. Why are the shades down? And the lights off?"

"I like it. It's like I'm at the movies," Sophia said.

Rose was flipping up light switches. "What are you talking about?" Rose turned and looked at her for the first time since she came in. "Sophia, are you okay?"

"I'm fine, Mom. Are you okay?"

Rose was watching Sophia with wet brown eyes. "I wish you wouldn't go at your Uncle Julie—he only means what's best."

"Mom, you're the only person who doesn't see how insane he is. He's going to kill somebody with that temper of his. Probably has, and the cops covered it up."

Because Rose's face was so thin, her eyes seemed darker than they were. Shadows. On her face. In her life.

Rose held up her hand. "Sophia, stop. He's family. When your father died in the war . . . you know, something died in Julie. He always looked up to your father . . . Julie felt responsible, I think . . ."

"Responsible for what?" Sophia asked.

"I don't know . . . Julie was younger." Rose was frowning, thinking hard about something.

"Mom, what are you saying?" Sophia wanted this to end. Maybe Rose did too, but it seemed to keep running inside her, a third voice in their conversation.

Rose said, "It eats me up to watch you and Julie go at each other. I know it's not all your fault, what with my having to raise you alone . . ."

Sophia's voice grew loud. She was trying to be heard inside her mother's head. "You're doing fine. It's that crazy man. I'd do fine if Julie would stay out of my life. He's got four kids—let him give them shit and leave me alone."

Rose's face softened. When no one else was around, it could be nice. Sophia liked her like this. It never lasted long.

"Shh, shh. Don't use such language, even if it's just the two of us. Julie thinks you shouldn't dance on that TV show, the one that Eddie Greene has. Says it puts thoughts in your head—thoughts you're too young to have."

Sophia felt the grin on her face.

Rose begged, "Please don't laugh at me."

"Mom, I'm sixteen. Look at me. I'm not a little girl. Men look at me and see a woman."

Rose put a hand on Sophia's mouth, pushing the words back. "Don't talk that way. You're not a tramp. Don't talk like one."

Sophia lifted her hands in front of her breasts. "Mom, look at me."

Rose kept her eyes on Sophia's face. "Please, Sophia, what is it you want from me? . . . Why did your father go off to that war?" Rose was crying, her voice helpless as a five-year-old.

"What did you say?" Sophia asked.

Rose held her hands out, showing Sophia they were empty. "Nothing . . . please promise me you won't get pregnant. I couldn't take that. Your father would never forgive me if that happened."

Sophia hugged her. "Mom, it's okay. I'm okay. Where are you going?"

"I need to lie down. I need to be by myself. It's quiet in my room. I just pray that when I close my eyes I won't see your father giving me that look."

Rose scared Sophia when she talked like that. "Mom, let's do something together. Take a walk outside. It's sunny. Our last chance before it gets cold again."

"You go. I'm too tired." Rose was bent over as she shuffled into her bedroom, closing the door behind her. Sophia felt Rose's heaviness on her shoulders. If Sophia didn't go out she would hurt her, at the very least with words.

Back on the street it had clouded over, and the wind was picking up. The day had turned raw. Sophia walked the four blocks to Ninth and Christian. The shop windows were clouded. Monday through Saturday the dust, truck exhaust fumes, grime of the city, would be sponged down and scraped to a clear sparkle with squeegees on long wooden handles. But on Sunday, the neighborhood grit colored the glass an off-yellow.

Here were the cheese stores, vegetable stands, butcher shops, bakeries, all closed. There were no brown-crusted breads with waffled surfaces, no sides of beef, no bright red legs of lamb. Those would come out fresh tomorrow, along with the women, the women who spoke as loud with their hands as with their voices. It felt so empty on Sunday. But the cheeses were there, yellow, white, tan, round and sausage-shaped.

Sophia's family felt like the market—familiar, something she hungered for, but when she was with them it was Sunday, closed to her, something she watched from the outside.

Sophia turned up Ninth Street and stopped at Teresa's. Her mother came to the door. "Come in, Sophia. Quick, before the cold gets in."

The dinner smells were familiar—a gravy of tomatoes, onions, oregano, and sausage. It was too warm inside; Teresa's parents were in their sixties. Her sister was fifteen years older than Teresa. When the older women were alone, they joked that Teresa should have been named "Whoops."

"Teresa, Sophia's here."

"Have her come up," she yelled back.

The narrow stairs were a few feet from the front door. At the top was the hallway all the bedrooms opened onto. Sophia walked down the worn gray runner and opened the second door on the left. A single bed was against the wall, with a small table holding Teresa's record player with the thick spindle for forty-fives. Scattered on the floor were a dozen or so in their paper sleeves.

Teresa had her hair tightly wound in curlers. She wore a loosely tied flannel bathrobe. She had cotton balls wadded between her toes, waiting for the nail polish to dry. Jungle Red. *Who thinks up these names?* Sophia thought. At school they were forbidden to color the nails on their hands, but the nuns didn't have them take off shoes and socks for inspection. Teresa had her left foot on the bed, fanning it with a forty-five. Probably not "At the Hop." When Danny and the Juniors were on *Varsity Dance,* Teresa had them sign the record sleeve. It was now a holy relic.

Sophia asked, "Do you have a date tonight?"

Teresa looked up. "No, I just want to look good tomorrow on *Varsity Dance.* Sophia, do you know any of these new girls on the show? They look older. I ask around, but no one seems to know them. Or what school they're from."

"What about their skirts?" Sophia asked.

Teresa now had both feet on the floor, and frowned.

"I know," she said. "That's funny too. It's Saint Agnes'. I thought I knew everyone."

Sophia had nothing to add. Besides, Teresa hadn't answered her question. "So, what's with the curlers?"

"The camera's never on me," she said. Teresa looked up at the ceiling, blushed, and went on, "One of the guys said he doesn't think I'm on the show."

Teresa had Sophia's interest. "Does the guy have a name?"

"Jimmy, Jimmy Vennotti." Teresa's blush darkened.

Sophia told her, "I've been watching who the cameras are on. Teresa, and it's not their hair. It's those pointed bras. Christ, they're like Cadillac bumpers."

Teresa giggled and flung open her robe. Sophia was staring at a bra ad.

"Teresa, if the sisters catch on, they'll slice your fingers off."

She flapped a hand at Sophia and said, "I'm not wearing it to school. I'll change in the bathroom at *Varsity Dance.* Do you think the camera guys will notice?"

"You better hope they're the only ones who do, them and Jimmy Vennotti."

Teresa's face reddened more, and then the color drained. She gasped: "Your uncle's not going to be there?"

"God, I hope not." With her thumb Sophia pushed her nose to the side, and said, "No, I was thinking of some of those guys that stand next to the camera men."

"What's with them anyway? Where did they come from?" Teresa asked.

Sophia shrugged. She had learned in Little Italy not to ask too many questions about some guys. "Don't know. Anyway, tell me about Jimmy Vennotti."

Teresa held her hands behind her back. "Nothing to tell," she said, twisting her shoulders from side to side.

"Teresa, look at me. Either I'm your best friend or I'm leaving."

Teresa held her right hand up. Lowering her voice she said, "Swear on your mother's eyes you won't tell anyone."

"Yeah, yeah."

Teresa's voice was louder, insistent. "Say it."

"I swear on my mother's eyes. Teresa, this better be good."

Leaning toward Sophia she whispered, "I'm thinking I may not be a virgin when I turn seventeen."

Sophia shouldn't have been surprised, but she was. "Meaning you're one now?"

"That's what I want to ask you. You know more about men, and what they like, Sophia."

Sophia felt the heat in her face. "Is that what everyone says? I'm easy?"

Teresa put her hands on Sophia's shoulders like she was moving her away from a fight with one of the religious girls. "No, no. But the men look at you. You know it's true. I think we're best friends because they don't look at me that way. I don't mean to get you going. Anyway, Jimmy looks that way at me. If no one's looking, he puts his hand on my . . . you know."

"Your ass?"

Teresa grinned. "Yeah."

"Sounds like you're doing great without any help from me," Sophia told her.

"Well, I think a lot about how to let him know . . . I'm interested." Teresa was grinding her big toe into a worn spot in the carpet.

"Watch out! You'll get polish on the rug," Sophia said. Then, softer, "Look, Teresa, why don't you just tell him?"

Worry lines shot out from Teresa's eyes. "Don't laugh. I know I'll go straight to Hell if I say it." Teresa turned red again.

Sophia's laugh sounded more like a snort, and Teresa complained, "Sophia, don't make fun of me!" Teresa's forehead crinkled into an angry frown. Sophia thought, *Is it me?* Whoever she spoke with got ticked off.

Sophia asked, "What are you talking about?"

"You know, lifting your eyebrows," Teresa said, "like I'm crazy. Anyway, I've been thinking about how to show Jimmy, without saying the words. Tell me what you think."

Teresa lay down on her bed and spread out her arms and legs. Sophia burst out laughing.

"What's so funny?" Teresa demanded.

"Teresa, you look like you're making an angel in the snow."

Teresa started laughing too. Every time they looked at each other, the laughter erupted louder, their faces pink and wet, eyes squeezed together.

"What are you girls laughing at?" As her mom opened the door Teresa sprang up, pulling her robe around her. Sophia told Teresa she would see her tomorrow and kissed her mom goodbye.

Outside, it was gray. It was close to five. In another half hour, Sophia would head home to make something for supper. Neither of them would be hungry, but Sophia was scared to let Rose keep sleeping in her room, scared she'd slip away, die when Sophia wasn't looking.

It started feeling cold. Part of Sophia wanted to run back to the house, run into her mother's room, make sure she was alive, make sure she could open her eyes and see Sophia. Rose had told her that when Sophia was a kid, four or five, if she fell asleep Sophia would climb up on her. Some days, Rose was so tired she wouldn't wake up. Sophia would lift her eyelids, and Rose would see Sophia studying her. Twelve years later, and Sophia still wanted to do it.

Jesus, what is with me? she thought.

Chapter Two
Blueberry Hill

His cousin Eddie's call could not have come at a worse time. Naomi mumbled, "David, who's that?" He smelled the sour warmth of her breath. It was two in the morning in the Greenberg bedroom six blocks from her parents, Sol and Ruth. It would be years before David could have bought a Georgian brick home in Cheltenham on what he made. Sol had said that at the closing.

The Christmas party had ended at eleven. In 1957 there still were blue laws about Saturday "entertainments" ending before midnight. David was uncomfortable that a Jewish law firm held a Christmas function. But Bloomie, the managing partner, had said that the party was for the secretaries, and they were Catholic. All the partners had been in tuxedoes. David had heard of big firms in Washington that had women partners, but this was Philly. The wives had worn heavy silk dresses from Nan Duskin. Naomi had brought home two Schiaparellis and asked which he had liked. David had picked the pale yellow. Naomi had said the other was the color Schiaparelli was known for: "shocking pink." David told her it reminded him of flamingos, and they had laughed.

She had left the sales slip on her vanity. "I could buy a car for what these cost," he had said.

"David, it's okay. We have the money. Please don't get angry."

"You mean you and your family have the money," he had said.

She had run a fingernail down his cheek, opened her mouth and kissed him. Her other hand had cupped David's crotch.

"At the end of the day it's just you and me," Naomi had said in her high-pitched child's voice.

At the party Bloomie's wife had said, "I saw your dress at Duskin's, but with three tuitions at Friends Select . . . well, it was out of the question." David had given Naomi's hand a squeeze and made an excuse to move along to another group.

His secretary, Catherine Marie, had come up and gushed about Naomi's dress. David knew that the nagging voice inside Naomi told her she'd paid a price for her indulgence. Catherine Marie had worn a navy dress with a white collar. Without asking, David had known it was her dress for Sunday Mass, weddings, funerals, and the firm's Christmas party. He liked seeing the secretaries in different clothes than what they wore in the office, clothes he didn't picture with steno pads. But there was always the insurmountable distance between scraping by and money, the cold knowledge that life was not fair. The sensible gabardine fabric was shiny at the cuffs. David wondered whether Catherine Marie had dreams of frivolous pastel dresses filling her closet. It would be the same nightly escape in which Cary Grant lit her cigarette. At least she had not made oblique comments about their being childless.

David had passed through the evening in a blur of scotch. His drinking hand had never been empty. He wasn't an angry drunk. Smiling and nodding became more natural. David had watched Naomi's face as a man in the Arctic reads a thermometer. She had been at ease; he must not have embarrassed himself.

Toward the end, Naomi had brought him coffee. When people had been with them, she had smiled and mentioned that she preferred not to drive at night. Once she had leaned close so no one could hear and had said, "I'd like to pick up where we left off." Naomi had looked pleased with herself, like a little girl who had won the spelling bee. A little girl in a heavy-breasted, wide-hipped woman's body. Naomi's physical elegance was lavished on her face—high cheek bones, cocoa eyes, and thick curly hair the reddish brown color some trees turn in the fall.

In bed she had been moist. David had been limp. First he had rerun the Packard memory, seeing Naomi's seventeen-year-old breasts, the waterfall of snowflakes outside the breath-fogged windows. The images had not worked their magic. David had known Naomi needed him to want her. He had squeezed his eyes shut, and Havana had appeared, Mary Beth the succubus, the resemblance to Naomi amplifying her desirability. Mary Beth writhing with Eddie in front of the window. David had entered Lilly as he and Eddie stared at each other. Naomi's breathing had been strong and hoarse beneath him, and then she had spit out "Damn," and David had known that tonight he would not grow hard.

Naomi had refused to let him use his fingers, had pushed David off, rolled away, and had fallen asleep with her back toward him.

An hour later the phone rang. "David, I've got to see you now."

"Eddie, it's the middle of the night." Naomi's hair tickled his face; she moved closer straining to hear what Eddie was saying.

"Please, David, I'm in trouble," Eddie whined.

"What kind of trouble?" he asked. David's head pounded.

"What time is it?" Naomi asked. "Why is Eddie calling? Why does he think he has the right to call at"—Naomi's body rolled away from David, and he saw the shadow of her hand lifting the clock on her night table—"at two in the morning."

"Eddie, call me tomorrow at the office."

He was lowering the receiver to its cradle when Eddie's voice shrieked at David: "No, I need to see you now. I'll be dead by tomorrow. This is out of control."

He brought the phone back to his ear. "Lower your voice, Eddie. What are you talking about?" David felt the sheets moving on Naomi's side of the bed.

"You've got to come here now," Eddie insisted.

David was distracted by the clicking of Naomi's slipper heels on the bathroom's tile floor.

David was more awake. Eddie was panting, short of breath. David asked, "Where's here?"

"Blueberry Hill."

What was Eddie talking about? David asked again, "Where?"

"It's near Cherry Hill," Eddie said, "in Jersey. Go down the main drag in Cherry Hill. A mile out of town there's a private road on the right. Take that. It's just beyond the top of a hill, through a gated entrance. Better write it down. You're not great on directions." Eddie was calming down.

Naomi returned from the bathroom. "David, either hang up or take the call in your office." She made no effort to soften the sharpness in her tone.

"Ok," David told her. "Eddie, hold on." He put his hand over the mouthpiece and said, "Naomi, hang up when I'm back on."

Downstairs at his desk he said "Hi," listened for the click, and then said, "What the hell is going on?"

"Let me go over how to get here."

David hadn't put on a bathrobe. He missed Naomi's warmth under the blanket. He told Eddie, "No. Tell me what this is about or I'm hanging up."

"Do you know who Julie Rabelli is?" Eddie asked.

"No, should I?"

Eddie's voice became testy. "You do a lot of work for Pyramid, right?"

"Eddie, get to the point." David rubbed his calf to get the blood circulating. If Naomi hadn't been so put out, he would have taken the time to find his robe.

Eddie hesitated a moment and then said, "*Varsity Dance* is making money hand over fist for Pyramid. Rabelli is the head of the Philly Vice Squad. He's taken it into his head that *Varsity Dance* is corrupting . . . Look, I can't talk about it on the phone—who else can I call?" Eddie's voice was loud again. Loud and panicked.

"Ok. Enough," David said. "Give me the directions again."

He was not alone on the roads. There were some cars but more trucks, mostly eighteen wheelers. From Cheltenham to Cherry Hill there were lots of streetlights, to the effect that David was aware of the darkness but not in it. That changed once he turned onto the private road. It was paved but unlit. David was the only person on the planet. Had he taken a wrong turn? Eddie had said the road rose and fell and it would take five minutes before David saw the place. He came to a high point, the headlights shooting into the sky like a movie premiere. As the car tilted down David saw a three-story house defined by soft light from rows of what he assumed were curtained windows. If it were in New York the mansion would have occupied a city block. He learned later that the estate had been built in the 1890s by a beer baron.

At the bottom of the road were metal gates a story high, attached to a fieldstone wall. Inside and off to the left was a guardhouse. Discreet lights were built into the gates, just bright enough for the man on the other side to see David's face but not so strong that they were visible from the crest of the road.

David rolled down the car window and leaned out. There was enough light to see the holstered gun on the guard's hip. The man asked: "What's your name?"

"David. David Greenberg. My cousin Eddie called me. Tonight. He called me tonight. To come here."

The gun. That's what had David scared. And made him sound like a fool.

The guard's voice relaxed, a hint of recognition in his next question, "You got a driver's license?"

David showed it to him.

"Back it up. The gates open toward you. Drive to the front entrance. They'll take your car."

The crunch of the tires sounded like the driveway was made of oyster shells. It was less than an hour to the Jersey shore. As David walked up the stairs he heard his car being driven off. He turned and saw it disappear behind the house.

The man who opened the door seemed uncomfortable in his clothes. The open collar of his dress shirt overflowed with the thickness of his neck, and the jacket pulling across his belly threatened to launch the middle button.

In the entranceway music played. A male Negro sang, "I found my thrill, on Blueberry Hill . . ."

The gravelly voice was accompanied by a piano with an old-time blues sound. New Orleans blues. A top forty hit was out of place in the stately mansion, like the bottles of ketchup at the formal dinners Hearst had thrown at San Simeon.

"Hi, I'm Sophia, your hostess at Blueberry Hill."

At first David thought the young woman was in her twenties. She was sheathed in a strapless satin dress the color of a ruby, her breasts puffing over the top. His eyes rose to her face. Though heavily made up, underneath she was a teenager, angry red acne floured with powder. She was watching David, like a salesgirl figuring out his taste in ties.

"I don't remember you. Is this your first visit to Blueberry Hill?" she asked. "Was there a particular girl you saw on the show that you would like to spend time with?"

"I have no idea what you're talking about," David said. "I'm here to see Eddie Greene."

Sophia never lost her composure. She asked, "Is he expecting you?"

"Yes, he called me an hour ago. What is this place?"

Eddie appeared behind Sophia. At five foot six he was her height. He placed a hand on her shoulder as if she were a show dog, more to draw attention to her than a gesture of affection. That same hand held a cigarette dangling ashes. Sophia lifted Eddie's hand, slid to the side, and let his arm fall. Silver rain fell on his tie; a few embers flared and burned pinpoint holes in the red silk. Eddie didn't brush at the tie. He seemed too drunk or too preoccupied.

"Hi, David. Sophia, this is my cousin David, the big-time attorney."

When David looked again at Sophia, he imagined a secretary fresh out of parochial school, recommended by the Mother Superior as the top in her class in shorthand, her feet pigeon-toed in sensible shoes, her breasts fully covered and de-emphasized in a loose-fitting dress, any lipstick or rouge roughly wiped off in the ladies' lounge by Catherine Marie before introducing Sophia to the partners.

David followed Eddie into a room larger than a high school gym set up for senior prom. At the four corners were bars staffed by Negro men in maroon jackets, white shirts, and clip-on bow ties. David clung to the lie that he had never seen a colored man who knew how to tie a bow tie. Naomi would become piqued when he said that; he believed it was because she knew he was right.

In the lit room David studied Eddie's face. The dark curly hair was speckled with gray; his cheeks protruded as though stuffed with food. Eddie was not the sleek panther he had been in Havana.

There were a handful of men in coats with hats on. Eddie said good night to one and offered to have another driven home.

Large sets of photographs hung on the wood-paneled walls. On one side a high school girl was doing a popular dance, long hair swinging, plaid skirt rising with the movement of her body. These were paired with photos of the same young women facing the camera, naked from the waist up. Their faces were professionally made up: pouting mouths enlarged with greasy lipstick, heavily rouged cheeks, artificial eyelashes. A gallery of adolescent whores. Their eyes looked fearful and sad. David wondered whether that was intentional. Under each set of photographs was a name in large block print: Sue, Claire, Marge.

"Eddie, what the hell are you into?"

"I can explain everything," he said. They were still in the room with the photographs. It must have been a ballroom when the beer baron lived here. Eddie walked behind the nearest bar and opened a door in the wall. David followed.

"David, sit down." Eddie pointed to a chair, and David thought of the talk leading up to their last night in Havana. He did not sit down.

"I've found a gold mine," Eddie said. "*Varsity Dance* is a showcase for ambitious girls. What's with the face? I don't force any of them to do anything. These girls surprise even me. They come up with things we never dreamt of. David, please sit down. You're a lawyer—whatever I tell you, well, I'm your client."

It bothered David that Eddie's shirt spilled over his pants.

"Eddie, this is crazy. Underage girls? What's in your head? Another thing: I'm not a criminal attorney, but I remember a little from law school. If you tell me about an ongoing crime, there's no protection— I'm obligated to tell the police."

Eddie's right eyelid fluttered. "What're you saying? You'd turn me in? Come on, David. It's me, Eddie."

How could Eddie do this to me? "This is—I don't know what you expect from me. You've put me in an awful bind. You know I do work for the TV station. No one at Pyramid knows what you're up to, right?"

"David, stop pacing around and sit," Eddie's voice was loud. "Now listen. If this breaks, I'm in the crapper. And *Varsity Dance* is too."

David stopped and looked directly at Eddie. "Just tell me, is anyone at the station in on this?"

"No. Keep your voice down. Now will you listen? The hostess, Sophia, is she a walking wet dream or what?" Eddie's tongue licked the corners of his mouth.

"Eddie, you're out of your mind. You're not making any sense. Look, I came here because you said you were in the biggest trouble of your life, and all you can tell me is that the teenage hostess gets you hot? You have one minute to tell me why I'm here. I'll find a good criminal lawyer and maybe he can help."

Eddie reached out. In David's imagination the extended hand was covered with boils. He could not help his cousin without catching his disease. David stepped back. Eddie lurched forward, grabbing David's shoulder, pulling him closer.

He said, "Sophia's uncle, Julie Rabelli, is head of the Philly Vice Squad. He's got a thing about me. He hates Jews, and he's violent." The sweat popped on Eddie's forehead. "He's sniffing around," Eddie said. "If he catches on, he'll destroy the show, and that's who's paying you and your fancy law firm. Don't you get it? I want you to tell your client what's happening. I don't have the clout to call off Rabelli. Pyramid does. I think this guy's crazy enough to kill me."

Were those tears? Was Eddie that scared?

"This is insane, what you're telling me and what you're asking," David said.

Eddie's fingers tightened on David's shoulder. He shook him once, hard. "David, calm down. Use that brain of yours. You're my only hope. Look at your fucking hands, shaking like a leaf."

Eddie must have pressed a buzzer. David smelled a heavy expensive perfume . . . Joy. Naomi put it on when she wanted to make love. David turned around. Sophia was leaning against the door. Her mascara had run, a raccoon mask on an underage pinup.

"Eddie, everyone's gone," she said. "I'm going to change for school. Drop me off at Teresa's. I'll sneak in before anyone's up."

Waving Sophia in, Eddie asked, "Are any of the girls around? I thought we'd have a nightcap with David. It's only three-thirty. We have an hour before we have to go."

David said, "Eddie, I'm leaving."

Sophia looked at David and made her sales pitch. "Claire's still here. You'll like her. She's wild."

Eddie took his hands off him, and said, "David, stick around. It'll be like the old days. Claire will make you think you're twenty again. Come on. It'll be a time you'll never forget. Claire does things—she's the best."

Sophia was pressing against David's back. She reached around and unbuttoned his topcoat. "Feels nice," she said. "Cashmere? If you ask her, Claire will get into your coat naked and then come into the room."

Sophia rubbed the back of her hand against the lining while her nails marched lightly across his shirt. She had her lips against David's ear. Her voice sounded like it was coming from inside his head. "David, when Claire has nothing on, it will be cool on her skin and her nipples will get hard. That's how it works for me. I bet you can imagine my breasts with hard nipples. It's getting you hard."

Her other hand brushed across the front of his pants. "Oh my," she said. "I think you've undressed me in your mind."

He stepped forward, out of her reach.

"Do you need another girl for this party?"

David turned around. Standing in the doorway was a tall blonde. Her face was apple-shaped, with a slight upturned nose and large prominent teeth. One of her blue eyes stared at him; the other was locked at a sharp angle seemingly focused on the office's shadowed corner.

"I overheard you'd like me to model your overcoat. Navy is my best color. Don't you agree?" As Claire spoke she pulled her white blouse up, reached under and behind it with both arms. Her good eye never left David's face. He shook his head to clear it. He needed to understand how big a mess Eddie was in.

Sophia pushed a chair behind David. Claire faced the door. He heard the snick of a lock. Claire bent over. David watched the pleated skirt rise up her dark knee-high socks, watched the skirt lift like a curtain on the back of perfect white thighs. Sophia's hands were on David's shoulders, insistent, suggestive, and he lowered himself into the chair. Claire turned, her strapless bra moving in a short arc, a metronome for a rhythm the four of them heard.

Claire's mouth was exaggerated with tomato red lipstick, an animal caught in mid-feast measuring David for the next kill, her walleye helplessly frozen on the darkness. "David, men like schoolgirls," Claire said. Claire's long fingers unbuttoned her white blouse, a button for each of the well-practiced sentences: "My breasts are bare under my blouse. I have large breasts. A grown woman's breasts."

Her blouse was open to the skirt. David saw the shadow between the breasts, the outline of her nipples. Claire moved closer and leaned down. Her mouth was open. He saw the white of her teeth, felt the warm cigarette breath. David smelled Eddie behind him, a mixture of sweat and Canoe, part of what was arousing him, part of what was forbidden.

"Look down David, look down at my breasts."

He did.

Then Claire straightened, and took a few steps back. She lifted her plaid skirt, lifted it slowly over schoolgirl thighs, lifted it to blond pubic hair.

"How do you like it, David?" Claire asked. "Do you want me facing you, David? You need to take your pants off, David, if you want me in your lap, facing you, sitting on it, David, pressing down on it. Is that what you want, David?"

Claire took a step toward him. She lowered her skirt. With her breasts covered in white cotton, her pale blond hair concealed beneath the parochial plaid, she was a diva singing behind the curtain.

"This is mad. You are all crazy," David said. He was having trouble hearing his own words.

Claire was speaking again, in control, ignoring his protest, "What age do you want me to be, David? Do you want me older? Twenty or twenty-five?"

Eddie's voice broke in, "Just don't be forty. Right, David? Naomi just turned forty."

David stood up.

"What're you doing," Eddie whined. "Take your coat off. David, I swear I won't open my mouth again. Please? Where are you going?"

"Eddie, have them bring my car around. Call or whatever you do. Do it now!"

"Okay, okay. Calm down, David. You're scaring the girls. Christ, you're scaring me. I'm sorry you're so upset. You'll still help me, right? I was just trying to say thank you. You know I'm no good at this. David, promise you'll talk to—you know, the people that can save—David, don't walk out on me. You don't want my death on your conscience."

David was tired. The last twelve hours washed against the back of his eyes like wet sand. Weighing on him. Scratching. David poked his finger into Eddie's chest, harder than he intended. As Eddie winced and stepped back David said, "Eddie, no one's going to kill you. Close this place down. Tell your girls to wash up and go home."

David unlocked the door and walked into the great room. A light or two were on, softening the darkness to gray. He could not see the photographs, but knew they were there. Claire was on the wall. A billboard Claire in a whirling skirt, a Claire with breasts a foot across. A silent Claire. David's heels echoed off the parquet floor. He opened the front door and stepped into a cold black morning. The Packard's engine was running, headlights painting the oyster shells a harsh white.

Chapter Three
Homecoming

David came upstairs after the call from Eddie. I asked, "Why are you getting dressed?"

David turned on the light in his closet. With his back toward me, he took off his pajamas. Black hair was thickening on his back. I had told him it was to make up for his going bald. "I have to see Eddie, Naomi. He's terrified of something."

"It's the middle of the night," I said. I wasn't sure David heard me.

There was a long pause as he pulled on pants, shoehorned into his tassel loafers, and took a shirt off the hanger. "I know," he said, "I don't know why—I'll be back soon as I can." He held a tie against a jacket.

Why could Eddie make David jump at the snap of his fingers?

"You don't have to look just so," I told him. "Listen to me, David. Don't go. Not now. See him at the office tomorrow."

David's voice was exhausted. "I tried. God knows I tried. I'm the only one he's got. I can't let him be alone. Not when he sounds this way."

"What are you talking about?" I asked.

David rolled his collar down. With his back to me, he continued talking into the closet. "I swear, Naomi, this is it. I'll be back soon. You'll see. This is the last time."

"I don't see. Nobody sees. Only you and Eddie see."

He was pleading with me, "Please—please. Don't get angry. I'll talk to him—it'll be okay."

"If I need you," I asked, "can I call you at Eddie's?"

"He's not there. He's in Jersey," David said.

"What?" I didn't understand what David was doing. It scared me.

David finally faced me and said, "He's at a place near Cherry Hill."

"What place?" Damn Eddie.

"Blueberry Hill," David said. He was walking out of the bedroom, his back toward me.

The last thing I said was, "Is there a phone number?"

David was going down the stairs. He never replied. Maybe he really hadn't heard me. I turned off the light and watched the dark. I don't know when sleep came or when the dream appeared.

I was inside my parents' house. My hand moved a white curtain to one side of a window. Reflected in the glass, the curtain was a bridal veil. There were wrinkled cheeks; gray hair like a Brillo pad. Fingers mapped with blue veins touched my lips. I looked through my mirrored face and saw Daddy on the front walk staring at the sky. David and Eddie were with him. Why were they so young? I passed though the front door, transparent as the bridal curtain. Daddy turned around.

"Hi, Princess. We've missed you."

"Daddy, what is everyone watching?"

"Look at the moon, Princess."

The moon was swollen. Across the pale yellow surface, gray canals throbbed. Pudgy hands with tiny fingers reached out. A head, a tiny foot. The gray was a watery home to thousands of fetuses. Eyes opened, staring at me.

"Daddy, I never knew the moon was babies."

"Unborn babies, Princess."

I looked back, and the moon burst like a dandelion blown on by God, scattering pink-gray bodies in the night sky. Some would land in women and grow; others would circle in the black to wither into frozen dust.

I woke in the unlit bedroom as alone as one of the fetuses whirling in the void. Reaching out, I knocked over the table lamp. My heart was pounding. Leaning over too far, I fell hard on the floor. I needed light to wake up, to see the dream was over.

I was sitting on the edge of the bed when David walked in, turning on the overhead light. He stared at me, bent over, and put the lamp back on the nightstand. What could I say, what would he think if I told him about unborn babies watching me? David sat down, put an arm around me. I leaned my face into his chest, tired, craving David to move me back and forth, gently, slowly, to rock a frightened child.

David kissed my forehead; his lips brushed my eyelids. His hand was on my breast, stroked my nipple, pressed it between his thumb and finger.

"Gently, David. That hurts." I looked at David's face, glimpsed sadness, a flash of rage, like lightning flickering in a cloud, so quick I was not sure I had seen it.

"Naomi, stand up, a few feet from me."

I thought of asking him what was going on, but decided to wait.

David rose and shed his clothes like a snake moving into its new skin. He was aroused, in full erection. "Naomi, do you have anything on under your nightgown?"

"No," I said.

"I want you to seduce me," he demanded.

"David, you already have a full head of steam." I wanted him to laugh, to ease up. He blushed.

David was a director telling me, "I want you to lift your nightgown to your waist. No, don't pull it over your head. Hold it there for a moment."

"This isn't fun for me, David. It scares me. What's gotten into you?"

David scowled, a little angry boy. "I'm aroused by my wife. Just my wife. Is there something wrong with that?" He bit off the words as he spoke.

"No," I said, "of course not. It's just that—"

He didn't see how his anger cheapened me. Something else, someone else, was all he heard. He commanded, "Naomi, I don't want an argument. I don't want to lose the moment. Take off your nightgown. Don't fold it."

"David, lower your voice. Why are you angry at me?" I took a step back. Did I think David would hit me?

"I'm sorry," he said. "I didn't hear my voice. Let's forget it. I'll shower, get ready for work."

"David, no. Tell me what you want. Please—"

"Put your hands under your breasts. That's it," he said. "Like a young girl's. They are as firm and lovely as the night I met you."

"Oh, David, I'm glad you believe that. It's not true, but it's nice you believe that."

He was shaking his head from side to side. I hadn't read my lines right.

"Naomi, tease me. Act like maybe you'll have sex with me, maybe you won't. It's all in your control. It's a favor. Make me want you."

What had happened tonight? No matter what I said, he would be angry. I bent forward holding my breasts. David suckled. Felt good. Tongue. Teeth.

"Ow!" I cried.

"I'm sorry." Was he?

"Just your tongue," I said, "good." I took his face in my hands and moved it to the other breast.

"Not just the nipple," I had told him this before. Why did David forget? I guided his face lower, his tongue against my belly, my navel.

"Naomi, move back. I want to touch you, but have you out of reach. Smile. Laugh at me."

"David, this isn't helping me. It feels like you're in your head with another woman. I want you here—with me."

David's eyes narrowed. He said, "I am. I swear to you I am."

I moved forward. David kneeled on one leg. His hands cupped my bottom, squeezed, pulled me toward his mouth, kissed my pubic hair.

I needed to remind him, to teach him again. "Use your tongue—Easy . . . Better. Not just one spot. . . . Nice—Nice . . ."

David was down on both knees.

"David, move around. Not just my vagina. I don't want to come yet. Move around. Do different things."

David stood up. His hands were on my shoulders, turning me around. He pressed against me. I felt his hardness, heard his labored breath. His lips were dry on the back of my neck. I touched myself, felt the wet between my legs, but did not want sex. Whoever he was making love to, it wasn't me. I wanted it over, to be alone. I needed to cry. I tried to turn around, to have him come inside me, to have it end. David needed to flush his anger, to pass it to me so that he could become quiet inside himself. I longed for him to walk out of the movie inside his head and return to me. David's hands would not let me turn. Within me the sadness simmered into anger. David mistook it for arousal. He pulled over a straight-back chair and sat down.

"Naomi, I want you to straddle me. Face toward me. Ease down on me." He continued directing, and he was the only one with the script. Damn him!

He was inside me. His sounds grew louder. I moved up and down, pushing down with greater force. The anger inside me tightened, squeezing David harder. It satisfied his rage. God, why didn't he come?

David put his hands under me and stood up. He carried me to our bed, laid me down. He stayed in me, fearing that once he withdrew he could never re-enter, sensing I would not let him. We were sweating, our bodies wet, the hair on his head slicked down. I smelled his day on him: cigarettes, red beef, onions, garlic, scotch. David thrust harder.

"David, maybe we're too tired. It's been a long day."

I looked at his face, red with effort, mouth set, stress lines spreading from the wings of his nose.

His words came out in short bursts.

"We must do this," he said. "I can do this."

I saw rage howling inside him, smashing everything within its reach. I heard again Dr. Stern's measured words, the wound that was always fresh: "Mr. Greenberg, you produce dead sperm. It's not your fault. It just happens. Have you and your wife considered adoption?"

Stern had suggested that David get professional help, grieve through his anger, mourn the child we would never have. But David clung to his rage.

"David, stop. This isn't enjoyable. It hurts, damn you!"

David rammed harder and harder, not hearing my words, feeling only his own pain.

Making love was now something we worked at and failed to enjoy. When had it become a task, as necessary and joyless as getting out of a warm bed on Monday? When we had learned David would not father children? Dr. Stern had told us I could conceive. Why hadn't Stern just given me the information? I would have lied, assured David that I was the problem, that I couldn't get pregnant.

The violence in David's lovemaking had started earlier. I couldn't pinpoint when. The news from Stern had made it worse, much worse.

David's gasping, his "Ohs," were louder: My cue. I began to moan, first softly, rising, lower, then louder than before. David couldn't come unless he believed I had reached orgasm.

I was sore by now. David rolled off. In the lit bedroom, I saw his red face, and heard his panting. When his breathing became more even, he propped his head up on one hand and asked, "Did you have an orgasm? Please be honest."

"I always tell you the truth," I said. "Yes, a small one. I was tired." I took a Kleenex from the night table and turned back. Wiping David's face, I moved it until he was looking at me. "David, what happened in Havana?" I asked.

"What—?" David's brows lifted, pulling up the lids, enlarging his eyes. He was startled, and there was something else. Guilt? My high-pitched voice was calm, strong. Insistent.

"I want you to tell me," I said.

He asked, "What made you think about Havana?"

I knew David well enough to recognize the tone of his voice, stalling for time. Tonight I did not back off. "Tonight you were with Eddie. You know—"

David, louder, "I don't know. You're not making any sense."

"Don't get angry," I said.

"It's not very flattering. Do you think about Eddie when we're making love? Does that excite you?"

David was using a lawyer's trick, attacking me, distancing himself from what I had asked. Something had taken root in me tonight. Surviving David's assault? Feeling angry without apology? I said, "No, nothing like that."

"What then?"

I knew the answer to his question. Could I confront him? Calmness flowed in my mind, in my belly. "It's just that—When you came back from that trip, well, our lovemaking was different. You were different. And—you were that way again tonight."

David turned his head away, scared I would read his face, and know. When he looked at me again, he said, "You're always telling me to take the lead, that you like it when I do. But when I do, there's this complaining afterwards." He rose from the bed, his back toward me.

I wrapped my fingers around his hand. He still did not look at me. "Where are you going?" I asked.

Turning, David pulled his hand out of mine. He looked down at me. "I have to shower and go to work."

I raised my back against the headboard as I said, "David, please sit down. Talk. I need you to talk. Let me know what you're thinking."

His eyes, those beautiful hazel eyes, were wet. "Damn it, Naomi, I can't do this."

"You're crying. I'm so sorry, David. I should just keep my mouth shut." I stood up and hugged him, stroking the back of his head. Bending over, David buried his face between my neck and shoulder. I rubbed his back, massaging the words out of him.

"Naomi, sometimes I feel so worried about Eddie. He's really not bad. But he gets himself in trouble."

I snapped, "I don't care about Eddie. I care about us, David."

Under my fingers I felt David's muscles tighten. He lifted his head, his mouth pulled tight. "Why are you so angry?" he asked.

David walked into the bathroom. A moment later I heard the water running in the shower.

I felt the sadness dragging on me. I needed to have David go. To be alone. Not really alone. Liz would be here by nine. To clean up after us. I'd have a drink. Liz knew.

David was never here when Liz was around. Even if she wanted to, she couldn't tell David how much I drank. Liz knew I'd fire her if she talked to David. No one kept a maid who told what she saw. Even if Liz were white I'd fire her. I'd love to be a fly on the wall when the maids got together. Bloomie's wife, Sarah, fired her new maid a month ago. Bet that's what the colored girls called her: "Maid-A-Month Bloomenthal."

David's voice broke in. "Naomi, let me in on the joke." I hadn't heard him return or begin dressing. David pushed the top part of his tie through the loop, pulling it down while he pressed an indentation under the tightening knot.

I crooked a finger on the tiny silken valley, stroking it as if it were Cary Grant's perfectly achieved Windsor knot, trying to vamp like a movie star, an intelligent beauty, Kate Hepburn. "What's this called again, David?"

"A dimple," he said.

"It's elegant," I told him.

Color rose in his cheeks. Why couldn't he be this David all the time?

"Naomi, what was so funny?"

"A private thought. About Sarah Bloomenthal. You don't want to hear it. Catty."

David was gone and Liz was not here yet. I poured some gin into my orange juice. Easier for Liz to pretend if she didn't see it happen in front of her. The day stretched ahead of me. Too long to get through. I couldn't go back to bed and sleep. People got scared when I did. Mommy. Daddy, too. David stared at me, trying to see inside my head, trying to find an answer there. Sometimes I laughed when I saw David's Clark Kent stare. Of course, David was not the Man of Steel. He was the Man of Secrets. Eddie secrets. Havana secrets. David always asked, "What's so funny?" I didn't know how to explain because David would think I was crazy.

When I heard David close the front door I put on my bathrobe and walked down to the kitchen. Everything in this bright room was small and white: the stove with its four electric coils; the refrigerator that was my height; the sink scrubbed until no trace of food smells remained, just the antiseptic smell of gritty cleansers. It reminded me of a hospital room.

Exhausted, I pulled out one of the chrome-backed chairs and lowered my heaviness. My hand trembled in the strong morning light. Stabbing light reflected off my diamond ring and made me squint. I was married to David. Was he married to me?

I looked into the backyard. The ground was gray-brown from the cold, glistening where the last of the frost resisted the sun.

Here at the kitchen table my face was wet with sadness. I swallowed the remaining gin and orange juice. When had I poured it? I heard footsteps. Liz was in the doorway, a thin woman the color of coal ashes. Taking off a worn spring-weight coat, a hand-me-down from Mommy, Liz vigorously rubbed the tops of her hands. She looked worried.

"Are you okay, Liz?"

She smiled and said, "I'm jes' fine." Liz's voice lifted the cold damp that lived in me. I warmed to the cadence of her words; was soothed by a presence that demanded nothing from me.

Liz walked over and pulled the bathrobe up to my shoulders. "Miz Greenberg, don't be sittin' here undressed. Nevah' know when someone could be in the yard lookin' in."

I laughed at the thought that anyone would want to look at me naked.

"Bin drinkin'." It was not a question. "L'es go upstairs, get dressed," Liz said. "Figger out what you doin' today."

Chapter Four
The Engagement Party

Catherine Marie put the cup of black coffee in the center of the desk blotter. "Is there anything else, Mr. Greenberg?"

"No," David said. "Thank you. I didn't get much sleep last night." He moved the cup to the upper right hand corner of the blotter. His voice buzzed in his head like a wasp. *I always keep it there. I can reach for it while reading a document and not knock it over. Catherine Marie knows that. Why didn't she place it there?*

He looked up and saw the door close, wondering whether Catherine Marie had read his thoughts.

The angry voice prodded David again. *Why does Naomi always throw Havana in my face? It wasn't my idea to go there. Sol came up with that at the engagement party.*

By 1939, Sol's Packard dealerships and his movie theater had made the Luntz family wealthy. Sol and Ruth's backyard had held a hundred guests that night. The freshly mowed lawn had given off a night perfume. Torches, fastened atop seven-foot-high metal poles, had swirled flames and oily wisps of smoke.

Naomi and David had been standing in a group of six, including Morris Chumsky. Rumor had it he had made his first fortune running bootleg during Prohibition. Before the party Sol and David had been alone, watching the tables being set up. Sol had gone over the guest list, making comments about people David had not met. When he came to Chumsky, David had asked whether the story was true.

"David, I'm in a group that invests in real estate. Every December Chumsky visits his friend Meyer Lansky. When he comes back, he tells us he and Meyer sold some property." Sol had poked his index finger into the palm of his hand, pausing after chosen phrases.

"Chumsky comes to the lawyer's office with fifty thousand dollars in cash—he wants invested through the group. *Vershtay?* In cash! I don't ask. Once he volunteered that he and Lansky came from the same town in Poland—and that's why they do business together. Am I nuts? Would I question?"

Later at the party, David had tried not to stare at Chumsky. His head was a bulldog's, square with powerful jaws. The rest of his body was small, a compact frame with tiny hands and feet. He had been wearing a suit and shoes that Sol said were custom-made for him in London. Chumsky had looked at David and said, "Sol tells me you're in the top of your class at Harvard Law School. What are you doing this summer?"

"Interning at Schmidt, Harris, Cardozo & Green," had been David's answer.

"Good firm." The bulldog head had nodded approval. "I use them for some of my business. I'll keep an eye out for you. Maybe we'll have lunch." Chumsky's voice had been a rasping growl.

"I'd love to," David had said.

David swallowed black coffee and felt his stomach congeal into a lump, as it had eighteen years ago with Chumsky. He moved the fountain pen to the top of the blotter, parallel to the letter opener.

At the party Sol had said, "David works too hard," while looking at Chumsky. "Naomi says he's tired all the time. I tell him to take a week off before he goes back to school."

"Except Daddy doesn't want David and me spending a week together," Naomi retorted.

Sol had looked down.

Naomi's Aunt Ida had broken the silence. "This is a lovely turnout. The fact that people came up from the Jersey shore in the middle of such a gorgeous weekend is a complement to Sol. Ruth too, of course."

Naomi had stiffened, stared hard at her aunt, taken David's hand, and led him to the bar. A woman had walked by carrying a tray of cocktail wieners in puff pastries. The browned skins had been shiny with fat. Naomi had looked at them, her mouth opening. She had put her hands behind her back. David had told her, "You look great."

"Thanks," she had said. Naomi had begun dieting two months earlier. He had not asked how much she had lost; she took such questions as hidden criticism. With the slimming of what she had called her "chipmunk cheeks," her face had become voluptuous: her eyes had grown larger, high cheekbones had been revealed, and her neck was now swan-like. She had still fretted about the loose flesh under the top of her arms, her "batwings."

Both of them had ordered a fresh gin and tonic. Naomi had concentrated on finishing hers, and had ordered another. Sol had watched. "Naomi," David had said, "your father is staring."

"Let him! Why does he let Aunt Ida talk to Mommy that way? 'Ruth too, of course.'"

"Your aunt is a little tactless," he had conceded.

"David, don't you start," Naomi had fumed. "The woman thinks because she's Daddy's sister she can get away with anything!"

The last thing the party had needed was a scene between Naomi and Ida. "If you say something it will embarrass your mother," he had said. "She really looks like she's enjoying herself."

Naomi had held David's face, and had kissed him hard and long. Though the diamond in her engagement ring had been "no bigger than a grain of rice" according to Ida, it had had a liberating effect on Naomi, unleashing public displays of affection. Several people had looked over. Naomi's cousin Ronald, David's roommate at college, had begun to clap and whistle.

That's when Eddie had walked out of the house and boomed, "You guys better save it for your wedding night!"

Everyone had laughed; Naomi giggled. Sol had walked over to Eddie, and David had feared he would deck him. Instead Sol had said something, and they had both walked over to Chumsky.

As the party had ended, Eddie had found David standing alone. Eddie swung his jacket in one hand; a dark food stain had trailed down his tie. "David, I'm going to Havana the last week of August. Come with me, it'll be great. I was there a year ago. You can't believe the women. It'll do you good. You can go back to school relaxed. And you won't be so tense around Naomi."

"Who says I'm tense?" David challenged.

Eddie had draped his jacket and hand on David's shoulder. "David," he had said, "you're a gentleman. Everyone knows that. No one questions the package won't be unwrapped until the wedding night. But you've got to be paying a price." Eddie had made the gesture, jerking his hand up and down like milking a cow.

David had looked around to see if anyone else had caught this pantomime. Everyone had seemed frozen in conversation. David's movement had not been lost on Eddie. Eddie had taken his hand off

David's shoulder, reached for a rye and ginger on a nearby table, smiled and said, "Shit, there I go embarrassing the best cousin I have," he had said. "David, I've never steered you wrong. If it wasn't for me your mom would've made you into a sissy. Who taught you how to fight? Who showed you it was fun to break the rules?" Eddie had gulped down half his drink.

"Listen, I already have a room at the *Nacional,* the ritziest hotel in town. A suite—two bedrooms. I can't sleep in both at once. It'd be fun—just the two of us."

Eddie had finished his drink, dropped his jacket on the ground and put his hands back on David's shoulders. Torchlight had played on Eddie's sweating face. Had he been feverish, or had it been the liquor and the lingering summer heat? Had David imagined something in his stare? Eddie's fingers had dug in, forcing David to concentrate on him. Eddie had said, "Naomi's going to have you the rest of your life. Give me this last week. Like old times."

David had known he would go with Eddie, but had needed to say something else, something he could use to defend himself later. "Naomi will feel hurt. Besides, I don't have the money for plane fare or anything else."

Eddie had known the rules of this game. "I've got some loose change burning a hole in my pocket. If I don't spend it on this trip, I'll spend it on something worse."

David had felt Naomi's presence, the questions she would hurl at him. "Eddie, is this your money? I didn't think you made that kind of dough. Is Sol behind this?"

The knocking on David's office door grew louder, more insistent.

"Who's there?" he asked.

"Catherine Marie. May I come in?" she was opening the door as she spoke. "Mr. Greenburg, its Mr. Luntz. He says it's urgent. He's on line two."

David picked up the receiver and pressed down the button.

"David," Sol said, "Ruth and I are at your house. Liz called us. Naomi is hysterical. You better come now." There was a click and the line went dead.

Chapter Five
Dr. Flynn

After David's middle of the night visit to Eddie I cried all the time. Liz could not get me to stop. She telephoned Mommy and Daddy, and they called David.

Mommy cradled me as we sat on the sofa. I kept slipping deeper into her arms. She held my head next to her breast, well protected by her stiff bra and tweed jacket, as though we were both waiting for me to suckle.

Daddy marched back and forth. "Princess," he asked, "just tell us what has you so upset."

I didn't answer. It wasn't safe to talk about last night.

"David," Daddy said, "she's your wife. You must know what's going on."

He does know, I thought. David wouldn't look at me.

He said, "Sol, I wish I did."

I glared at David.

Mommy propped me up and said, "Naomi, I'd like to speak with you alone." Standing up, she put her hand under my elbow and walked me to the kitchen. With Liz there, it felt crowded. Liz handed me a glass of water and walked out.

Mommy said, "Take a swallow. Not big. It will help stop the sobbing. Slowly." I did, and the contractions in my throat eased. Mommy waited while I sipped again, and then said, "Can you talk now?"

I nodded.

Mommy told me, "Say anything. Let yourself hear that you can. That you're in control."

"Thank you," I said. "It's better."

"Naomi, can you tell me what's going on?"

Mommy was my height, but weighed half as much. I wasn't aware that I was pinching my batwing. Mommy's hand covered my thumb and finger and stopped me. Minutes passed. I looked at her and shook my head from side to side.

She said, "If you can't talk with me, we need to find somebody you can."

After Mommy and Daddy left, David went back to work. Liz made me a cup of hot chocolate. She held her mouth close to the rim and blew on the rising steam. After handing it to me, she said, "Hain't your friend Rachel become one of those head doctors?"

"I can't do this with her," I said, "it would feel too uncomfortable. Daddy would ask her about me all the time."

"I ain't thinking she should be the one. Rachel must know a good 'un. That's what I'm sayin'."

Rachel recommended a Dr. Flynn, and talked to him before I called. An appointment was set for Thursday, five days after David's visit to Blueberry Hill.

Flynn's office was in his house in Chestnut Hill, a forty minute drive. I allowed myself an hour. I was distracted guessing what we would talk about and made two wrong turns. Even so, I was in his waiting room ten minutes early.

Two chairs sat behind a coffee table covered with copies of *The New Yorker,* some in a pile, others strewn about. I was thumbing through a December issue and stopped at a cartoon of Santa Claus in his flying sled. One reindeer commented, "For a sweet old man he's quick to use his whip." The corner of the page was bent down, a message from a patient. I smiled, and then thought I couldn't tolerate anyone else getting angry at me. I took the check I had made out at home, put it on the table, and stood up to leave.

The door between the waiting room and the office opened. A man just over five feet, slightly built, was staring at me. The olive-gray suit looked professorial. Tortoise-shell glasses reinforced the academic look. Rachel had told me Dr. Flynn was thirty-two; nonetheless I was startled that he was clearly younger than me.

He motioned for me and walked into his office. I grabbed my check off the table and stuffed it into my pocket.

Standing in front of a black leather chair, he gestured for me to sit in a matching chair. It felt too close. I moved my chair back and sat down, putting my pocketbook by my foot where I would remember to take it when I left.

"I am pleased to meet you," he said. "Rachel Cohen speaks highly of you. Tell me what brings you here."

I thought he would say something about my keeping my coat on, but he appeared not to notice. I started blubbering and felt like a fool. A Chinese garden seat to my right held a box of Kleenex. Grabbing a fistful, I held them to my eyes. When I lowered the moist wad, I found he was looking at me, nodding.

I pointed to the garden seat and said, "That's a fine example. Are you a collector?"

Dr. Flynn moved his head from side to side, and remained mute.

I looked around the room. He had some first-rate Oriental rugs. The one between us was a faded maroon Bokara. I was pretty sure he would not respond to a verbal inventory of his office.

I said, "I guess you're waiting for me to tell you about my mother and father. And my childhood."

Leaning forward, he asked, "Is that what has you upset?"

I stared down at my shoes and began to tap one foot. Without looking up, I said, "No, it's my husband. He's acting strangely. At least, I think it's not normal. Maybe it is and I'm the problem. I'm not very worldly. I know men have—have appetites."

I refused to raise my head, afraid that I would find Dr. Flynn shaking his head in disbelief at my naïveté.

I expected to hear sympathy and a trace of condescension, but the latter wasn't there. "Would you prefer to be called Mrs. Greenberg or Naomi?"

"Naomi."

"Naomi, let's talk for a moment about some of the rules of therapy," he said. "The privacy you can count on. Even if you've heard some of this from Rachel or others, it's important that you hear it from me."

Dr. Flynn waited, and I raised my head. He smiled and said, "Good. Everything you tell me is just between us. If anyone, your husband or your parents, were to ask me what's happening in our sessions, I would not tell them."

As he talked, the smile faded, replaced by a firm set to his mouth. I thought he was girding himself for a call from Daddy.

He went on. "I am not here to sit in judgment."

I arched an eyebrow, silently challenging the good doctor.

"Naomi, this is very important," he said. "I cannot do my job, I cannot help people, if I'm judgmental. It stands in the way of my understanding them, of helping them to understand themselves. I know it was hard for you to call me. It was hard for you to come here today."

I expected him to keep talking, but he stopped. I couldn't speak while I looked at Dr. Flynn. When I did I concentrated so hard on his reaction, on whether he approved or thought me a fool, I lost the thread of what I was trying to say. So I lowered my head and talked to the floor.

"Last night my husband made love to me. No, that's not right. It was ugly. There was no caring in it. He was angry. It hurt." I paused, and then, almost in a whisper, "I mean physically as well."

I felt so ashamed, telling this stranger about David. I picked up my pocketbook and rose hurriedly from the chair. My hand was on the doorknob when Dr. Flynn said, "Naomi, if you decide you want to see me, call. I'm here."

Chapter Six
Julie Rabelli

Four men were in the office. Rabelli was the only one sitting. A gray sport jacket hung on the back of his chair. Rabelli looked at the three men standing around his desk. Terry Synge was dressed like he had just come from a college class, a blue striped shirt with a maroon knit tie.

"Let's hear it," Rabelli said.

"I'm wearing the druggist's white coat when the guy comes in," Synge said. "He looks at the sleeves and sees they're way too short. So he asks, 'Where's the owner?' I'm thinking the guy's got smarts, and he's about to leave, so I say the linen service gave me the wrong coat, and how can I help him. He gives me a prescription and asks if he can wait for it. Like he's still checking me out. I tell him it'll take a few minutes, and go back and hand it to the owner. He's heard everything and starts to put it together. While he's doing that I ask if he's ever seen the guy before. The owner peeks out, tells me he's never been in, but fits the description the liquor store owner gave him."

Rabelli's fingers did a drum roll on the desk.

"Terry, get to it."

"Yeah, right," Synge says. "We chew the fat, and the guy asks have I ever watched *Varsity Dance?*"

Rabelli saw that Synge was into it like he was a movie star. "Terry, I'm sure you and the D.A. will whip up an affidavit Judge Schultz will love," Rabelli said. "Cut it short."

"Okay, okay," Synge said, "keep your pants on."

Everyone laughed. Terry resumed, "So the guy says, 'You got a TV in back?' and I'm praying the owner is listening, and getting out of sight."

Rabelli held his hands out and opened his eyes wide. "Terry, let me guess. You turned on the tube and there's *Varsity Dance?*"

This time Rabelli got the laugh.

"Right, right, Julie. Why you getting pissy with me? Anyway, the guy says watch for the tall blonde with the big tits. You see her? Name's Marie. And he opens this briefcase. Did I mention the briefcase?"

Rabelli rolled his eyes. "No, but you and the D.A. will get that into your affidavit."

"Right," Synge said, "right. So he takes out this big photo album."

Synge took the album from behind his back, slapped it onto Rabelli's desk, and opened it. There were black-and-white photos on both pages. On the left was a teenager with a ponytail, wearing a short-sleeve white shirt buttoned up to the neck and a plaid skirt. A thin chain with a delicate crucifix hung around her neck. One eye faced the camera; the other did not. On the opposite page the same girl was naked to the waist, holding up large breasts in her hands, the cross hidden in her cleavage.

Rabelli turned the pages, his face becoming the color of blood spilled on mud. As he studied each photo, veins corded on his neck. "Synge," Rabelli asked, "you recognize any of these plaid skirts?"

"I asked around," Synge answered, "some are from Saint Agnes. The rest no one knew."

Rabelli's voice came from a grave, "Saint Agnes is the school my daughters and niece go to."

Synge's left eye flickered.

Rabelli said, "They're not here."

The posturing had seeped out of Synge's body. "I'm sorry. I had no idea your girls went there."

Rabelli's slamming of the album sounded like a pistol shot. "Synge, where's the guy?"

"He's in a holding cell," he answered.

"D.A. been called?" Rabelli asked.

"Yeah," Synge replied, "said he'd get someone there in an hour."

Rabelli smiled.

"Good. Synge, come with me. Let's see what that bastard can tell us about *Varsity Dance*. Johnson, you and Tate cover over the nude photos. Then go to Saint Agnes and get the names of the girls in the book. Get their addresses. Tell the sisters to keep it to themselves. Make up a story."

Rabelli stood, loosened his tie, slipped the noose off his neck and laid it across the gray jacket.

Synge rubbed his left eye; the twitching continued. Johnson and Tate stared at the floor. Sound had been sucked out of the room. Rabelli's breathing grew heavier. He marched to the door and flung it open. Tate caught it before it hit the wall. As he followed Rabelli, the back of Synge's neck glistened yellow from the overhead fluorescent light.

Tate watched Rabelli and Synge grow smaller and then turn the corner. He looked over to Johnson, who nodded. "Better call the D.A.," Johnson said.

Tate picked up the black receiver, put his finger into a hole on the circular dial, and moved it around. "Ever notice how a telephone dial looks like the bullet chamber in a handgun?" Tate asked.

"Anybody ever tell you you're crazy?" Johnson shot back.

Tate turned away, and said, "Hi, this is Ned Tate, over at Vice. I need to speak to the D.A.—No, this can't wait. Look, where's the regular girl? Put the phone down, walk over to Sue, and put her on. Move it, this won't wait. I promise if you don't get Sue on in the next thirty seconds, you can kiss your job goodbye."

Tate's fingers tapped on the desk. "Sue, this is Ned. We got a Rabelli problem," Tate scowled. "No, I don't want to tell you. I want you to walk into his office and get him on the horn now. Thanks."

Tate broke into a smile, the salesman seeping into his voice. "Hi, sorry to break in—yeah, it's that important. The guy Synge picked up peddling ass from *Varsity Dance*—yeah, I know, but we ain't got an hour. The hookers in the book—yeah, he had a book of photos he was selling from—tit shots—some of the girls are from Saint Agnes. Rabelli's kids go there. He just left with Synge to do some questioning— the guy's in a cell by himself—yeah, the one Rabelli uses for 'interrogation.'"

The holding cell was ten by ten. Three grimy cinder block walls were covered with scrawled messages: "for the best lawyer call Manny Black, DE7-1267"; "call Honey for a good time, DE8-6969." Steel bars formed the fourth side of the room.

Synge said to the man in the cell, "Nice to see you again. This is Lieutenant Rabelli. He has some questions for you."

"I got nothing to say."

Rabelli's voice was flat. "I'm going to ask questions, and you're going to answer."

The man was two inches taller than Rabelli. His six-foot frame was clothed in a dark brown suit and a white shirt like a two-hundred pound fudge sundae drizzled with marshmallow. The police had taken his tie, belt, and shoelaces. He backed away from Rabelli, feet sliding in and out of his untied brogues.

Rabelli began, "What's your name?"

"Johnny Furtado."

"Johnny, it sickens me you're Italian. How does it work?"

Furtado's face became a question mark. "How does what work?"

In a matter-of-fact voice Rabelli said, "Give Detective Synge your suit jacket."

Furtado began to shrug off the jacket. Synge grabbed it and pulled down hard trapping his arms behind him. Then he angled Furtado's side toward the Lieutenant. Rabelli's fist slammed into his kidney. A puddle spread across Furtado's crotch.

Rabelli said in a patient voice, "Johnny, stop screaming. You won't hear my questions. If you keep yelling, I'll have to keep hitting. Before long your insides will be gravy. *Capiche?* Just nod. Breathe normal. It won't stop hurting, but it'll remind you of the rules. I ask and you answer. Blink if you get it Johnny—good. Ok, let me break it down. Who tells you what to do?"

"Some guy."

"What's his name?" Rabelli asked.

Furtado shook his head from side to side.

"Johnny, look at you. Blubbering like a baby. I hate to see Italians like you." Rabelli's fist caught Furtado in the chest, just over his heart. "Johnny, don't force your breathing," Rabelli said. "It makes it worse. God, your lips are turning blue. Terry, help him breathe again."

Synge spread his hands under Furtado's rib cage and pulled lightly, released, and pulled again.

Rabelli put his thumb, thick as a carrot, on the white shirt. Furtado winced.

"Johnny, if I push, it'll hurt like hell. You'll piss in your pants again, maybe shit. Your nose will be full of your own stink. I'm asking again. What's the name of the guy giving the orders?"

"Vince, his name is Vince. I don't have a last name."

Rabelli nodded. "We'll come back to that. Do you know Eddie Greene?"

"The guy on TV?" Furtado smirked.

Rabelli's open hand shot out. Furtado's mouth and eyes popped. He shrieked, "Oh, shit! Why'd you do that? I'm answering."

Rabelli tapped his finger against Furtado as he spoke. "Johnny, I hate guys who give me lip, especially Italian guys who give us a black eye. I want to know if Greene is part of the group."

Furtado's tongue licked the mucous off his upper lip. He replied, "Greene's never talked to me. I've seen Vince and him talk."

"What about?" Rabelli asked.

"They always talk away from me."

Rabelli's hand grabbed Furtado by the throat.

"Johnny, listen to me. You can't breathe. I'm going to squeeze your life in my hand. Then when I let go, and you get some air, you're going to tell me everything you know. I won't ask another question, and you'll be scared to stop talking." Rabelli's hand grew white as he tightened his hold on Furtado.

"Hear the pounding in your ears?" Rabelli said. "Feel the pressure on your forehead? Your heart's beating like a rabbit. The thing is, I could make a mistake here, choke you too long. Happened once. Autopsy showed the guy had a stroke. You don't want to die, Johnny. I'm going to let go now."

Furtado slumped in Synge's arms. Synge whispered, "Christ almighty, you killed him."

Rabelli put his ear next to Furtado's mouth.

"There's a little whistle. He'll live. This time. Johnny, shake your head when you can talk. Don't make me do this again."

The skin on Furtado's neck fluttered.

"Take your time, Johnny," Rabelli said. "I want you to talk slow and loud. Terry, go and get a steno for Johnny's statement."

Furtado whispered, "Don't—"

Rabelli leaned close to Furtado, who looked toward Synge. "You. I want . . ."

"Terry, he wants to say something to you." Synge lowered him into a straight chair and came around in front, blocking Rabelli from Furtado's sight. His voice was inaudible, but Synge read his lips.

"Don't leave me." Furtado's tongue flicked out and back.

"Lieutenant, Furtado here is going to have a heart attack if I leave."

"I won't touch him until you get back," Rabelli said. "He understands the rules."

Synge hesitated and then said, "What about you walk with me outside the cell and wait until I get back? Furtado won't forget you're here. Give him a chance to put his thoughts together."

Synge was walking back to the cell. Next to him was a white-haired woman in a gray skirt that went to mid-calf. Her green cardigan was buttoned up to the neck. Synge stopped and put his hand on her elbow; her steno pad was shaking.

"Mrs. Kelly, are you going to be okay?" Synge asked.

"Yes, I'm fine," she said. Her head kept bobbing up and down after she stopped talking, jiggling the loose flesh on her cheeks.

"The stories about Lieutenant Rabelli . . ." Synge said.

"I'm fine," she repeated. "You'll have a transcript of everything that Mr. . . . Mr. . . ."

"Furtado," Synge offered.

" . . . Furtado says." The sound of Mrs. Kelly's sensible shoes echoed off the cement floor.

Furtado looked up, a street dog waiting for the next kick.

Synge said, "Lieutenant, this is Mrs. Kelly."

Rabelli nodded, opened the cell door and followed them in. Facing Mrs. Kelly, with his back to the prisoner, he said, "Mr. Furtado was arrested today by Detective Synge. He has decided to make a statement. This decision was voluntary. Mr. Furtado, do you agree with what I just said?"

"Yes."

Rabelli turned around and put his hand on Furtado's shoulder. Furtado flinched, moving the chair away in frantic mouse steps.

"Take it easy," Rabelli said. "Mrs. Kelly needs to sit while she takes down what you tell her."

"It's not necessary," she said, and took a step back.

Furtado recited his name, address, age, and told about showing Synge the book of photographs.

Rabelli asked, "What did you say about the girls in the photographs?"

"That they would perform sexual acts for a fee," Furtado said.

"What else?" Rabelli asked.

"That these girls could be seen on *Varsity Dance*."

Rabelli smiled at Furtado, a teacher pleased with a prize student.

"Do these girls attend high school?" Rabelli asked.

"That's my understanding," Furtado said.

"Who told you that?"

"On the show," Furtado replied. "It's said on the show."

Rabelli frowned. "Who says it?"

Furtado's face pleaded with Synge and Mrs. Kelly, but they looked away. He turned back to Rabelli. "Eddie Greene. He says it during the show."

The cell door opened and a man in his late twenties walked in. He was five feet tall, in a navy vested suit, white shirt, and red striped tie. A freckled moon face was topped by hair the color of a blood orange. In the D.A.'s office he was called Howdy Doody. His mother had trained him to grin in the belief it minimized his harelip. He held his hand out and said, "Lieutenant Rabelli, I'm John Sullivan."

"You don't look like a heavyweight champ." Rabelli looked at the hand, but didn't extend his.

Sullivan forced a bored grin and turned to the man in the chair. "Mr. Furtado, I'm an Assistant District Attorney."

Sullivan lifted Furtado's chin and looked at the outline of fingers on his throat.

"How'd you get those bruises?" Sullivan asked.

Rabelli stepped in front of Sullivan and kept on moving, bellying him away from the prisoner. Sullivan slipped to the side. "Lieutenant, what the hell's going on?"

Rabelli spoke loud and slow to Sullivan, as though giving street directions to a man with no understanding of the English language. "Let me do my job. Why don't you go back to your office? I hear the paperwork's drowning you guys."

Sullivan circled Rabelli and kneeled down, looking at Furtado's face. As he stood up, he said, "Let me talk to both of you outside."

Synge took a step toward the cell door. Rabelli did not move.

"Terry," Rabelli said, "you talk to the champ. I'm going to help Mrs. Kelly get the rest of Furtado's statement."

Sullivan's voice rose, "Lieutenant, you need to hear me now!"

"You've got nothing to say to me," Rabelli boomed.

Sullivan walked over, stood on tiptoes, and spoke into Rabelli's ear, "We got a call from Morris Cohen just before I left the office. Said he was on the way and bringing a photographer. Made a point of saying any statement beaten out of Furtado wasn't worth spit."

Rabelli's neck darkened. "Damned *shyster* lawyer. Whose side you on, Sully, the good guys or the kikes?"

"I'm on yours," he said. "You've got an ironclad case. Synge is great on the stand. I understand there's a book of photos. Don't blow it."

"Who cares about Furtado?" Rabelli said. "Its Greene we want. Terry, walk Mr. Sullivan back to his office."

Rabelli turned around.

"Mr. Furtado, you mentioned Eddie Greene, the guy on *Varsity Dance*. Mr. Greene has a place in Jersey called Blueberry Hill. Is that where these underage girls perform sex for money?"

"I'm not saying anything," Furtado said, "until I talk to my lawyer."

Rabelli grabbed Furtado by the hair and yanked him out of the chair.

"You'll answer my questions now!" Rabelli said, loud enough to be heard over Furtado's screams.

Sullivan yelled, "Lieutenant, it's over. Get out of here, now!"

Rabelli released Furtado, who fell back into the chair. Spinning around, he grabbed the lapels of Sullivan's suit in both hands and ran at the wall. Sullivan took a deep breath, raised his head, and looked at Rabelli. One side of the lieutenant's lip was raised exposing grayish yellow teeth.

Synge was behind Rabelli wrapping his arms around him. Rabelli's elbow snapped back. Synge dropped like a doll thrown on the floor. Mrs.

Kelly scuttled to the cell door, opened it, looked at her empty hands, and then at the steno pad on the cement floor. She ran down the hall.

Rabelli glared at Sullivan. "Damn you!" Rabelli lifted him again and butted his forehead against the harelip. For a moment Sullivan's mouth was colorless; then bright red spurted on Rabelli's face, on Sullivan's lips and chin. Rabelli's fingers opened. Sullivan slid down the wall until he sat on the gray cement floor, his back against the wall.

Chapter Seven
Pyramid

Bloomie walked at a pace David had trouble keeping up with. They were on their way to see Jay Karp, the president of Pyramid Communications, which owned *Varsity Dance.* Bloomie stopped and turned. "David?"

"I'm right here," he said. Cars on Chestnut Street accelerated, honked, braked. David feared Bloomie was lost in his monologue, but he didn't step into traffic.

Bloomie continued. "I reminded Jay that you and Eddie were cousins. He insisted that you come. Asked me where your loyalties were. I told him with the firm, and that meant Pyramid."

Bloomie stopped talking. At five foot six he was shorter than David, and thinner. Maybe it came from some part of him always moving. If he was in a chair, his right leg bounced up and down; if he sat for ten minutes, he got up and paced. David saw the top of his bald head a lot, as everyone did, for Bloomie always stared down, as though he saw a kaleidoscope on the toe of his shoe. Before starting his day Bloomie swam a mile. David's theory was that he needed to burn off enough physical energy to concentrate. Golf was barely tolerated; Bloomie reluctantly went if it was a business necessity. Because he was rarely out-of-doors his skin was pale, and his watery blue eyes faded against this whiteness.

It was eleven in the morning. The brightness of the winter sun hurt. David had just entered the office, back from what he considered the burden of Naomi's hysteria, when Bloomie had said to come with him. In David's view he was carrying Naomi's emotional weight and Eddie's. How did they do that, shift it to him? To David each one in his or her own way was Willie Loman lifting a sample case filled with a life they couldn't sell to anyone or buy themselves. David chafed as he opened each bag to look in.

The walk from the law firm's building to Pyramid's offices was seven blocks. Waiting for the light to change, Bloomie said, "Loyalty and smarts. That's what Jay wants from us. You're sure you're okay with that?"

David nodded.

Bloomie returned to alternating between watching the traffic signal and being lost in the light racing up and down his shoe cap.

Bloomie didn't talk much about the past. From the corporate work David did for Pyramid he knew Bloomie and Morris Chumsky went way back with Pyramid. He had also seen Sol's name, along with a few others, on shareholder lists.

A few years ago Naomi and David had been at her parents' for Thanksgiving. Spurred on by the need for an artificially joyous holiday, David had opened both bottles of wine they had brought. Sol had enjoyed the chardonnay, but not the wooziness, so he and David had gone for a walk before dessert.

Sol had placed an arm on David's shoulder to steady himself and had asked, "You work on the Pyramid accounts, right?"

"More and more," he had replied.

Waving his other arm, Sol had said, "It's become very large. Bigger than I ever imagined. So, you know we have money in it."

"I know all the investors," David had said. "Bloomie and I do. Others work on the account, but the list of shareholders is kept in a safe in Bloomie's office."

"Why is that?" Sol had asked.

David had been surprised. "You don't know?"

Sol's eyes had focused. David wondered whether the slurred speech at dinner had been a ruse. "Maybe," he had replied. "Why do you think?"

"This is just between us? I'm sorry. I shouldn't have said that." David could have kicked himself, but he had kept on talking. "Because Morris Chumsky's name is on the list."

Sol had pulled him closer. When Naomi had told Ruth that they couldn't have kids, Sol had distanced himself. The physical closeness had felt good. Maybe Sol had forgiven him.

Sol had then said, "Years back, things were hard. To make something of yourself—well, you had to be tough. Do whatever had to be done. Some stuff got into the papers. You don't want Chumsky's name connected, you know, to remind people."

They had walked two blocks and had reached a bus stop. Sol had pointed to the green bench and said, "David, sit. This will only take a few minutes. The cold air feels good."

Sol had buttoned his heavy cardigan all the way up. Clapping his hands together, he had leaned closer. "Where was I? Oh, yeah. Manny Karpinsky had come to this country as a child and dropped out of school in his teens to be a numbers runner for 'Fat Tony' Porchetti. By the time he was eighteen, Manny had a dozen kids running numbers for him and $50,000, a fortune in 1912. He was at a restaurant when Fat Tony was gunned down coming through the door. On the spot Manny decided to go legit. David, you know this already, right?"

David had shaken his head. "No. No one talks about any of this, if anyone knows."

Sol had leaned back. "By the time Manny's son Jay came into the business in the forties, Pyramid owned a radio station in Philly and a newspaper in Jersey. Jay had shortened the family name to Karp. Like he's a fish, not a Jew." Sol had laughed at his joke and had looked to see if David had grinned. Satisfied that he got it, Sol had picked up the thread of his story. "Teamsters tried to organize the drivers for the paper, beating up anyone who wouldn't sign on. Manny and Jay met with Chumsky, who agreed to bust the union in return for a piece of Pyramid."

David had never known how Chumsky had become a shareholder. He had felt himself smile.

Sol had said, "Remember this is between you and me. Family. *Vershtay?* So a street war broke out and the union was voted down. Chumsky did what he had promised. Some time passes. Then a well-insured warehouse, owned by Pyramid, burned down. During the investigation the teamsters produce a witness who said he was present when Jay paid a man to torch the warehouse. Jay was convicted. Am I going too fast? You still with me?"

Sol had known he had him. "I never knew what the connection was between the Karps and Chumsky," David had said. "I'd heard rumors of Chumsky being a union buster. Nothing about Pyramid."

David had started to get up. Sol had put his hand on David's shoulder and said, "Hold on. Don't you want to hear the rest? About Bloomie and Jay Karp?"

Sol had leaned in close again. "That's when Bloomie came into the picture. Old man Cardozo was the smartest trial attorney in the city, and Bloomie was his right hand man. They were hired to get Jay out of prison. Bloomie got the names of the jurors, and began interviewing them. He obtained sworn statements from two that they had received anonymous threats against their families if Jay was not convicted."

Sol had paused to let this sink in. Then he had gone on. "Old Man Karpinsky wanted to go for a new trial. Bloomie had noticed brand new cars outside the homes of the two who had given him the affidavits, in a neighborhood filled with junkers. When he brought this up, the Old Man's only comment was, 'Damn fools!' Bloomie was sent to the prison to speak with Jay, who agreed to have the statements used to cut down his sentence to time served. Since then Jay Karp has never made a decision that wasn't cleared through Bloomie."

Bloomie's voice broke into David's reverie. "David, you've been quiet. I won't ask you what you've been thinking about." David did not remember walking into the Pyramid building or getting into the elevator marked "Private." A light on the wall went off, "PH," and David followed Bloomie onto navy carpet so thick he thought he would lose his balance.

They were ushered into Jay's office, a triangle formed by two floor-to-ceiling windows joined at a right angle. The hypotenuse was a rosewood wall with the door they had walked through. David was struck that Jay could look out on Philadelphia with a clear view of Billy Penn atop City Hall, but nobody that worked for Jay could see into his space.

The man behind the desk was forty years old, five foot six, same as Bloomie, and must have weighed three hundred pounds. His custom-made suit made his body appear powerful. But Jay's face told it all. His cheeks burst like ripe peaches, and his eyes were sunk in pastry pockets of flesh. He was a mean fat kid living in an adult body.

His desk appeared eight feet wide. Jay came around to the front in a graceful movement. He shook Bloomie's hand and then David's, saying, "It's good to see you again. Bloomie speaks highly of you. You did good work with the licensing agreement. This is a little different. More important. Involves your cousin." Pausing, lids lowered until David couldn't see his eyes, pouring all his energy into a command, he said, "Tell me now if there's a problem."

David's lips were dry, stuck together. He felt the sting of torn skin as he opened his mouth to speak. "Look, I'll be frank. Eddie and I are close. We're different. He gets in trouble once in a while. Sometimes he looks for me to bail him out. If I can, I do. He's family."

Jay had not let go of his hand. "David, none of us knows what's going to happen tomorrow. If we can work it out to help both Eddie and me, that's how it will go. I'm hoping that Eddie will see it that way. If you're in, the odds are better that Eddie will be with us."

Jay's tone grew harsh. "But I have to know that if he tries to hurt me, poses a threat to the business, you're on my side." Jay's other hand sandwiched David's in the middle. Jay's eyes opened, cat's eyes watching the bleeding mouse.

"I'll do everything I can to make it work out for everyone," David told him.

Jay's hands dwarfed David's. They were as dry as a baker's who worked all day with flour. They held his attention; made David look at his face, at his thick wet lips, at his eyes watching him, reading him.

"That's not good enough, David," he said. "Once you're in, you're in. Right, Bloomie?"

Bloomie's head bounced as he said, "David understands."

Jay had not released my hand. "I want to hear it from David."

"You're my client, not Eddie," David told him.

Jay's hands opened. David took out his handkerchief and patted his mouth. When he looked down there were two spots of blood on the white cotton. David folded it over, and put it back in his hip pocket.

Jay took a step back, and spoke to both Bloomie and David. "We have a problem. Eddie is running a string of teenage hookers using *Varsity Dance* as a movie trailer. Cops busted one of Eddie's people, with a book of photos."

"What's at stake?" Bloomie asked.

Jay replied, watching David. "Worst case? The whole shooting match. Story comes out, *Varsity Dance* folds."

Jay took off his jacket and put it on a wooden valet. His dress shirt glowed like a white sheet flapping on a clothesline. He extended his arm toward Bloomie. David saw a blue monogram on his French cuff.

"We're in the middle of negotiations to go national. Right, Bloomie?" As Jay spoke he continued reading David's face, like he was talking to Eddie, making sure Eddie was getting it. "The TV station is the future. Bigger than newspapers, bigger than radio."

Bloomie tried to step between Jay and me. "Let's move Eddie out. Get a new face for *Varsity Dance*, a Mr. Clean," Bloomie said. "You know, a Pat Boone. If we keep playing rock 'n' roll, all that colored music, we'll keep the kids. Pat Boone will keep the advertisers."

Jay walked behind his desk. With his back toward them, he said, "I have someone working on that. If we can keep the lid on this until a new guy's in place, fine."

Bloomie looked up. "What's the problem?"

Jay lowered himself into a wine-colored leather chair, releasing a sigh from the cushion. His right hand knotted into a fist. "Julie Rabelli!"

Bloomie's face didn't react.

Jay said, "Name doesn't register? He's head of Vice."

"Call in your markers," Bloomie said.

Jay's head swiveled as he spoke, sometimes watching Bloomie, sometimes David. "Reason I know we got a problem is I got a call. Rabelli's a nut case. He was in seminary and dropped out. Priest with a billy club. Cops picked up one of the guys showing photos of these girls—one shot of them on TV, one with their tits hanging out. When Rabelli sees the pictures he figures out some of the girls go to St. Agnes, where his daughters and niece go."

"Shit!"

David wasn't used to Bloomie using street language. Both Jay and Bloomie were watching David to see what he already knew.

Jay went on, "Right. So Rabelli uses the guy as a punching bag, trying to get him to say he works for Eddie."

Bloomie looked up from his shoes. "So he hasn't given up Eddie?"

"Not yet," Jay said. "Assistant D.A. walked in and tried to stop it. Rabelli busts him up."

Bloomie's jaw dropped. "He attacked an assistant?"

Jay's hands rested on his stomach, fingers laced together, and said, "Rabelli's out of control."

Bloomie walked in a tight circle, and looked up at Jay. "Why don't the cops get rid of him?"

"Rabelli's got lots of support," Jay said. "Italian community. Neighborhood priests and nuns. If the cops go after him, he'll scream they're on the take." Jay stopped. His voice lowered to a whisper, "We've got to do the job."

Bloomie frowned. "Don't. This is out of your league. I don't care what's at stake."

Jay stood up behind the desk. Since the conversation had shifted away from David, Jay could not stay in one place for more than a minute. His head bent over from an unseen weight.

When it came back up, Jay looked at Bloomie and said, "I know that. I've set up a meeting with Chumsky tonight. Seven. At his office. I told him you were coming."

"Why?" Bloomie asked, irritated.

"I want another set of eyes and ears," Jay said.

Bloomie shook his head from side to side. "I can't. This isn't a meeting I can be at."

"How much do you bill Pyramid?" Jay asked. A nerve twitched on Bloomie's forehead.

Jay's hands patted down the air in front of him. "Okay, okay. Relax. There will be others. Lee Steinhardt . . ."

"Steinhardt?" Bloomie's eyes widened.

"Is he blueblood enough for you? You know he owns ten percent of Pyramid. Hell, you reviewed the original papers for Old Man Cardozo. Chumsky insists that the major players be there. Oh David, your father-in-law will also be at the meeting."

Jay's head turned away from Bloomie and faced David, his voice loud. "Did you know what Eddie was doing?"

"Not really," David said.

Bloomie arched an eyebrow. Jay scowled and said, "What does that mean?"

"Eddie called me," he said, "in the middle of the night. Really scared. Gave me directions to Blueberry Hill."

Bloomie asked where Blueberry Hill was, and David told him. Jay filled in that it was the place in Jersey where johns met up with the girls. Both Jay and Bloomie were focused on David, and Jay told him to continue.

"Eddie said he was terrified of Rabelli. He told me to tell you what was going on, that his interests and yours were the same."

Jay nodded. Bloomie cleared his throat, opened his mouth to speak, stopped, and looked down at his shoes.

"You can still walk away," Bloomie said to David.

Jay's face grew pink. His eyes narrowed, but Bloomie held his stare and said, "Tell him, Jay."

"David, you can leave now," Jay said. "If you hear from Eddie, tell him you're out of it—he'll need to speak with me or someone I tell him to talk to."

David used his tongue to moisten his lips. "He'll panic," he said. "He's not good under pressure. He's really a kid who looks like a man. I'm the only one he'll listen to."

Jay nodded. "I think that's right."

Bloomie broke in. "David, go back to the office. Tell the girls to find you if Eddie calls. When you talk with him, find out where to reach him tonight and tomorrow. If you don't hear from him by one, call him. Whatever you learn, tell me. Everything. I'll be the judge of its importance."

Jay interrupted, "Keep him away from the studio. We'll make an announcement that he's sick. Lots of flu going round."

It was clear that Jay and Bloomie would only tell David as much as served their purposes. It wasn't just that he was on a short leash; he was also blindfolded. As he let himself out, they were huddled together. Their voices were too low for David to follow, except when Jay raised his, "You're right. David has a future at the firm."

He knew he was meant to hear that. David knew he had just sold out Eddie. He had sold himself as well.

Chapter Eight
Julie, Sophia, and Eddie

"Lieutenant, it's the Captain," her voice quavered.

"I'm not here." Rabelli walked over to the woman holding the phone. His hand shot out. She winced and closed her eyes. When the moment passed, and there was no physical contact, she opened one eye, leaning away from the Lieutenant. His finger, white at the tip, pressed down on the phone cradle.

She was sniffling; her words came out faintly with long pauses.

"Speak up, Mrs. Wolf," he said, "I can't hear you."

"The Captain said—he was in the District Attorney's office—he said you were to come right over."

"Mrs. Wolf," Rabelli said, "go to another office and call them back. Tell them you can't find me."

She held an embroidered handkerchief to her nose. It covered most of Mrs. Wolf's face. Her words were muffled.

"Damn it," he said. "Move that doily away from your mouth or talk louder. I can't make out what you're saying."

"I—I told them you were here," she said.

"Get out," he said. "Now!" Rabelli turned around. A tape recorder the size of a loose-leaf notebook sat on his desk. The man standing next to it had a red-veined nose, bluish purple at the tip. Sour smells of dried Thunderbird and vomit came out in waves as he spoke.

"Lieutenant, you okay?"

"What's with the concern for me?" Rabelli asked. "Oh, I get it. Don't worry Jimmy, I'll protect you. So, what've we got here?"

Jimmy rocked from side to side. "I did like you said. Went to that apartment. Who lives there?"

"You don't need to know," Rabelli said.

"Anyway, the guy's a slob. Expensive place. Doorman. Had to get a Philly Electric uniform to get in." Jimmy grinned. "Reddy Kilowatt. Cost me ten bucks."

One of Jimmy's hands did a pantomime of counting out bills.

"I'll cover it," Rabelli said. "Tell me where you put it."

"Under the bed. There was so much dust, dirty socks, even mouse shit." Jimmy pinched his nose. "And dark, real dark. Even if someone lifted the sides of the sheets, he wouldn't see it unless he moved the bed."

Rabelli prompted, "Go on."

"So I left, went to the garage entrance and waited, like you said. The guy in the photo shows up. Early afternoon. I swear I know him, but I'm having trouble remembering. You know how it is, Lieutenant. If you've been on the hooch since you was eight—well, your brain is fried."

The man talking to Rabelli had snow white hair and no teeth. His eyes were like smashed blue marbles, white threads appearing where the glass had shattered. Rabelli reminded himself that the man was only thirty-three and a step away from the morgue.

"It's better you don't know who he is," Rabelli said. "If it comes to you, forget it."

"I getcha," Jimmy said. "Anyway, he pulls up in this Caddie convertible. Robin's-egg-blue. Like the one the Phillies gave Robin Roberts."

"Damn it," Rabelli spit out.

"Okay, okay. Jes' wanted to show you I remember lots," Jimmy whimpered. "Anyway, guy gets out, and this looker gets out on the passenger side."

"Describe her," Rabelli said.

"Dark hair. Maybe five three. I think young, but she could pass. Terrific figure. What a set." Jimmy cupped his hands in front of his chest. "They talk and get back in the car. He drives in."

Rabelli knew the man couldn't go for more than a minute without being prompted, like a broken electric razor that needed constant recharging. "How long were they up there?" Rabelli asked.

"Long time. I had to pee bad." Jimmy held his crotch and bounced on his feet, grinning. "Held off as long as I could. I was scared I'd miss seeing them leave—scared you'd be angry."

He had stepped back from Rabelli. Jimmy whined, "Then I was thirsty. Got the shakes. I don't know how long I was in the liquor store, but I was back when they walked out. You're not mad, are you Lieutenant?"

"No," Rabelli said, "go on."

"I had a real good spot," Jimmy said. "I could see both the garage and the front. They come out the front. On foot. Headed into a grocery store. Figured they needed smokes or ran out of something."

Rabelli's face pinched into a frown.

"Jes' wanted you to know I was scared I wouldn't have enough time to get in and out," Jimmy said. "Told the guy at the desk I had left somethin'. Nervous all the time they would walk in on me. Thinkin' so hard what I'd say if that happened, I kept forgetting why I was there. And here's the tape, jes' like you wanted."

Rabelli pushed a button. The thin brown tape whirred from spool to spool. For a long time the buzzing sound was barely audible. Finally it had Eddie Greene saying, "I need a drink. It's been a long night. Crazy, the way David stormed out. How about you?"

Rabelli pushed another button and the spools stopped, the overhead light no longer dancing back and forth on the moving tape. His hand came out of his pocket holding a twenty-dollar bill.

"Ten's for the uniform, ten's for you."

Rabelli knew the man had stolen the uniform. If he'd had ten dollars it would've been spent on booze. He didn't have time to argue. The tape was here. Rabelli's breathing was rapid. He needed to play it, to hear Eddie Greene, but he had to do it alone. He had the door open. In another minute he would push Jimmy into the hallway. The man felt the rage coming off Rabelli like summer heat shimmering off the sidewalk. The pace of Jimmy's shuffling increased, and he was finally through the door.

When Rabelli started the tape again it was Sophia's voice: "Eddie, you drink too much. You do a lot too much."

Greene, annoyed: "What's that supposed to mean?"

"You think I don't know about you and Marie?"

Rabelli's fist slammed the top of the desk, making the recorder jump. The sound was garbled as the machine landed. It took a few seconds until the tape stretched tight again and the voices became distinct.

". . . has crabs."

Greene's voice in a comforting tone: "Sophia, cool it. I don't play around with any of the girls. Besides, they're all checked out regularly. I run a clean operation. Don't give me that look. What's set you off? You been thinking about this at school? How'd you get out so early anyway?"

Sophia, still pissed: "Don't try to change the subject. Last night Marie was saying you told her she was the number one girl."

"So?" Greene asked.

"Then she said she was number one with everyone and looked right at me. I told her to watch it or I'd scratch out her one good eye."

Rabelli thought Sophia had his temper.

Greene again: "I'll talk to her. She's got a big mouth. But don't you start up with her."

Sophia teased, "Why? Some of our customers would pay more for a girl with a black eye. Creeps who would like to hit a woman themselves."

Rabelli put a hand in his pocket.

"Sophia, you know the rules. Anyone starts a fight is out. Besides, Marie's a big girl. I wouldn't want you to get hurt. A face as pretty as yours shouldn't get messed up. Come on over here."

Sophia's voice, seductive: "It's hot in here, Eddie. Think I should take my clothes off and cool down?"

"Yeah." Greene's voice was softer now.

"Watch. That's right, Eddie."

The sweat on Rabelli's forehead glowed.

Greene's voice was low, raspy: "God, you get me hot."

Rabelli's hand squeezed through his pocket, wrapped around his penis, needing to strangle something.

"Do I, Eddie? Tell me. No, don't touch. Not yet. I'll step back. Let you look while you talk. Tell me, Eddie. Tell me what it's like to see me."

Rabelli's teeth bit his lower lip.

Greene's voice was syrupy: "It's like Elizabeth Taylor is in my bedroom. The dark hair; beautiful eyes. Come here."

Rabelli rolled his eyes.

"Keep going," she said. "You're a good talker. Makes me feel sexy."

Rabelli thought Greene's voice had aged from a love-struck adolescent to an over-the-hill seducer: "Did you see *Giant*?" Greene asked. "Loved her in *Giant*; I could see you in that movie. James Dean all nervous round you, 'cause you're such a knockout. Those big eyes. And you're small. She's small, too."

"Except for her tits." Sophia laughed.

Rabelli grumbles to himself, "Where'd she get that mouth?"

Greene: "Right. Same with you. Little doll with big tits."

Rabelli's finger punched down the off button. He felt dizzy and unbuttoned his shirt more, saying out loud, "I'll kill that Jew-bastard."

"Are you okay, Lieutenant? Need some water?"

A blond-haired man stood in the doorway.

"Tate, how long you been there?" Rabelli asked.

"I just came in."

The man swung a foot back toward the door. The threat in Rabelli's voice stopped him. "Did you hear the tape playing?"

"No, Lieutenant," Tate said. "Just you, loud and—you sounded real mad. Something I can help you with?"

"NO! I need to do this myself." Rabelli stood rigid as stone until he heard the door shut. He pressed a button and the voices on the tape began again.

"Marie's got big tits. Does she get you going?" Sophia mocked.

Greene sounded irritated: "Will you knock it off with Marie? She's not pretty like you. She's no Elizabeth Taylor. You're the one could be in the movies."

Rabelli's mouth opened, his tongue fell out, a man coughing up rotten food.

"Eddie, I want it to be special," Sophia pleaded.

"Me too," Greene assured her.

"Where you going?" Sophia asked nervously.

"I got a bottle of champagne in the fridge," Greene said.

Rabelli shook his head.

"I never had champagne." The excitement was back in Sophia's voice.

"I'll put a strawberry in it. I had it like that in Havana. A long time ago. The women there are the most beautiful in the world." Greene's voice was affected, his attempt at sophistication.

"More beautiful than me and Liz Taylor?"

Rabelli heard Sophia's laugh on the tape, soft and purring; his erection hurt.

"You and Liz would have been queens, even in Havana. 'Here's looking at you, kid.'"

Rabelli said aloud, "Your Bogart imitation stinks!"

"Whose voice you imitating?" Sophia asked.

"Bogie's," Greene said. "That's a toast he makes to Ingrid Bergman in *Casablanca*."

"I don't understand." Sophia, no longer seductive; now an annoyed child.

"It's a movie, maybe fifteen years ago. Very romantic. Bogie and Bergman were so sophisticated," Greene said.

"Eddie, get out of the old movies. It makes me feel creepy. Fifteen years ago I was a year old."

Rabelli saw Sophia and Greene in his head, like one of the hundreds of stag films Vice had seized over the years. Eddie would be walking back from the kitchen, a glass in each hand; tiny bubbles floating up as if the strawberries were breathing. Eddie would notice lipstick on the rim of one of the glasses. He would twirl it until the speck of red faced him and stretch out his arm to Sophia with the other glass.

What was with Greene? If he had to diddle kids, why not coloreds, or his own kind? Maybe what Rabelli had heard was true, about Jews' hunger for white Christian girls.

Greene's voice came back on: "Okay. I was complimenting you. I've never used the line before. Saving it for a special woman."

"Cut it out," Sophia bristled. "I hate it when men think I'm so dumb I'll buy any line."

"What's eating you?" Greene said. "I've brought out champagne. You said you were in the mood, and when I say something nice you're insulted."

"I'm sorry. Sometimes it gets to me that you're so much older. You're as old as my Uncle Julie."

Greene: "Now that's a name that can ruin my day."

Rabelli smiled.

"Fill up my glass again," Sophia asked. "I'm getting back in the mood."

Rabelli heard a clink. Had Greene tapped his glass against Sophia's? The sound on the tape was now background noise: shoes dropping, human sounds that were not words, a faraway police siren—were they so nuts that they'd left the window open?

"Eddie, you're too heavy. Roll over. That's better. . . . Is there anything you want me to do that your wife won't?"

Rabelli lifted the tape recorder and smashed it on the floor. Jumping on it with both feet, the machine's shell cracked into more and more pieces. He slowed down, panting, and bent down to the recorder. Gripping the tape, Rabelli jerked hard. It unraveled but did not rip. He tore the spool off the spindle and stuffed everything into his front pants pocket. He was no longer hard, and was angry that he'd noticed.

Rabelli's shoes crunched on the plastic strewn on the floor. As he yanked on the doorknob, the latch caught, vibrated and popped free. The door flew open, crashing against the wall. Frosted glass shattered and pinged on the floor like hail.

In the hallway Mrs. Wolf froze. In large letters she block printed on her steno pad "ASK HIM WHERE HE'S GOING" and held it up to Tate, who shook his head, mouthing "Not now."

Chapter Nine
At Eddie's

"Hi, Sophia. How's it going?"

Sophia had left Eddie's apartment and was walking past the doorman. She didn't want to talk. This afternoon with Eddie hadn't felt right. While he talked a good line, he wasn't with her. She wondered whether he was he getting ready to dump her. Everyone whispered that Eddie and Sophia were doing it. If she was history, she would be dog meat. Only losers would sniff around her.

When she came out of the building, she forgot to check who was on the street. Sophia didn't see Julie. That brick of a fist caught her off guard. At first she felt a burn spread through her cheek, teeth, lips. The numbness left and the pain set in. Her gums and jawbone shrieked. Sophia touched her lower lip and jumped back. Holding her hand under her chin, she saw blood. It kept dripping, making ripples in the red already in her palm. If she could catch the blood, hold it, not stain her clothes, she would be all right. She squeezed her fingers together. Watching the blood, Sophia didn't know what to do with it. It was such a bright red. She put her other hand under it and caught the overflow, thinking, what would she do when the second hand dripped?

Sophia smelled Julie. First the Old Spice, sweet, pleasant, not at all what she thought of him. Underneath was his scent: dried sweat so strong it made her step back, the stench inside the zoo building with the—what were those dark little animals?—ferrets. It was worse than garbage stewing in the heat. It stunned.

She forced herself to look up and saw him staring at his fist. "Why are you—here?" she asked. He was saying something, but the ringing in her ears made the words unclear.

Julie's mouth was moving again. "I should have been a father to you. Had you and your mother move in with us. I should—"

"You're a monster," she whispered and spit at him. Her blood dotted his shirt.

"You don't know what you're saying," Julie cried. "How can you say that to me?"

Sophia watched his eyes. The fury always started there, moments before his fingers closed into weapons. His eyes were no longer wet. A drain had opened, and they were drying into rage. Her voice was loud. She had to keep talking, so he couldn't.

"Move in with you? So you could beat me? Ohhh shit, this hurts."

He spread his arms to hug her.

"NO! Get away! You should be locked up."

Julie tilted his head to one side, a puzzled dog. "Look at me. My face is ruined. Get away, you bastard. I told her. I told her you were crazy. We should have moved to another state. Changed our names."

She watched his lips draw away from yellow teeth. The hurt sunk deeper, and she felt nausea rising. As Sophia wobbled, he reached out and grabbed her forearm.

Jumping back, she screamed, "Get your hands off me!"

He cocked a fist. Sophia's hand jerked in front of her face, bloody palm out. Julie whined, "It's not me. It's him. The Jew."

"What are you—?"

He pointed at her. "Can't you see what he's turned you into?" Julie's hand pointed up to the fourth floor.

The doorman had come out and said to Sophia, "Are you okay, Miss? I'll call the police."

Julie was howling, "Look! Look!"

She followed Julie's pointing finger. Eddie was standing at the window, buttoning his shirt. Julie reached under his jacket, and his hand came out holding a gun. The window above Eddie's head exploded. Glass slivers flew. A few splintered into Eddie's forehead. Eddie looked down, his hand moving toward his face. The next bullet spat against the building wall. Eddie moved back.

Julie kept firing at where Eddie had been. The gun was clicking even after it was empty. Julie ran into the lobby. Sophia was right behind him.

Julie shouted at the doorman, "What is Greene's apartment number?"

The doorman's face was pale against his gray coat, but he didn't back away. "I've called the police."

Julie put the gun's barrel against the doorman's eye and pulled back the hammer.

"Four-B."

The revolver was still cocked. "Stairs?" Julie demanded.

The doorman pointed to a red EXIT sign.

"Don't call up," Julie warned.

Sophia waited until he was out of sight and then told the doorman to call Eddie.

When she reached the fourth floor, Julie was smashing into the apartment with a fire axe. Sophia shouted "Eddie" over and over. There was no answer. She heard Julie slamming doors and swearing. Eddie was gone.

Sophia stumbled down the stairs to the garage, missing steps, grabbing at the handrail, just missing falling headfirst, the pain stabbing with each movement.

The garage was wide as a city block. She watched Eddie jump into his car and yelled to get his attention. He didn't hear her or see her coming. The engine finally caught. Eddie's Caddie hit the front of a parked car, crumpling the Jag's grill.

Eddie's voice was loud as she got closer. "Old man Stone's. Shit, I've got to get control. This is nuts. No sleep. Getting smashed with Sophia. Now this!"

Sophia was incredulous. He was blaming her! Why didn't anyone own up to making the crap in his own life?

The Caddie drove away. It stopped at the attendant's booth. She tried to run faster but each time her foot came down her teeth and gums screamed, a crowbar slamming against her mouth.

Eddie shouted to the attendant: "Tell Mr. Stone I'll take care of everything. Raise the damn bar! Got to get out of here."

"Mr. Greene, are you okay to drive?"

Eddie's voice was a shriek. "Don't I give you fifty bucks at Christmas? Push the damn button! I can't waste time arguing."

It was painful for Sophia to breathe. Her chest hurt; it killed behind her eyes. She knew she couldn't get Eddie to hear her. If she could just get to him, she would open the door and fall into the car.

The engine made a piercing whine. Sophia watched the car explode through the cross bar, smoke swirling off the tires.

Chapter Ten
Eddie at the Firm

"David, are you okay with all of this?" Bloomie asked.

"It's the lack of sleep," he replied. "What with going to Jersey in the middle of the night—and things at home—"

Bloomie's voice was flat. "That happens. Anything else?"

"Why do you keep asking?" David heard the fear in his voice and thought, "Damn, damn them all."

Bloomie raised his voice. Not much. Just enough to pierce through the fog of David's exhaustion. "This is important. I vouched for you. Come through on this. People remember. I remember."

He wondered what Bloomie and Jay had talked about after he left. David knew they both used people; got what they wanted, and then spit them out, like cats clearing hairballs. But David would know where the bodies were buried. Could he use it when the time came?

David remembered a conversation with Naomi: "David, don't become one of them. It scares me." He had asked who she was talking about.

"Bloomie, Chumsky, the Karps."

And he had said, "They succeed. They win."

Naomi had held his face in her hands, holding it so he had to look into her eyes, willing him to know the truth as she saw it. "David, inside they have turned to ice. Don't do that to me—or to yourself."

He had kissed her forehead, had looked above Naomi's hair, had escaped her eyes, and she had tilted his head down, back to her. He had smiled and said, "Your father succeeds, and he swims in the same water."

He had been surprised to see Naomi's face fall in on itself, her lips fluttering like a child shocked by pain, and she had said again, "Don't do that to me."

"Who's talking to you?" Bloomie asked.

"What?" David said.

"When you have conversations with yourself, your lips move," Bloomie said.

He felt the heat in his face.

"David, if you can't do this, get out now. It's only an opportunity if you can deal with it."

"I don't know what 'this' is," he said. "What am I supposed to do with Eddie?"

"Just what Jay said." Bloomie nodded as if Jay could hear. "Know whose side you're on, if it comes to that."

David thought better of pushing Bloomie. They both knew that if he kept on questioning he was off the team.

As they walked into David's office, his phone rang. It was the receptionist, whispering.

"Mrs. Howlin, speak up," David said. "I can't hear you."

"Mr. Greenberg, there's a man here asking for you," her voice a bit stronger. "Says he's your cousin. His face is bleeding. He's shouting at me." Her tone was outraged. "He's scaring people. The Vollmers are here, waiting for Mr. Schmidt."

He heard Eddie screaming that Rabelli had tried to kill him.

"Mrs. Howlin," he told her, "put him on the phone."

"David, that madman shot me!" Eddie yelled.

"Eddie, I'll help you, if you do exactly what I tell you."

"David, I—"

"Don't talk," David said. "Listen to me. Are you seriously wounded? Just yes or no."

Bloomie looked at the receiver as though it were a cobra coiled around David's ear.

"He tried to kill me," Eddie said. "The window splattered in my face."

"The answer's no," he said, as much to Bloomie as to Eddie. "I'll meet you in the hallway. The receptionist will come with you. Put her back on. Don't talk, just hand her the phone. . . . Mrs. Howlin, lead Mr. Greene toward my office—Yes, he is my cousin. I'll meet you halfway. You must get him out of the waiting area, away from the Vollmers. They're important clients."

Bloomie held out his hand and David gave him the receiver.

"Mrs. Howlin, this is Mr. Bloomenthal. . . . I agree, this is terrible. Just do what Mr. Greenberg told you. I'll come out and talk to the Vollmers. I'm going to hang up now. . . . Don't let the dizziness get to you. Take a deep breath and lead Mr. Greene toward Mr. Greenberg's office. We're on our way."

The hallway's thick carpet absorbed sound as though they were in a forest.

"David, get Eddie in your office," Bloomie said as they walked. "Do whatever you can for him, but don't let him leave until I tell you. I know you have work to do. Farm out anything that's urgent. Your priority now is Eddie. Bill the time to Pyramid."

Bloomie and David turned the corner. Eddie was trailing behind a round-faced woman in her fifties. Her hair was in bangs, cut to look like Mamie Eisenhower's. Mrs. Howlin had once said to David in a critical tone that the last name was originally spelled Eisenhauer but had been anglicized during the First World War. Then her eyes had widened and she had gasped, "Not that Germans are to be admired. My brother told me what they found when they liberated the camps."

Eddie's face was cobwebbed with blood. Glass shards were lodged in his forehead. He was unaware of the effect he had on people. Grabbing David's hand with both of his he blurted, "David, I told you. He's crazy."

Bloomie, a smile working its way onto his mouth, walked past Eddie and Mrs. Howlin. She turned and fell in behind him.

"Eddie, come with me to my office," David said. "We'll take care of your face and you can tell me what happened."

Eddie's hand reached for his forehead; he flinched as he touched a spike of glass.

Bloomie's voice drifted in from the reception area. "Charlie and Liz, so nice to see you."

David could not make out the rest of what he said. Undoubtedly a reassuring explanation of why, among the leather chairs and Persian carpets, there was a person who looked as though he had just stepped out of a car wreck.

"Have you talked to Jay?" Eddie asked. "Something's got to be done. Even if I close Blueberry Hill."

Eddie's voice grew louder. Office doors slammed. A foreign infection had entered Schmidt, Harris' bloodstream, and the firm was sealing it off, isolating Eddie and David.

David's voice was a harsh whisper. "Eddie, for God's sake shut up. I can only help if you stop until we have some privacy." His tone softened. "We're almost there."

"Will they do it?" Eddie asked. "I have to know, David. If they won't, I'm a dead man. Ow! Why'd you do that? Let go of me. David, stop it. Just talk to me."

David's fingers squeezed harder.

"David, you're choking my arm. What's funny?"

Eddie, in his shock, had it right. David wanted to choke off his words, keep them from the lawyers and secretaries who didn't want to hear, who should not hear.

David kept his grip on Eddie's arm, walking faster, knowing Eddie had no control. The panic made sweat pop on Eddie's skin and dilated his pupils like a horse trapped in flames.

"Damn it, David. Just say it's okay. It's not, is it? Why are you hurting me? Does Jay want me to disappear?" Eddie raised his free arm, and with his thumb and forefinger made a gun at the side of his head.

Was there no way to shut down this verbal hemorrhage?

"It's okay," David said. "You'll be protected. But you've got to stop talking until we're in my office." They were in front of his secretary's desk. She had pulled her chair back until it was against the wall.

"Catherine Marie, please get the first aid kit and bring it to my office," he told her.

"First aid kit?" she asked. Her face was bloodless. David wondered if she was in shock.

"It's a white box with a red cross on it," he explained. "About the size of a large book."

"I know," she said in a robot voice.

"What's the problem?" He heard his anger. "I believe it's kept in the secretaries' lounge."

"I know," she said.

Her irises seemed unusually large as though an ophthalmologist had dilated them for examination. Were you supposed to slap a person hard or wrap them in a blanket, he wondered. David wasn't prepared to do either.

"Catherine Marie, please go now and return as quickly as possible. My cousin's bleeding."

"I know."

"What is the problem?" David demanded.

"I have no training," she explained. "I think you should take your cousin to a hospital. I'll call for an ambulance or the police."

"Please!" David yelled, then lowered his voice. "Please do what I ask, and nothing else. Get the kit. Knock at my door and give it to me. I'm not asking you to play nurse. Do not call anyone! Can you do that?"

Catherine Marie scuttled away from them. As David pulled Eddie into the office, he looked one last time. Catherine Marie crab-walked with her back against the wall. Her eyes never left Eddie.

David closed the door and Eddie asked, "Don't you have a mirror? I need to see. By three I have to be at the studio." Eddie's hand circled in front of his face and he said, "Makeup will cover this. Can't wear these clothes. Do you have a shower here?"

David shook his head from side to side. Eddie wasn't paying attention. He went on: "Have to tell everyone to keep Rabelli out. David, my face—will it scar? What's going to happen to me? David, look at me. I can see it in your eyes. I'm already dead. You're looking at a corpse. Talk to me. Say something."

David pulled Eddie's hand down and said, "Don't touch your face. I'll take the glass out. Everything's going to be fine."

David pushed on Eddie's shoulder until he sat in one of the chairs. The Chivas bottle David kept in his desk was half-full, and he poured three fingers.

"Drink this," he told him.

"Don't you have some ice?" Eddie said.

"Drink it," David repeated.

Catherine Marie knocked at the door, and David took the kit.

He asked her, "Do you have tweezers in your purse?"

"Tweezers?"

David thought, *Why does she repeat everything I say?*

"The ones for plucking eyebrows," he explained.

"Yes, but . . ." *Is she deaf to every request I make?*

"Get them now," David put some force in his voice. "Please do it quickly."

He heard Eddie refilling his glass.

David said to Catherine Marie: "One more thing. Take the Ortlieb rezoning file to Dan Shuster and tell him to complete the variance application. I'll review it. If he has any questions, call me. He's not to call the Ortlieb people without checking with me first."

"Can he come into your office if he needs to?"

Her irises looked smaller. *Am I the one in shock?* David thought.

"No. No one is to come into the office. I'd rather not be disturbed at all, but if it's urgent, you can knock on the door. Go look in your pocketbook now."

Catherine Marie returned with the tweezers. She brushed each pincer, blew something off her finger, and handed them to David.

"Thanks," he said, "please don't mention my cousin's appearance to anyone."

He knew she would talk about nothing else the rest of the day.

Eddie was on his third glass of scotch. With one hand David held his jaw so Eddie couldn't jerk, and David began. "You should have been a doctor," Eddie said. "You've got good hands. Steady. I can hardly feel it when you take out the glass."

"I wish I could take all the credit, but I have Dr. Chivas to thank. Don't move. I've taken care of the large slivers. Now it's all the tiny ones. Lucky nothing got in your eyes." David's hands were tired. He put down the tweezers and rubbed his fingers.

Eddie said, "I was staring at the bastard. You should have seen his face. A rabid dog. Couldn't believe the gun. Shut my eyes when I saw the puff of smoke. I was so scared I wet myself."

"What was this all about?" David asked.

"I told you—he's a Looney tune."

Shaking his head, David said, "Loonies have something that sets them off, even if it doesn't make sense."

"Got me," Eddie said, but looked away.

"I heard you've been pimping some of the girls from *Varsity Dance*," David said. "Is that true?"

Eddie looked up. "Where'd you hear that?" he asked.

"Sophia and Claire—are they on your show?"

"What do you know about Sophia?" his voice petulant. Eddie had put his hand on David's wrist, pushing the tweezers away. Eddie got up and circled David, holding his hands in front of his face like a boxer in the ring.

David answered, "Just a guess. She greeted me when I came in as if I were at a club. Asked if I was looking for a particular girl from the show. How old is she?"

Eddie tried to put some anger in his voice, but it came out a squeak. "Will you stop already? What's all this interest in Sophia?"

David put his hand on Eddie's shoulder and pushed him back into the chair. Most of the glass was out. David stretched the skin on his cheek to see if he had missed anything. Eddie looked relieved that David had stopped questioning him. Then David asked, "Does she go to St. Agnes?"

Eddie's mouth opened. "What—?"

"Hold still," David said. "I can't do this if you're moving around. Here, take my handkerchief. You're sweating like a pig. It's getting too slippery to use the tweezers."

"Then shut up," Eddie said, "and stop giving me the third degree."

"I heard Rabelli has daughters and a niece at St. Agnes." Eddie's head snapped back, and David said, "Jesus, don't do that. Look what you've done."

Eddie leaned his face into David's stomach. He felt Eddie crying against him. Eddie wrapped his arms around David's waist.

"David, it's all so crazy."

"What is?" David asked.

"Rabelli. Everything's falling apart," Eddie sobbed.

David stroked his hair, fingers wrapped in the curls. For a moment David thought it was Naomi, and he jerked his hand out, scared by the illusion. Eddie didn't notice.

David said, "It'll work out. Rabelli will be taken care of. I don't know how, but he will. You've got to do your part. Close Blueberry Hill."

Eddie's muffled voice rose up, "Sophia is Rabelli's niece."

"What?" David didn't hide his anger.

Eddie whimpered, "She's his niece."

David asked, "Are you pimping any of his daughters?"

"No," he said.

"So when you close Blueberry Hill, that'll end it."

His voice was an undertone. "It's not that easy."

"Eddie, I'm having trouble hearing you." David took Eddie's head in his hands, and tilted it up facing him. David's shirt was wet and smeared with blood. He still felt the warmth where Eddie had been against him. Eddie's face was fleshy now, not lean and handsome as it had been in Havana. As Eddie cried, his lips puckered and trembled the way a child's do when sobbing blurs their features. David kissed his forehead.

Eddie said, "David, I love Sophia."

"What?"

"I love her. I'm thinking of marrying her."

He feared Eddie had taken leave of his senses. David reminded him, "You're already married."

Eddie said, "I'll leave Thelma," sounding as though he believed this was a reasonable plan.

"Damn it, Eddie, Sophia's a child."

"You've seen her," he said, a smile playing at the corners of his mouth. "I wake up in the morning and see a fat old woman in bed with me. I haven't had sex with Thelma for a year now."

"Eddie, I don't want to hear this. When the Rabelli problem is over, you'll see a shrink, work it out."

"Why?" Eddie whined.

"Because it's sick when a man in his forties is only aroused by a teenager."

"Bullshit!" he said. "If I'm sick so is everyone who comes to Blueberry Hill."

David tried to inject sympathy into his voice. "I think this is tied up with your drinking problem."

Eddie scrunched up his face as though David was speaking a foreign language he was trying to follow. "What drinking problem?"

"This isn't getting us anywhere," David sighed.

"David, I'm so tired."

David stepped back and looked at Eddie. A blue dress shirt clung to his belly, leaving gaps between buttons where flesh poked out. A watch sunk into his wrist, wiry black hair curling around the gold mesh band. Breathing was labored. Eddie's heart was drowning.

"You're killing yourself," David told him.

Eddie said "Go to Hell" in a tired voice. He had given up on himself.

David asked, "When was the last time you saw a doctor?"

"I've got a wife, David. I don't need this from you."

"Okay, okay. Forget it."

Eddie held his right hand up to his face.

"Is it really two? What does your watch say? I've got to go to the studio."

David told him, "Relax. You're not going on the show until we know it's safe."

Frown lines formed on Eddie's forehead. "What are you talking about? If I'm not there it'll be a disaster."

"Jay is taking care of it," David said. "There'll be an announcement you have the flu. With your luck there'll be so much sympathy the show's audience will double."

"Fat chance!" Eddie grinned. He picked up the Chivas and poured his fourth glassful. David reached over, taking away both drink and bottle.

Eddie got up and paced in front of the desk.

"What do you hear?" he asked. "Is Jay looking to replace me? It'll never work. Tell him that. The kids love me. I'm worth every penny he pays me, every penny. Believe me, it's not as much as people think. Well, you know—probably drew up the last contract."

Eddie wiped the saliva off his mouth with his wrist. Some wet the cuff, darkening the blue. David was thinking it was funny how people's bodies reacted differently to fear; with himself, it turned to cottonmouth.

Eddie kept talking. If David tried to stop him he knew Eddie would bury his fears inside where they'd ripen and grow.

"I got expenses," Eddie whined. "I got a wife to support. Two boys. I'm messing that up. I'm just a kid myself. That's why they love me. Eddie Greene's one of them, just larger. They love the car, the jewelry. It's like Elvis. I can't sing. I don't mean like Elvis that way. But it's like a magic wand was waved over one of them. That's how they think of me. Know what I mean?" Eddie watched David's face. "Guess not."

He became quiet. David thought it was over. Then Eddie jabbed a finger into David's chest, and said, "I hear rumors. I got friends. You tell Jay *Varsity Dance* will go in the crapper without Eddie Greene." He was close to shouting, "Tell him that!"

Eddie stared at the wall, shuffling his feet. David thought he was about to throw a tantrum again. Then Eddie's face sagged. "Shit, if I'm canned I'm in trouble. I owe a ton of money. With Blueberry Hill and the show I just manage to break even."

Eddie studied him. "You don't believe me," he asked. "Well, you don't have my needs. My needs are expensive, David, real expensive."

He held out his hand to David, the light catching the diamond pinky ring. In David's head he heard Naomi, her voice freezing each word as if they were clunking out of an ice tray, "He's so tacky, David," she had said. "I don't want him in the house. I feel mortified."

David stepped closer to make sure Eddie heard what he was about to ask, "Eddie, who runs Blueberry Hill?"

"I do," he said.

David shook his head. "Where'd you get the money to set it up?"

"I got associates," Eddie answered.

David was scared to ask the next question. "Chumsky?"

"Don't ask questions you know I won't answer." Eddie walked over to the wall and ran his finger around David's law degree. He stared at it, and then turned around.

"You're just like me, David. As long as we're useful, they feed us. Like the joke about the farmer and the sheep."

"Eddie, you're your own worst enemy," David said. "You know that?"

Eddie's voice was steady, a teacher reviewing a lesson that would be on the final exam. "You may have brains and be married to money, but you're still a sheep." He looked at David. "Maybe you don't know the joke?"

"No, but this is not the time," David told him.

Eddie, louder, worried David was ignoring him: "Oh, yes it is. If you don't get anything else I'm saying, you better get this.

"A farmer walks into a bar with a three-legged sheep on a rope, and asks for a whiskey for himself and a bowl of water for the sheep. After a few rounds, the bartender asks him: what's the story? The farmer says, 'This is a special sheep. A year ago I fell off the tractor and this sheep carried on until the wife came and got me to a hospital. A few months back, the sheep woke us up just as a fire was starting in the barn.'"

Eddie watched David and said, "You listening? Pay attention. Anyway, the bartender says: 'That is a remarkable animal, but what's with him only having three legs?' and the farmer says: 'A sheep like that you don't eat all at once.'"

David asked, "Everything work out with the Vollmers?"

Bloomie looked up. "Hmm? Yeah, fine. How's Eddie?"

"Passed out," David said. "I'd like to have him checked out by a doctor. I don't think he's seriously hurt, but I'd feel better."

When Catherine Marie had called to tell David that Bloomie was back, he had locked a sleeping Eddie in his office and walked around the corner to Bloomie's suite.

Bloomie's voice broke into David's thoughts. "For now he's not to leave your office. Later, if you're still concerned, take him to a doctor. Did he say anything?" He waited to see if there was more to tell, letting silence build up the pressure.

David offered, "Eddie will close down Jersey."

"The sooner the better," Bloomie said. "Shepherd him—make sure he does it."

David started to say it wasn't legal work, but stopped. The need to slip away to where there was no one telling him what to do seemed so reasonable. When had this weight attached itself, this cantankerous infant whose demands David could never meet? *That call from Eddie,* he thought. David felt again the physical pain from the shrillness of the phone ringing, his throat parched from night breathing. The voice inside David's head asking, was he now doing something to Eddie for which there was no forgiveness?

"David, did you hear me?" Bloomie was tapping his toe.

"I'm sorry," he answered. "Say it again."

"Did Eddie tell you anything we don't know?"

"Like what?" David asked.

Bloomie scowled.

"Cut it out," he said. "We can't protect him unless we know everything. Come on. Getting blindsided by something a client doesn't tell you is a disaster."

David said, "I'm not comfortable about Karp or Chumsky."

"You're going to have to trust me to use my best judgment," Bloomie threatened. "If you won't do that, I've misjudged you."

"Of course I trust you," he said. Bloomie's face smoothed.

"What haven't you told me?"

"Eddie's involved with Rabelli's niece," David said.

"Involved? Involved like he's *shtupping* her?" The lines reappeared on Bloomie's forehead, cutting deeper than before.

"Yes," David admitted.

"And she's a minor?"

"She goes to St. Agnes," David said.

"A Jew in his forties is having sex with a girl at a Catholic high school?" Bloomie's voice was incredulous. "Maybe he should be dead."

"I told him to get help when this was over," David said.

Bloomie's lips had drawn in; his mouth was a knife-cut. "In the old days he would have been castrated." Bloomie found nothing wrong with that.

David pleaded, "Eddie needs to be helped, not punished."

"Anything else?" Bloomie asked.

"Nothing," David said. "He kept on wanting to go to the studio. I didn't let him."

All of Bloomie's energy concentrated on him. "Is he a drug addict?"

"No, he drinks."

Bloomie bounced up and down on his toes. "That's how you put him to sleep?"

"Yeah," David answered. "Oh, he kept on asking me to be his lawyer. I tried to explain that the firm represented Pyramid, and his interests and Pyramid's might be at odds. He didn't follow that. Kept on saying we were cousins. Asked if I had told Jay that protecting him protected Pyramid."

"This isn't a class in legal ethics. We made that clear in Jay's office."

He hoped Bloomie was okay with his silence. Repeating another time that he was on the team was more than he could do. Bloomie picked up the phone and told his secretary to get Jay Karp on the phone.

"Hi, Jay. Wanted to bring you up to date. Eddie's here. Passed out. . . . Yeah, in David's office. David's here with me. . . . Right, just the two of us. Eddie's going to shut down the place in Jersey." Bloomie inhaled, held it for a moment, and let it out as he said, "Eddie's been sleeping with Rabelli's niece." David heard Jay bellow "Oh, shit!" and then Bloomie: "I know. It's crazy."

Bloomie's head puppeted up and down, punctuated with, "Yeah," all the while staring at David.

"Jay, listen for a second. I know . . . I know. But we've got to protect you and the show, even if it means protecting Eddie. . . . What do I mean? If Rabelli's around, it'll come out about Eddie and the niece, about *Varsity Dance* and Jersey, and the headlines will be 'Pyramid Corrupting Innocent Catholic Girls.' . . . I know it's a lie, but . . . Listen, we can't put a lid on it as long as Rabelli's around. If Rabelli's out of the picture we have a chance. It'll buy us time. Eddie will either clean up his act or we ease him out."

Bloomie rolled his eyes to the ceiling and turned his free hand palm up. "You're right, Eddie's not going to change. That's not our problem today. Rabelli is. No, I don't know what to do. The more I think about it, you were right to call Chumsky. . . . Right. Don't say anything else."

Bloomie stared at David, anger lines at the corner of his mouth. "Don't worry about Eddie. David will keep him here until we decide what to do. Eddie wants David to be his lawyer. . . . Yeah, it is a good idea. . . . Right, we'll know what the bastard's thinking. Look, we'll talk more tonight. Do you want me to pick you up? . . . I swear that's all I know. . . . You'll be the first to hear when I learn anything. . . . Right, you're the only one I'll call. I swear. . . . I'm sure it'll work out."

"Tell you what," Bloomie said into the phone, "I'll cancel my two o'clock and come over. We'll talk. . . . I know this is important. We can't talk about that now. . . . See you in a few minutes."

Bloomie hung up. He picked up a pencil and tapped it back and forth in a short arc. The rat-a-tat-tat slowed, and he looked up at David. "I haven't heard Jay like this since the warehouse mess. Don't let Eddie out of your office. On the street he'll be dead in an hour, and the whole stinking mess will spill over."

"I—"

"What?" he demanded.

David asked, "How long are Eddie and I supposed to live in my office? How am I going to do that? I—"

Bloomie's finger punched the air, underlining each word. "David, you don't want Eddie to die."

He nodded.

"You have to do whatever is needed to keep him in your office. Make sure he doesn't call out and talk to anyone. Get back in there before he wakes up."

"What if Rabelli gets into the building?"

"There's the check-in desk in the lobby."

"Come on," David said.

Bloomie heard something in his voice. "Okay. I spoke to Chumsky. One of his guys is sitting with security. Dressed in a uniform. There's a second guy on this floor."

"Where?"

"David, enough. I've got to get over to Jay. Go back to Eddie. I promise you will hear from me tonight."

"When?"

Bloomie put a hand on David's shoulder. "Whenever there's something to tell. Get back to your office. Have Catherine Marie get some dinner for both of you before she leaves."

Bloomie had on his coat and hat. He held the door open and walked with David to his office. Neither of them spoke. David was trying to figure out when Bloomie had spoken to Chumsky. He concentrated on when; he didn't want to guess what they had talked about.

Chapter Eleven
Havana

Eddie was stretched out on the floor, his head resting on the crook of one arm, the other arm between his legs. Flesh flowed down his cheeks and settled on the floor. His lips contracted and relaxed like a nursing infant.

David walked around the sleeping body and sat down behind his desk. Pulling out the top drawer, he lifted the notary seal. It rested on an old match box. He ran his thumb over the raised gold lettering: Hotel Nacional.

The casino at night had been filled with men in white dinner jackets and women in evening gowns. There had been wealthy Cubans with oiled black hair and star-white teeth, gamblers from the States, from Canada, a few from Europe. In 1939 everyone had spoken of Hitler, Germany's claims on neighboring countries, and inevitable war. Most had said the Nazis could be dealt with, and they would clean out the Communists, the real threat. David had been right to be frightened. Starving dogs, ribs outlined like swallowed knives, attack any animal eventually no matter how large.

A crowd at the craps table had watched the pregnant girl. Her mahogany skin had been vivid against a different white dress every night. She had not been more than fifteen. David had heard her called The Bride With Child, though she wore no wedding ring. Her pile of chips had melted down like the ice in her glass. Then a wrinkled man in a dark suit, old enough to have been her grandfather, had appeared at her side. The croupier had brought out fresh dice and the piles in front of her had grown to twice their original height. They had cashed in and left. He had imagined the old man was the head of the Secret Police, but never asked.

Women had approached them: expensive call girls, young women whose aging husbands had been in gambling frenzies until the casino had closed at three in the morning. Eddie had not paid for sex, but had never turned away a bored wife. David had been stroked and grabbed by professionals and amateurs and had gone up alone to the suite. Eddie had been next door with his catch of the night, coyotes howling at the moon.

Two days before they had left, David had been drinking at the bar. He had watched Eddie leave with a redhead and had waited to allow them time to settle into the bedroom. A pair of white women, one taller than the other, had sat on the piano bench, the man between them a dusty shade of bark.

While David had been wondering whether Negro men had larger sex organs than whites, a Cuban woman had run at the three of them, a machete raised in her hand. The man must have seen her as well; he had jumped up and pushed the women off the bench.

Bouncers had swarmed over the Cuban woman. The machete had dropped on the carpet. Everything had happened at once: thick-necked men had lifted the ebony woman and rushed her out of sight; the two white women had been helped to their feet; and the piano player had held his hand against his shirt, the blood between his fingers black in the dim light.

It had been their sixth day in Havana. Eddie had been walking back and forth in white silk boxer shorts. Curtains had been drawn against the afternoon heat. The ceiling fan had offered little relief. In the room's dusk, the white silk had reflected whatever light there was.

Eddie had said, "David, Naomi's supposed to be the virgin. Not you."

His anger had flared. "Five nights of trying to fall asleep after the Hallelujah chorus ends. And you're criticizing me?"

Eddie had opened the bathroom door, turned on the light, and walked back to the now visible chairs. Lowering himself into one, he had gestured to the other. "Sit down. Don't get on your high horse. There are women here who would love to teach you."

Still standing, David had said, "I won't go with a whore!"

Eddie had shaken his head slowly from side to side.

"David, no one's asking you to."

He had pointed at Eddie. "Those women you bed, they're whores too."

"David, David. Calm down."

Eddie had patted the empty chair. "Come on, relax. You need to hear what I've got to say."

David had slumped into the chair. With a finger under the chin, Eddie had lifted David's head. He had laughed and Eddie had said, "That's better. So here's what I've been trying to tell you. Last night I met these two society dames. Sisters. Beautiful. I could smell the wildness."

Eddie had twitched his nose, and David had laughed again. He went on. "Good. Okay. They were playing roulette, losing on every spin. They tried to take me away from the woman I was with. Almost had a fight on my hands. Crazy! The point is both of them were willing to go with me. Two on one. You get what I'm saying—gorgeous and willing to try anything."

He kept talking, "I got their names. Called them earlier. They're meeting us at nine. This is our last night. Don't back out on me. If we play this right, you'll have a meal from soup to nuts."

He had grinned, and Eddie had said, "Thank God you still get a joke."

It had worried him that he was enjoying the fantasy Eddie had spun out. He had felt the panic and had blurted out, "Eddie, these women have slept around. We'll get syphilis or something."

"David, David, these are classy women. Would I let my cousin get in trouble? But we'll play it safe. Here, come to the bathroom where I keep supplies."

With his hand on the bathroom door Eddie had turned to him. "One more thing. Don't wear that old black suit. No one swoons over an undertaker. Wear my other dinner jacket."

The sisters had called themselves Lilly and Mary Beth. David had been shocked to recognize them as the two white women from last night's violence.

Eddie and Lilly had been drawn to each other, a study in contrasts. At six feet she had been six inches taller than Eddie, with corn silk hair.

Eddie's raisin-colored curls and swarthy complexion had led more than one croupier to address him in Spanish. Lilly had looked like she was recovering from a long illness. Her skin had little pigment and the veins had been visible on the top of her hands.

Mary Beth, her half-sister, had been almost a foot shorter and thick-bodied: heavy arms, full breasts, and broad hips. Her hair had been dark and coarse, visible on forearms and plucked eyebrows. Though her face had lacked Naomi's refinement, from the neck down she seemed familiar. David had felt ashamed. Eddie must have seen something. He had stared hard at David until he turned back to Mary Beth.

Lilly and Eddie had exhaled as they talked, words and smoke drifting out together. Mary Beth's lips had formed a crimson circle, puffing out a coil of evaporating "O"s. Her open mouth had stared at Eddie.

Lilly had said, "The Nacional's show is good as far as it goes, but I've heard that in the Old City there are entertainments—well, that cannot be found anywhere else." She had looked at Eddie.

"I've heard of them," he had said.

David had not known what they were talking about, but the Old City at night was said to be dangerous.

"I think this is a bad idea," he had said.

Mary Beth's hand had squeezed his thigh.

"It's our last night here. Lilly and I want to see everything, but it's not safe for girls alone. Go talk to someone. The maitre d' . . . give him some money. If people know about it, there must be a way."

On the stage the women's breasts had risen and fallen; their pubic hair had glistened purple-black. Behind the women, men had stood at waist high drums, upper bodies drenched. The music had been as dense as the tobacco smoke in the room.

A man and woman had performed sexual ballet. He had lowered himself to his knees and she had climbed on to his shoulders, facing him. She had tilted her head back and opened her mouth soundlessly. Mary Beth's face had been riveted on the couple.

The naked dancer had wrapped her legs around the man's chest and had slid down until she rested on his hips. He had pulled her toward him.

Again she had leaned her head back, and this time sounds had broken, long moans punctuated by the morning cries of birds.

Returning to the hotel in a horse-drawn carriage, the four had been glued to the leather seats in the leaden heat. It had been past midnight.

Lilly had said, "I think it must be at least ninety. Nothing cools me. Not taking a shower. Not being naked."

Lilly had grinned like the Cheshire cat.

Mary Beth had put her head on David's shoulder and leaned back, searching the sky. Seated in front and above had been the driver and the bodyguard selected by the maitre d'.

The route had snaked through the old city. Hooves echoing on old stones had been the only sound. In front of closed markets chickens had slept in cages. Nests of apartments, a few glowing dimly, had risen above the storefronts.

A full moon had lit up the block: wooden sidewalks, a red cooler with the white Coca-Cola script. Coins had dropped into the slot; they had heard the lid raised. A light inside the cooler had made the escaping moisture gleam; it had drawn their attention like a magic lantern show. A grinning mulatto boy had toasted them with a Coke bottle. From the other side of the street a man had leapt into the carriage. His hand had wrapped itself around Lilly's necklace and pulled. Pearls had scattered. The bodyguard had smashed the heel of his hand into the attacker's nose, and they had heard the snap of bone. Red had spurted onto Lilly's dress. The attacker had swung back wildly; his hand had opened and bloodied pearls had fallen.

While the fight had continued, Eddie and David and the sisters had squeezed against the opposite side of the carriage. Lilly's face, a few inches from David, had looked past him at the snarling, bleeding men. Her mouth had opened and closed with shallow breaths.

One of the attacker's eyes had been swollen shut, and he had been unsuccessful in trying to wrap his arms around the bodyguard. Their man's arms had been jackhammers, pounding, pulling back, pounding. The attacker had doubled over and slid to his knees. With one hand on his throat and the other gripping the front of his belt, the bodyguard had lifted him into the air. Flailing, the attacker had grabbed the bodyguard's shirt as he was thrown out of the carriage. Shirt buttons had popped, fabric had ripped, and the assailant had rolled across the street. Their champion had stood panting, upper body slippery with sweat. Musk from the fight had been overwhelming. The driver had kept the horses flying to the hotel.

"Eddie, can't you make it cooler?" Lilly had purred.

He turned off the overhead light and the lamp on the table. A white triangle remained, flowing from the bathroom door, widening until it had reached the sofa.

"How's that?" Eddie had asked.

"I'm still hot. And sticky."

Lilly had unbuttoned her dress and let it fall to the floor. "I'm going to take a shower. Eddie, make me a gin and tonic. I'll be out soon."

David had said, "We could all use a drink. I can't believe what happened tonight."

"The show or the fight?" Mary Beth had asked.

"Both."

Eddie had brought frosted drinks to him and Mary Beth. Droplets had gathered on the outside of the glass and trailed down. She had extended a small pink tongue and licked hers from bottom to top. Looking up at David, she had patted the sofa. He had sat down. Mary Beth had undone his bow tie and opened the top shirt button. Slipping her fingers under the shirt, she had held the mushroom shaped stud. The back of her hand had moved softly against his chest, sliding out the golden cap.

David had pointed toward the curtain. Eddie and Lilly had faced each other in silhouette; they had not heard her return. Both had held gin and tonics. Eddie had been in his formal pants and shirt; she had been wrapped in a towel. Lilly had taken her free hand, lifted and pulled the corner tucked between her breasts, knelt down, and laid the towel at Eddie's feet. When she had stood up her fine hair had glowed white forming an aura around her head, a Madonna in a medieval painting. In profile her breast had been small with a prominent nipple.

Eddie had leaned over and kissed her on the mouth. She had taken a step back, lifted a breast and held the icy glass against it; biting her lip, she had placed a hand behind Eddie's head and pulled it down.

Mary Beth had asked, "Which room is yours?" As they had walked away, David had watched Eddie and Lilly moving to his room. Mary Beth's hand had cupped David's crotch. He had looked down. Her face had been tilted up. "That's better," she had said.

"Leave the light until I get this damn thing on," David had told Mary Beth.

"I think it would be easier if you took off your pants and boxers first." She had laughed.

He had felt the heat in his face. David had felt mortified by his clumsy efforts to pull the Sheik over his erection, rising he had thought like a little flagpole from the open fly.

David had been sitting on the bed. Mary Beth had been next to him.

She had kissed him on the mouth. He had tasted the gin on her breath. Her lips had moved up to his eyes. David had held her face in his hands, feeling a sigh rising in his throat. When she had turned around, he had unbuttoned the back of her dress. As he had reached the last one, she had reached behind and squeezed his erection. "Making sure you're still here."

She had stood up and the dress had dropped. Underneath had been a corset.

"I need help getting out of this," she had said.

David's fingers had been clumsy as he had struggled with the tiny hooks and eyelets. Maybe it had been the night's drinking. It had felt more like work than seduction.

At last she had been naked. She had turned around. The sight of Mary Beth's pubic hair had startled him. Naomi had never revealed that part of her body. When David had imagined Naomi naked, he had visualized a smooth rising of skin. No thicket of hair. No vagina.

"I see I have your attention," she had said. "It's all fun from this point on." Mary Beth had pressed against the erection with one hand and had pulled down on the waist of his pants with the other. "How about giving a girl some help?"

David had lifted his hips. Pants and boxers had slid to the floor. He had tried to undo the remaining shirt studs, but his fingers had slipped. Mary Beth had yanked the shirt over his head.

"David, let me have a Sheik. You'll have more fun if I do it. Put the others on the night table."

He had handed Mary Beth one. She had rolled it up, and had put the cap over the head of his erection, which had taken some effort.

"I feel like I'm going to explode," David had said, hearing the boast in his voice.

"Not so fast, big boy. We're both going to enjoy ourselves." Mary Beth had watched only the Sheik and his erection.

His voice had floated above her, "Does it have to be this tight? Maybe this is the wrong size."

Mary Beth had been unrolling the Sheik. Sometimes it had slid off her fingers and snapped like a rubber band.

"Ow!"

"David, it's got to be tight," she had said. "I'll be more careful."

He had a naked girl with her hand on his swollen member and had blushed because she had said a tight condom was a blessing. In his head he had heard Eddie laugh.

In his office David walked around the desk to check on Eddie. He heard a sharp snore and Eddie's head rose from the floor before settling down. Returning to his chair, David felt an erection tangled in his underpants. He rearranged it to a more comfortable position before sitting down.

Mary Beth had lifted their drinks off the night table, handed David one, and then had eased sideways onto his lap. She had slowly rocked her bottom, and said, "What do you like?"

He had stared at the beading on her upper lip, had leaned forward and licked it.

"David, you are a treat. I'll tell you what I like. I'll show you what to do. I'll try things with you. If you don't like them, tell me. I'll do the same."

Mary Beth had slid off his lap, and lay down on her back. With both hands she had framed David's face. "Kiss me gently like it feels when rain begins."

He had wondered where she had read that line. Guided by soft pressure in one direction, then another, David had kissed her forehead and beneath her cheekbone. He had tasted the sweat that had gathered at her collarbone, the saltiness on her skin. With his ear above her breast David had listened to the drumbeat of her heart.

His tongue had reached the outermost of Mary Beth's pubic hairs. After a moment, she had drawn his face close to hers and had said, "Not yet."

Licking his mouth, she had said, "I taste myself on your lips."

He had said, "I love how you taste and smell."

"Not all men do. What's it like?"

David knew he could never have talked to Naomi like this. It would have been shameful. But this *shiksa's* boldness had freed him.

"Salty. Smells like moist earth," he had said. "Fresh, rich."

She had followed his finger inside her with one of her own, had moved David's finger and pressed softly, teaching him.

"Now, David. Now."

Mary Beth had moaned, urged: "Come inside me."

Commanded: "Now!"

He had been held in her warmth and in her wetness, had felt her hips rise and fall, had heard himself, had heard her, had remembered Eddie and Lilly.

"Rest now," she had said. "I want you again."

The travel clock on the night table had read 2:15. The plane was scheduled to leave that afternoon. Smoke had swirled from Mary Beth's lips, had curled up from the cigarette in her fingers.

Eyes open, David had dreamed. On the roof of a tall building, he had stared at a billboard of a woman smoking. Her mouth had been as large as the Lincoln Tunnel. Clouds of smoke had puffed out and blown away. His hat had flown off, turned upside down and vanished. The wind had strengthened, pulled the jacket tight against his back. He had been lifted off the roof and had stared at dots moving below. Weightless, David had been drawn faster and faster toward the gargantuan face. Close up the lips, red as a fire truck, had been speckled with whitened billboard where paint had peeled. He had spread his arms and legs wide in a useless effort to avoid being swallowed.

"David. Stop! Wake up." Mary Beth had been shaking his shoulders. "David, are you okay? Look at me. Do you know who I am? You were having a nightmare. Pushing against me. Saying 'no, no.'"

At first he had not replied, frightened he had woken into the dream, not out of it. "Sorry," he had said. "I'll go splash some water on my face."

Eddie had been in the bathroom toweling dry.

"David, take a shower. Women don't like to smell another woman on a man."

"What—?"

Eddie had kept on talking. "We're going to switch. Lilly's great. You're going to love it. She does things with her mouth and hands— she'll take you to the moon. How's Mary Beth?"

"Eddie, these aren't prostitutes to be passed around."

Eddie had held a finger to his lips. "David, David. Take it easy. Keep your voice down. I'm not asking you about Naomi. Lilly and Mary Beth are on a fling. Don't you get it? They came to Havana to do things they'll never do again. We mean nothing to them. Nothing."

"I—I can't do this," he had said.

"David, when they're eighty with blue hair they'll still remember Havana. Get in the shower. I'll talk to them."

It had been the second time David had soaped himself. He had turned the water on as hot as he could bear. His body had turned pink as a newborn's.

Wrapping himself in a towel, he had opened the bathroom door. He had seen the silhouettes and had heard the sounds, but had been puzzled—was he looking at two or three people? There had been two women facing each other, squatting down, torsos rising and falling. David's eyes had adjusted and he had seen a third body on the floor, feet extended toward him. One of the women, he had assumed Lilly from her slimness, had been at the far end where Eddie's head would have been. The body that he still tasted had been astride the midsection. Eddie had raised a hand high in the air and had waved David over. Mary Beth had turned her head and had said, "Come here, David. We need you."

Lilly stood up and had walked toward David. Mary Beth and Eddie had rolled over. He had tried to look away, but with each groan from Eddie, David had been drawn back. His erection had returned, its dull ache intensifying. Lilly had been in front of him, un-wrapping his towel, turning her back to him, rubbing up and down against him, taking one of his hands and moving the palm across a nipple. She had turned around, slid down to her knees, took David in her mouth. His eyes had closed as he had moved into another warm wet place. Alone.

"Damn!"

Lilly's teeth had nipped. His eyes had snapped open. Eddie had mounted Mary Beth from the rear, rocking, pumping, facing David. A cloud had sliced halfway across the moon. Mary Beth had disappeared in the darkness.

The only light had been on Eddie's face, his brown eyes wide open staring at David, as they both cried out in release.

Eddie had suggested, "Let's walk Lilly and Mary Beth to their room."

"I'm exhausted," David had said. "I can't do it."

The three of them had stared at him. Eddie had opened his mouth, paused, looked at David's face, and then had said, "Suit yourself."

Lilly had held Eddie's hand and followed him to the door. Mary Beth had walked toward David holding her arms wide for a hug. He had turned and walked into the bathroom. The click of the lock had been loud in the gathering quiet.

When he had heard the door to the hallway close, David had come out and gone to his room. He had laid Eddie's spare dinner jacket on the bed, and had piled on the pants, cummerbund, bow tie, socks, garters, and white silk boxer shorts. He had tied everything together with the jacket sleeves and had called room service. "I have some clothes I want thrown out. I'd appreciate someone picking them up immediately."

He had left the studs and cufflinks on Eddie's bed. They were too expensive for him to replace.

On the flight back David had busied himself reading an old *Life* magazine. Eddie had said, "I don't get it. Throwing out my clothes. Why? I could have had them cleaned. What did you think? Naomi would look at them and see you getting laid in Havana? You're crazy. You know that, don't you?"

Eddie had never understood that it was David's feelings for him that he needed to hide from Naomi.

He was pacing in the office when he heard the groan. David turned to find Eddie's eyes open, mouth trembling.

"Eddie, it's okay."

Eddie was leaning on one hand, sitting up, flailing with the other. "Stay away, stop," Eddie said. His voice rose as he defended himself in the dream. David knelt down and put an arm around him, pulling Eddie against him, offering Eddie whatever safety he could, rocking him back and forth. "Eddie, wake up. It's all right."

Drool hung from his lips. David took the show handkerchief out of the jacket, dabbed and dried his mouth. Eddie suckled on one of the raised points. David jerked it away and blinked.

"Eddie?" he asked, "are you awake?"

Eddie looked down at the blood splatters on his shirt, then up at David. Eddie lifted both hands in front of his face, traced the outline of his forehead, and trailed his fingers down his eyelids and cheekbones. Shaking his head, he stood up. "I've got to get out of here," he said.

"Eddie, what's your shirt size?"

"What?" he asked.

"It's almost five," David told him. "My secretary can still make it to Wanamaker's. What's your neck and sleeve?"

Eddie shook his head, pushing the words aside and getting back to his own thoughts. "I've got clothes at the studio—it's five? Shit, the show's almost over."

"You can't go to the studio or anywhere else," David told him. "Rabelli is out there. Tell me the clothes you need and what you want for supper."

Eddie looked at the top of the desk, and then asked, "Where do you keep your scotch?"

David wasn't getting through. "No more," he said. "You've got to be sober tonight."

Eddie's eyes widened, "For what?"

"I don't know," he told him. "Bloomie's meeting with Karp and Chumsky. Others. He'll be getting back to us. If he finds you drunk— well, you know."

Eddie lifted each arm and sniffed.

"I stink. Is there someplace I can wash up?"

"Yeah. First tell me what you want in clothes. It's getting late."

David went with Eddie to the men's room. The attendant who turned on the faucet was over six feet, his dark hair oiled and combed straight back. As David took a towel from him, he saw that his oversized hands had white scar tissue on the knuckles.

David asked, "Where's John tonight?"

"Uncle John took sick. Asked me to cover."

"Did you box professionally?" David asked

"You this chatty with everyone?" he shot back.

David shut up. He and Eddie dried off quickly, threw the hand towels into the hamper and returned to the office.

Eddie and David sat at opposite sides of the desk, which Catherine Marie had cleared, putting the files, desk blotter and everything else in a corner, arranged exactly as they had been on the desktop. Then she had set it up like a dinner table at the Walnut Club: a linen tablecloth doubled over, china, silver, water goblets, and two serving dishes with domed covers. As David lifted one, a rich gravy steam rose.

He looked up and said to Catherine Marie, "You are a magician. How did you do it?"

"I called down to the Club. Mr. Bloomenthal's secretary suggested I use his name." She looked startled, then stammered, "I'm sure it would have been the same had I used yours."

"It wouldn't, and I'm glad you used your head. And thank you for Mr. Greene's clothes."

"Yeah, thanks, Katie," Eddie said.

The skin tightened across her cheekbones as she said, "Catherine Marie."

Her face softened and turned toward David. "I'm glad you're pleased. Is there anything else, Mr. Greenberg?" She was watching Eddie chew on a slice of roast beef that was larger than his mouth, resulting in it appearing partially in view and then disappearing.

"Thank you for everything Catherine Marie, I'll see you in the morning."

With an effort, Eddie swallowed. He held up his right hand and touched the button on the cuff of the dress shirt Catherine Marie had bought.

"I can't remember the last time I wore a shirt without cufflinks," he said. "And this tie. I look like an undertaker."

David laughed.

"Eddie, you look fine. She didn't mean anything bad. It's what she would buy for me or any of the lawyers here."

He said, "I guess so. She kept looking at me like something that needed to be scraped off her shoe."

"Relax. She's gone. Try to enjoy dinner."

"That's another thing," he said. "What's this supposed to be—the condemned man's last meal? If it is I want a cheese steak."

This time they both laughed.

Chapter Twelve
Meeting at Chumsky's

By eight that night the weather was cold and raw.

Lee Steinhardt was in the rear with a cashmere car blanket across his lap. The temperature inside the Cadillac was eighty-one. Sweat ringed the band inside the driver's cap.

"Leroy, does it feel cold in here to you?"

"No, Mr. Steinhardt."

"How old are you?"

Leroy Holmes answered, "Fifty-eight next week."

Steinhardt rubbed his hands; the blue veins sat on top like a city map. "I have a few years on you. You'll see. When you reach my age, you can't retain warmth. I'm always cold. Even in Palm Beach. But it's better there. Came home for the holidays. I should have been on my way back today. Jay called. Problem with someone who can't keep his pants on."

Holmes said nothing.

After a minute, the old man said, "Aggravation is how you know you're alive."

"I agree with you there, Mr. Steinhardt."

Steinhardt rambled, "When they decide you're useless they don't call you with their problems. Even if you own part of the company. They always call when things are okay. Want to take all the credit. Tell me how smart I was to put a million into Pyramid, and how it's worth ten times that now. Jay sure knows how to blow his own horn. Say that for him. But when something explodes, he wants me there *before* the hard decisions are made. Well, it's good to know he thinks I still have my marbles."

Holmes looked in the mirror. The old man was smiling. "Soon as this is over, I'm on the plane back. Day after tomorrow I've got a horse running at Hialeah, name of Hasmonaean Flame. Leroy, do you know who the Hasmonaean kings were?"

"No, can't say I do."

Steinhardt cupped his hands and blew into them. "The Maccabees. Great line of Jewish warriors. We'll see if Flame has the stuff. I love Hialeah. All those flamingos in the center of the track. A pink cloud."

Jay and Bloomie pulled into the parking area.

"Bloomie, pull next to the Caddie," Jay said.

It was after eight, and Keystone's employees had left for the day. Steinhardt's limo was there, parked next to the front door. The chauffeur wasn't in the car.

Jay said, "Must be wheeling Lee in."

Bloomie nodded.

Chumsky's Imperial was parked in the space stenciled "President"; black and gleaming like the Caddie, but more threatening. It was the gunsight taillights. Bloomie thought Chumsky shouldn't remind people of the rumors; he should buy a gray Buick, fade into the background. But Chumsky was a monster shark swimming off shore. He demanded others' fear as his just due. Take last summer. The group, Chumsky, Luntz, the Solomon brothers, had been walking around the hundred acres they had just bought from Henderson's Dairy to convert into an industrial park. The parcel was still used to graze cattle, ten miles west of the city. The dirt road had ended, and the group had followed the architect's finger from the site plan to a clump of trees. All of them had been dressed in suits. Bloomie had stayed on the road talking with a member of the zoning board. Chumsky, in his handmade shoes from Lobb, had stepped into cow flop as big as a football. His shoe had disappeared. Just a black silk sock growing out of a yellow-brown mound. Next thing Bloomie had known, Luntz and the Solomons had been on their knees pulling out their white handkerchiefs and wiping off Chumsky's shoe, all three of them wrist deep in shit. And sweating! They hadn't told Chumsky to step into it, but they had acted like it had been their own damn fault.

Bloomie didn't hear Sol drive up. He said, "Looks like we're all here."

Sol stood in front of his Packard. His voice was nothing like the booming salesman on the radio. Wetting his lips, he asked, "Why are we meeting at Keystone?"

Sol looked at Jay, over to Bloomie, and then back at Jay.

"This is about Eddie Greene and his TV show," Sol said. "So why aren't we at Pyramid? Or the firm?"

Jay's response was as quiet as Sol's question, the two of them sharing a secret in an empty lot. "We need some help from Morris."

"What kind of help?"

Bloomie broke in, "Let's not talk about it out here. You never know who's around. Sound carries at night."

Sol's voice was a plea. "Look, you don't need me. Whatever you decide, you got my vote." Sol tried to smile, but his mouth turned down at the corners.

Jay rubbed Sol's back with a circular motion. "Sol, it's okay," Jay told him. "We're all in this together. Like when we whack up the money in January. But it's not all fun. You know that. You're a businessman."

The hand on Sol's back pushed him toward the door.

The three men walked into the office. Steinhardt's driver finished arranging a blanket on the old man's lap and stood up, a soldier at his post. Chumsky smiled at the group and then looked at Steinhardt. "Lee, this is business. The *shvartza's* got to leave."

"His name is Leroy Holmes," Steinhardt said. "He's completely loyal."

Bloomie said, "Lee, Morris did not intend any insult to Mr. Holmes. He was just pointing out that we are here because of our ownership in Pyramid, an interest that Mr. Holmes does not share."

Chumsky stared at Holmes until he said, "Mr. Steinhardt, I'll be in the car when you need me. Just send someone to get me."

Bloomie told Leroy he would come out to let him know. Chumsky didn't appear to have heard any of the conversation that followed his dismissal of Holmes.

When the door closed, Chumsky spoke again. "Jay tells me Eddie Greene's using *Varsity Dance* to promote a cathouse he owns in Jersey. I like Eddie, but he's not smart. No one does this to me or the people I do business with. If this was all, a call would take care of it. But Jay says there's more and Bloomie's telling him it can't be over the phone. Why's that?"

Bloomie looked at Chumsky and said, "Certain things should never be discussed on a phone. Eddie Greene's sleeping with a sixteen-year-old. Sophia Rabelli."

"The cop's daughter?" Chumsky asked.

"His niece," Bloomie said. "Today Rabelli tried to kill Greene. Eddie's holed up at the firm with David Greenberg, his cousin."

Sol's face was turning gray green, the color of the outside of a hard-boiled egg yolk. He stood up, and Chumsky stared him back into his chair.

Lee Steinhardt's head was on his chest, but his parchment-dry voice was loud enough to be heard. "I assume we all agree that Mr. Greene is part of the package for *Varsity Dance* being picked up by a national network, which involves millions. Eventually, hundreds of millions."

The old man's voice wheezed on, "So, as much as we personally applaud Officer Rabelli's efforts, they are jeopardizing our legitimate business interests, bringing us to Morris."

The old man never raised his head. Sol looked everywhere except where Chumsky sat behind the desk. Only Jay looked at the bulldog head.

Chumsky began: "All of you look at me. That includes you, Lee."

Steinhardt's head lifted, lips quivering as he spoke, "Proceed, Morris. You have our attention. How do we remove Rabelli from the chessboard?"

"I can do that. It's not part of my obligations as a shareholder. I will be taking a great risk. It will be done tonight. Before Pyramid is worthless. In return Bloomie will deliver a document to me at home tonight, showing that my ownership in Pyramid is now thirty percent."

Jay's voice was a yelp, "Come on Morris. That's three times what you own! I agree we should show our appreciation. But thirty percent of Pyramid? That's a fortune. It might be appropriate if your interest grew to twelve percent."

Chumsky stood up. "I thought this was a serious meeting. However you'd like to see the situation, it boils down to asking me to kill a cop, an important cop, and to do it in a few hours. If you'd rather sit around watching your fortunes dry up, and being labeled child pimps, well you can see what's coming as well as I can. Priests, and the papers Jay doesn't own, will call you the Christ-killers who seduce children.

Remember Fatty Arbuckle? Didn't matter what was true. The stories killed his career."

Only Chumsky's eyes and lips moved; the rest of his body was stone still.

"Jay, no one will read your papers or turn on your stations.

"Bloomie, it'll be a race by your firm's clients to pull their business.

"Your showrooms will be empty, Sol, and no studio will let you show their films.

"Lee, you'll still be rich, clipping coupons, but all your blueblood friends will avoid you. They'll kick you off every board. Your grandchildren will change their names, and that will hurt more than if you became the first poor Steinhardt."

The bulldog jaw clamped shut.

Bloomie stood up and said, "This is not something we can respond to without talking. Can we use your office?"

Chumsky looked at his watch and then replied, "You can go into the hallway. You have ten minutes and then I'm leaving. If it's going to be done before *Varsity Dance* is worth *bubkes* that means tonight. I need to move quickly.

"When you've agreed, I want all of you back in here. It's yes or no. There's nothing to negotiate."

It took thirty-five minutes to drive from Keystone Liquors to the entrance to Steinhardt's estate.

When they drove out of the parking lot, Steinhardt's face was like a man with food poisoning. Holmes said nothing. When Steinhardt broke the silence, he was speaking to himself, his voice like a radio in the dark. "My mistake was underestimating Chumsky. Because of the silver ties. And the pinkie ring. I thought Bloomie would have some weight. He told Chumsky it would take several hours to do the paperwork. He offered to drop off the papers in the morning. Chumsky insisted that it be tonight; that the papers be delivered personally by Bloomie to Chumsky's mother's house.

"I was once at the mother's. For a charity event. Never again. Chumsky bought her a mansion on the Main Line and lives with her. That speaks volumes. Keeps a place for himself in center city if he wants a woman. The mother must weigh over three hundred pounds. She sat in the middle of the living room and passed gas like a dog eating from a garbage can."

Chapter Thirteen
David and Eddie; A Call From Sophia

David was pretending to work, to justify the time listed on his billing sheet. Squared off on a cleared portion of desk was the Ortlieb Brewing Company petition to the zoning commission. Black typing marched across the page, a determined column of ants. Finishing a sentence, he looked up to think about it and had no memory of what he had just read.

Outside his window the night sky was black. He walked to the door and opened it. The hallway was artificially bright. David heard the whirr of a vacuum cleaner in the reception area. It felt like high school, in detention with Eddie for setting off cherry bombs in the girls' bathroom.

They had been up to their ankles in water, scared and laughing. He had run behind Eddie to the janitor's closet. They had turned off the light and sat on upside-down metal buckets. The closet door had swung out, and the light from the hallway had framed them like suspects being questioned by the police. David had looked up at the teachers, then down to the floor where their wet footprints had been slowly drying. David had laughed, pointing at the trail ending where they had sat.

The principal, Mr. Horne, had split them up and had taken David into his office. "David, if you keep on being led around by Eddie you'll waste your life. Look at Eddie. He's seventeen and still in tenth grade. The reason you're both in the same class is that he's been held back twice. Don't follow in his footsteps. What is so funny? Why are you laughing again? Are you making fun of me?"

"David, what's so funny?" Eddie got up from the rug, sleep marks on his face.

"I'm thinking about Mr. Horne and the cherry bombs," he told him.

"Is that how you deal with this shit? Christ Almighty, get drunk or get laid, or both. I've got to get out of here. It's driving me batty."

"Eddie, sit down," David said. "Rabelli's probably across the street, waiting."

"You think so? David, don't bullshit me. Am I a dead man?"

There was a knock on the door, and Bloomie walked in with a guy running his finger under a shirt collar. His head was shaped like the working end of a shovel. It was attached directly to the collar-bone of his six-foot frame. Pepper-black hair, salted with white, was cut so short that the scar ending at his left eye was traceable to the crown of his head.

Eddie stepped back, staring.

"Gentlemen," Bloomie said, "meet one of Mr. Chumsky's associates."

David extended his hand, which opened uselessly without being shaken, and returned it to his side. Embarrassed, David asked him his name.

"Jack will do. Like jack shit."

His lips lifted over brown-yellow teeth. It was the best he could muster for a smile. David was sure his breath smelled like swamp gas.

"Which one of you is Eddie?" Jack asked.

Eddie slid back further.

Bloomie looked at me and said, "Jack is in charge. Whatever he says, you do." Bloomie turned toward the door.

"Where—where are you going?" David stammered.

"David, I told you. Jack's in charge. This is his show."

"Wait," David said. "What do I tell Naomi?"

Bloomie looked at Jack, who turned to face Bloomie as though Eddie and I were not there. "We figure Rabelli knows Eddie's here," Jack said. "We want the two of them"—Jack nodded at them—"to leave in a half hour and go to the lawyer's house. They should stay there another half hour and then head out. I'll tell them where to go. We'll know if Rabelli's following. Any luck, he will be. If not, we'll send them back to the lawyer's until Rabelli swallows the bait."

Eddie's face was shiny; his jowls moved in and out. Jack noticed and said to David, "Take your cousin to the head and let him puke."

David held Eddie's elbow, moving him forward. His legs buckled. David tried lifting him, but he felt like he was filled with wet sand. David turned to Jack. "Can you give me a hand?"

Eddie jerked away before Jack could touch him. Holding on to the desk, he pulled himself upright.

"I need to call Naomi." David heard his voice breaking.

Bloomie was walking through the doorway. Without turning around or stopping, he replied, "Let me. I'll tell her something has come up. You need to go to New York. Tonight. She should pack for two days."

Eddie's eyes were watering. Occasional gurgles like air bubbles in heating pipes were reminders of how close he was to throwing up.

Bloomie was down the hall. Jack moved to one side and signaled with his arm to get Eddie to a toilet. They just made it. David left him in a stall and lit a cigarette.

Today was the first time he had been alone with Eddie since Havana. In the past twenty years there had always been others around. Up until the night at Blueberry Hill, it was family: Thanksgiving, weddings, *bar mitzvahs*, breaking the *Yom Kippur* fast with Naomi's parents. If Eddie called to see if he wanted to go to dinner, David would come up with an excuse, usually work. Truth was, he felt uncomfortable, a little fearful. What would they talk about? *Varsity Dance?* The Athletics leaving in '54? Would Havana be brought up?

"Eddie, do you think about Lilly and Mary Beth?"

"Who?" he asked.

"Lilly and Mary Beth, the sisters in Havana."

Eddie bent over the sink. He splashed handfuls of water on his face.

"Eddie, do you ever wonder why Lilly and Mary Beth had sex like that with us?"

"David, is this what you think about?" he said. "Figures. Naomi will never do what those girls did. No offense. I get hard just thinking about that night."

"Naomi wouldn't because Jewish men are not exotic for her," David said. "What's so funny?"

Eddie looked up and shook his head like a dog drying off. "What the hell you talking about?"

At least he was distracted from thinking about Rabelli. "Eddie, I think we were white Negroes for Mary Beth and Lilly."

"Stop it," he said, grinning now, thinking he got the joke. "Do you know how much it hurts to laugh hung over? Come on."

David thought Eddie really was like a dog: if you put food in front of him, he ate; if he smelled a bitch in heat, he jumped her.

"Think about it, Eddie," he said. "They came to Havana to have a fling. Why?"

"You're crazy, you know. You think too much. David, some girls like it as much as guys. Sophia likes it. It gets me hot that she likes it."

"To Sophia you're a star," David said. "TV. Rock 'n' roll. Money. Colored music. But in Havana we were nothing. Not rich. Not famous."

Eddie scrunched up his face. "David, are you saying that two society dames came looking for nice Jewish boys? That's nuts!"

"I think they came for Negro music and sex," David said. "They came to Havana where no one knew them and when they got there, it scared them." In his head he saw Mary Beth and Lilly backing away from the wounded piano player and the woman with the machete.

Eddie didn't get it. He was talking to himself. "But Jews were safe," David told him. "Still exotic. You know, an oriental race. But safe."

"Why weren't we a risk?" Eddie asked. "They could bump into us back home. Didn't Lilly say they were from someplace outside Philly?"

"Not a risk for them," David said. "They could look right through us, like we weren't there. Invisible socially. Just like Negroes. White Negroes."

Rabelli was thinking he couldn't afford to miss again. He just had tonight to kill Eddie Greene. If that.

The Buick was parked on a side street across from the building where David Greenberg worked. Opening the folded scrap of paper for the tenth time he read out loud "David Greenberg" and the home address he had copied from the phone book.

There was a rap on the car window. Standing next to the passenger door was Paulie Tedeschi. Rabelli leaned over and unlocked it.

Tedeschi had been on the force with Rabelli for twenty years. Six months ago he'd been diagnosed with cancer. X-rays showed a cloud in his lung the size of a silver dollar. The docs gave him a year. At most. Rabelli cracked the window open and watched the smoke drift out.

"Paulie, want me to put out the cigarette?"

"What for? Won't shorten my life." Tedeschi's smile was as tired as the joke.

"What do you have for me?" Rabelli asked.

Tedeschi tried to read Rabelli's face. "Julie, this may be getting out of hand. You call me away from dinner to set up a tap on your sister-in-law. The wife's ticked off I leave without finishing. Your niece answers the door, and I thought she was going to call the telephone company to check me out. She would have if your sister-in-law hadn't followed her to the door."

"Paulie, I appreciate all you've done."

"No need for that," Tedeschi said, waving his hand away as if refusing cash. "But I keep hearing things. People say—"

"Say what, Paulie?"

"Like your temper. Sometimes it seems out of control," Tedeschi said.

Rabelli let out his breath. Here it was again. It wasn't just that no one else got it. It was something more. They didn't want to make the effort. And while they sat on their fat asses, Jews and coloreds and God knows who else were taking over the city.

"You want to say something, say it, Paulie."

"Why you tapping your sister-in-law's phone?" Tedeschi said.

"I can't tell you. I wouldn't have asked if it wasn't important."

Tedeschi took a step back. Rabelli hadn't heard his own anger.

"Okay, okay, Julie. Here's the tape," Tedeschi said. "You got something to play it on?"

"Not with me."

"I got the recorder in the trunk," Tedeschi told him. "It's got batteries, if you want to listen in the car."

Tedeschi was walking to his own car as he spoke, so Rabelli raised his voice to make sure he was heard, "Paulie, I need some privacy."

Tedeschi returned with a gray case the size of a radio, put it on the front seat near Rabelli, unsnapped the clips, and lifted the top off. The spools were set up.

"Thanks, Paulie. Why don't you take off? I'll get it back tomorrow," Rabelli said, and then added, "Don't worry about the bug on the phone. The next time I'm there I'll take it off myself."

Rabelli watched Tedeschi until he turned the corner, and then pressed the button.

The first call was answered by the TV station that broadcast *Varsity Dance*. Sophia was told Eddie was not there. The second call went unanswered, but Rabelli heard Sophia's voice in the background, talking to herself: "Jesus Christ, Eddie, answer. Where are you?" The third call was back to the station. Rabelli heard another receiver being lifted before anyone answered. Sophia had heard it, too: "Mom, get off the phone." There was the clunk of a receiver dropped into its cradle, and then: "WPHL-TV, tops in Philly. How may I help you?"

"Sandy, this is Sophia. Sophia Rabelli. I know Eddie's not there. Um, look. He called and left a message he needs to talk to me tonight, but he didn't leave a number. Did you take any calls from Eddie tonight?"

"Not from Eddie. But Nelson Bloomenthal, the lawyer, called. He was the one left the message; he said Eddie had some family business. Bloomenthal said if there was an emergency—he gave me a number."

Rabelli pushed a button to stop the tape while he got a notepad and pen out of his jacket. When he restarted the tape, Sophia said: "That's where he must have been calling from. He's had a lot on his mind. I know he'd appreciate you giving it to me."

"This better not get me in trouble!" the girl from the station said.

"Of course it won't," Sophia promised. "Eddie will thank you. You'll see."

"Okay, here it is. DE8-9255."

"Thanks Sandy, you're the best—wait—this is David Greenberg's number, right?"

Rabelli wrote down "Greenberg" in front of the phone number.

"Your guess is as good as mine," the receptionist said.

There was static for a few minutes and then the next call.

"Hello." The woman's voice was slurred.

"Is Eddie Greene there?" Sophia asked.

"Eddie? You have the wrong number."

"Wait. Please. Eddie called and left this number."

"Who is thith?" the woman asked.

"You don't know me. I—I'm a friend of Eddie's."

Rabelli rolled the window down more and flicked the lit cigarette out of the car.

"A friend? What kind of a friend?"

"I work with Eddie," Sophia told her.

"What kind of work?"

"Look, is Eddie there?" Sophia irritated now.

"Don't take that tone of voice with me!"

Rabelli nodded, thinking it was true what they said about Jewish women; they didn't take crap from anyone.

"Please, I'm sorry. I really need to talk to Eddie." Sophia sounded like a little girl now.

"I just bet you do. Okay, okay. Give me your name and a number."

"Thanks. You can't imagine how important this is."

"Okay, okay. Let me find paper and something to write with."

Rabelli heard a loud noise, and then Sophia's voice: "You all right?"

"I'm just ducky. Damn drawer's stuck and—well, some things fell. Here we go. Okay, give me your name. Slowly."

"Sophia, Sophia Rabelli."

"Slowly. I told you slowly. S-O-P-H-I-E."

"No. A."

"S-A-P-H-I-E. I've never known anyone named Saphie."

Rabelli wrote beneath the telephone number, "Mrs. Greenberg likes the sauce."

"Sophia."

"That's what you said before. I'm not deaf, you know."

"S-O-P-H-I-A. Sophia."

"Okay, okay. Look, do we have to do the last name too? Sounds tricky. Would Eddie know who it is if I just said Sophia?"

"He should."

Rabelli's lips pursed.

"You don't sound old enough to be leaving messages for a grown man. A married man. You know Eddie's married. Not that his wife's such great shakes. Never mind. My voice is high, like a little girl's. Did you notice?"

"It's a lovely voice," Sophia said.

"Don't try and butter me up. I'm no fool. One drink before dinner doesn't make me a fool."

"I'm sorry." Sophia sounded worried that Mrs. Greenberg was about to hang up. Rabelli thought it must be hell to be married to a woman with a mouth like that.

"You said that before. You're repeating yourself. How old are you, Sophia? What kind of business you and Eddie in? Monkey business? You can trust me. Old Naomi here's a well of secrets."

Rabelli sat up.

"Can I give you my telephone number?" Sophia asked. "You know, so Eddie knows where to call?"

"If Eddie knows you so well, he'll know your number. But—maybe I'll take the number. If you tell me how you know Eddie. Can't be too careful. Eddie may be a loser, but he's family. David's family. Maybe more. Who knows? Sophia, you still on the line?"

"Yes ma'am,"

Rabelli arched an eyebrow, thinking Sophia knew how to be polite when it suited her purposes.

"See, I knew you were young. Ok, let's hear what you have to say."

"I know Eddie from *Varsity Dance*," Sophia told her.

"What's that?"

"The TV show," Sophia said.

"I knew that. Just testing you. So what do you do on the show?"

"I dance."

"That's it?"

The woman had a way with one-liners, Rabelli thought. He wondered if she meant to be humorous, or if it just came out funny. Like Gracie Allen.

"Yeah," Sophia said.

"So why would Eddie call you? You and Eddie got something going on the side? Don't be afraid. Anything you tell me won't go any further."

"What's with the twenty questions?" Sophia snapped.

"Don't get on your high horse. You want me to do you a favor, right? I could hang up, and whatever's so important for you and Eddie to say to each other will just go unsaid."

Rabelli liked Mrs. Greenberg more and more, so long as he didn't have to deal with her.

"Is anyone else there I can talk to?"

"You got an attitude problem. You know that? Me, too. When I was a child, Maybelle—that was our cook, she was from Georgia—Maybelle would say to me: 'Miss Naomi, your personality's fine. It's your attitude that's the problem.' Now that's funny. How come you're not laughing? Sophia—bet you thought I forgot your name—Sophia, do you know about Eddie's business in New Jersey? Cat got your tongue?"

Jesus, what did she know? Rabelli wrote, "Bring in for questioning"—and drew an arrow to "Mrs. Greenberg." He put the tip of the pen to his lower lip and then crossed out what he had just written.

"No, Sister," Sophia answered.

"Sister? Did you call me sister? I'm not your sister. What a strange girl you are, Sophia—well, I'm drifting. You know what Mae West said: 'I used to be Snow White, but then I drifted.'"

Sophia laughed.

Mrs. Greenberg resumed. "Let's get back to my offer. Answer my questions about Eddie and Jersey and I'll tell Eddie you called—I'll even give him your telephone number."

"Thank you," Sophia said.

"That's better. Okay. Did you see my husband, David, and Eddie last night?"

Rabelli scribbled, "Greene & lawyer—December 20" and drew a second arrow to "Mrs. Greenberg."

"Yes," Sophia answered.

"Do you have any interest in my husband?"

"No, I swear."

"You better be telling the truth!" Mrs. Greenberg warned.

"Cross my heart and hope to die!"

"Why did Eddie call David last night?"

"I don't know," Sophia said. "They talked in Eddie's office alone."

Rabelli jammed the pen point against his note pad.

"What went on with David?"

"What?" Sophia answered.

"He came back this morning in a strange mood."

"What did he do?" Sophia asked.

"None of your damn business! I don't like you. I don't like talking to you. Maybe Eddie does want to speak with you. Maybe not. Wait. Someone's at the door."

Rabelli heard a soft thud. Mrs. Greenberg couldn't hold on to the phone—must have landed on a rug. He heard Sophia's breathing—soft, different than a drunk's. Then a man's voice: "Hello?"

"Eddie? I've got to see you," Sophia's tone was urgent. "Tonight. I'm going crazy. If I don't get out of this house—"

"I'd love to see you," Greene told Sophia, "but David and I have to go on a business trip. We'll be back in a few days. I've got to get off the phone."

"Wait," Sophia pleaded. "Talk to me. Where are you going? Give me a number to call."

"Don't have one yet." The line went silent, and then Greene's voice, "Yeah, Naomi, I'm almost finished. Naomi, throw in some extra socks and underwear for me, will you? No, I can't go to my apartment. I can't explain now. Please just do it. We have to leave in a half hour."

Rabelli turned on the ignition and pulled into traffic, yelling at a truck he almost hit.

The tape played on, Greene still talking: "Sophia. Sorry. Had to talk with Naomi. I'll call as soon as I get back. Love you."

Chapter Fourteen
Packing

I was replaying in my mind the call from Bloomie: "I'm sorry to give you such little notice, Naomi," as though I were one of the firm's employees. "I have to run," and he had hung up.

I stuffed each of the Evins slippers with a pair of argyle socks and then tucked them against the side of the overnighter. Pulling the suitcase sashes tighter than necessary, I creased David's freshly ironed shirts. Served him right.

I was thinking about Sophia. She sounded young, maybe fifteen or sixteen, carrying on with Eddie, a married man three times her age. When I was sixteen I played five-year-old Shirley Temple in Daddy's radio ads. God, she was important in our lives.

It had all started with going to the Mastbaum to see our first film. That had been 1932. The film, *Trouble in Paradise*, had been very European. All I remembered now was a nighttime billboard in Paris made up entirely of lights. There had been a man in a top hat standing next to a bed, with a half-naked woman under the sheet. Her arms had shot up in surprise, and there had been a bulb for each of her nipples. Some of the men had snorted and laughed; Daddy had cleared his throat.

It had played with a short film, Shirley Temple's first. She had been four years old. The rest of the cast had looked the same age. From the waist up, most had been in costumes. All the kids had been in diapers with giant safety pins, but had played adults. Shirley Temple had a long kiss with another child, and had pushed him away saying she had a husband and child. I couldn't wait for it to end. Daddy and the other men seemed to like it. They had clapped at the end. Mommy had not.

For the next six months Daddy had studied Shirley Temple's studio shots in *Photoplay* and picked one. He had wanted me to wear the same flowered dress, gloves, straw hat, and push the same baby carriage as we sat in the radio studio. I had been furious.

"Daddy," I had shouted, "I'm sixteen, not five. If anyone saw me, I could never face them again."

Mommy had taken my side. Costumes had no appeal for her. She had no need for make-believe the way Daddy did.

But he had insisted that unless we dressed up, people would not "see" the commercials. We had compromised. Daddy had carried a suitcase to the studio that held the Shirley Temple wardrobe. He had given up on the baby carriage.

There we were, "Looney" Luntz, the Packard King, and the Princess. My high-pitched voice sounded like a five-year-old. Daddy had boomed into the microphone, "My customers think I'm looney to sell Packards at these prices! But I love to see a man drive away in a purring Packard, King of the Road, with his wife next to him and his curly-haired Princess in the rear."

The station director had pointed a finger at me and I had giggled. Daddy had sworn families in their living rooms saw Shirley Temple, golden ringlets, dimples and all, sitting behind him. He had told me I had sold a lot of cars.

Daddy had been so taken with Shirley Temple he had built his own movie theater to show her films. People back then stood in breadlines. And in movie lines. We had grown richer.

"Naomi," David broke into my thoughts, "why are you sitting on the suitcase daydreaming?"

I snapped the overnight bag shut and pushed it toward him. "David, what's this trip about?"

His tone was dismissive. "Business. Just business."

"That clears it up," I chirped.

David looked at me this time. "I've got a lot on my mind."

"I'm sure you do."

"What's that mean?" he asked.

"What does Sophia look like?"

David held the suitcase in midair and stared at me.

I raised an eyebrow and twirled the ice in my glass. "That got your attention," I said. "Bet you thought I didn't know about Sophia. I'm not stupid. There's a lot I know about. Like Sophia and Eddie being in business together. Ah—got your attention again. So what does she look like, this girl who dances on Eddie's TV show? Is her face pretty, or do men never take their eyes off her tits?"

"Naomi!" David's tone was right out of a British comedy of manners: the long-suffering tolerance of a chief butler for a novice who couldn't be expected to understand all the nuances of the profession.

"What's the problem? That I used the word tits, or that you stare at hers? There was a time when you couldn't keep your eyes off mine."

"Naomi, what's got into you? This really isn't a good time for this." David's eyes darted about, unable to hold my stare.

"It never is," I said. "Damn. Look at that. Spilled my drink all over myself."

I patted my blouse. It looked like water. One of the advantages of drinking gin. David was watching me. His sadness made me want to cry. David spoke to break the spell, "Honey, I've got to go soon. Let's not end on a sour note. Anything happen today?"

"Nothing happens in my life, right?" I complained.

"Please. That's not what I said." David put the overnighter down and looked around the bedroom. "What's that on the chair?" he asked.

"Alumni news from Dover Hall," I told him. "Not important. Not like news about your anti-Semitic pals from Princeton."

"Come on," he said. "Ease up a little. I listen when you talk about Dover Hall. Anything about people you knew?"

David held my shoulders at arms' length. It wasn't clear whether it was to make sure I listened or to hold me at a distance. I put on my grown-up mask and asked, "Remember Elizabeth?"

"Sure. Married Smedley Industries." That would be what David remembered about Elizabeth. "I'd love to get him as a client."

"She committed suicide. He set up a scholarship in her memory," I said. "Are you listening to anything I'm saying? What are you looking at? David, what's outside?" David was lifting the right side of the window shade.

He went downstairs and I followed. At the front door, David took the glass from my hand and put it on the hall table next to the Venetian glass lamp, an expensive wedding gift from Morris Chumsky. He dropped the suitcase and hugged me.

"David, you're shaking."

"I'm tired," he said. "I get cold when I'm exhausted. I'll be okay. Take care of yourself."

Eddie walked out of the living room's unlit gloom and hooked his arm into David's. I looked at Eddie's face. It was different. Painted with Mercurochrome, brown dots and dashes, a message in a code I didn't know.

"Why are you made up like an Indian?" I asked. "Did you just do that?"

"No, I came in like this," Eddie told me. "Cut myself shaving."

"You shave your forehead?" I said. "You must be a werewolf."

I thought I was funny. No one laughed. David put his hand on my shoulder and said, "Naomi, you're tired. Get some sleep."

Chapter Fifteen
Leaving Philadelphia

"Can I give you a hand?" Eddie offered.

David carried the overnight bag to the rear of the Packard, threw it down, and heard it topple over. In the dark he felt for the lock, but the key in the other hand slipped around the keyhole. Eddie took it from him, opened the trunk, lifted the lid, and laid the overnight bag flat. Slamming the trunk shut, he said, "Maybe I better drive."

"Damn it," David insisted, "give me the keys back."

David flipped down the rear view mirror to the night position. The Buick across the street U-turned and fell in behind them. It made no effort to hide. At red lights it pulled up next to the Packard. The driver's fedora was pulled down in front, hiding his face.

"Eddie, does Rabelli drive a Buick?"

"How would I know? Why?"

"There's a Buick that's followed us from the house," David said. "Don't look around. Damn it, why are you turning the mirror? I can't see behind us."

Eddie said, "How am I going to see the car tailing us? You just told me not to turn around. Christ, will you let go of the mirror?"

He had his right hand on the mirror, twisting it against Eddie's two. The Packard wobbled erratically. Sweat soaked his undershirt. David knew he had to regain control of the mirror. He kept his eyes on the Buick, thinking that if he lost sight of the car behind them, he would slam on the brakes and jump out to see where it was. If it had vanished, the fear would be unbearable. He didn't see the Buick—

"DAVID, WATCH IT!"

The Packard smashed into the side of a truck. His mouth hit the steering wheel. Eddie's forehead cracked against the thinly padded dashboard. When he pushed off, his Mercurochrome tattoo was leaking red.

"Eddie, stay in the car."

"What?" Eddie croaked.

"Don't get out," David told him. "If they see your face, they'll want to get an ambulance. Take this handkerchief."

He stepped out and pulled the overcoat down in front, putting on his reassuring lawyer face. The Packard's front bumper hung loosely. Bathed in the overhead street light, the side of the truck advertised "Kelly For Brickwork" in three-foot-high letters. The door of the cab opened and a thickset man in a plaid shirt stepped down.

"What the hell . . . ?" he said.

"Sorry. You okay?"

The truck driver squinted to see David's face, his voice still loud, "Yeah. Are you drunk? Running a red light. Jesus!"

"I'm just tired. Long day," David explained. "But you're not hurt. How about the truck?"

The man said, "See if you can move your car. Then I can look."

David got back in the Packard. When the engine turned over, he let out his breath. Adjusting the mirror above the dashboard, David saw nothing behind them. He shifted to Reverse and jammed down on the gas. The heavy car lurched back in a deafening rip of metal. Putting it in Neutral, he grabbed the handbrake and pulled hard.

The truck driver announced, "It's your bumper. Fell off."

Eddie said, "David, stow it in the back."

"Put it in the car?"

"For Christ's sake, get this over with! Rabelli's out there."

David opened the door and walked toward the man in the plaid shirt, "How's your truck?"

"A little of your paint and some new dents. You're the one with the damage."

David reached for his wallet and took out a twenty. "I'd appreciate your forgetting this happened. You know—my wife thinks I'm working late at the office."

Embarrassed, the driver said, "No need for that."

"I appreciate how helpful you've been. Please. Take it."

As the driver tucked the bill into his shirt pocket, he pointed to his own mouth, "Your lip's puffy. Put some ice on it when you get home."

David opened the rear door and slid the bumper in.

"Eddie, I think we missed the turn," he said.

It had been twenty minutes since they left the Kelly truck. This part of Bucks County was farmland. There were no streetlights. He had trouble staying on his side of the road. The Packard's functioning headlight was askew and lit up only the right edge of the road and the shoulder. David could see little directly ahead. When the road curved to the left, the heavy car tilted as it slid onto dirt and then jerked back onto the paved surface. The Buick's headlights aimed at them.

"We're not there yet, David. Try to keep the car on the road," Eddie said.

"How do you know? The part of the road I see is the size of a postage stamp. Maybe we should stop and look around."

Eddie reminded him, "Jack was clear. We're not to stop."

He thought about Eddie's calmness about Rabelli. It only made sense if Eddie was more terrified of Jack. "I hate this," David said.

"Are your teeth chattering?" Eddie asked.

David felt drowsy, fighting to keep his eyes open.

"I'm fine," he told Eddie. "It'll be better once this is over. It feels like sand behind my eyes. The warmth leaves my body when I'm this way—like it must feel when you're dying."

"Jesus, David. I knew we should have brought some brandy or something. Let's see if you've got anything."

David told Eddie, "The glove compartment. I keep candy there."

The compartment cover clumped down. David heard something bounce out. It was the flashlight. He saw a wand of light moving around and then heard Eddie say, "Okay, here are some of those peanut chews. Goldenberg's. For us Jew-boys. Slow down. Here's the turn."

The Packard's headlight picked out the dirt road on the right.

A minute later the Buick took the turn, closing in on them. David couldn't tear his eyes from the rear view mirror.

From either side of the road, spits of yellow-orange-red ignited, as though the Buick were skidding through a gas oven. Windows popped. The Buick's engine went silent.

When David first heard the shots he stopped the Packard. He and Eddie turned around. Moving as slow as a hearse approaching graveside, the Buick rolled down the road's incline, tires thumping, flattened by bullets. David rammed the shift lever into Drive and mashed down on the gas, flooding the carburetor into a stall. His palms, slick with sweat, slipped on the door handle.

They heard a soft thud and saw the Buick resting against the Packard's trunk. Men were running toward them. Flashlight beams crisscrossed from both sides of the Buick. Eddie whispered, "Looks like searchlights in a prison yard. You know, Cagney running for the wall."

"Eddie, stop. Just don't talk."

A car door opened. "Pull him out." They recognized Jack's voice. Even though they had heard it for the first time that night, it was a voice you never forgot.

A different voice whined, "He stinks. Christ almighty, shit all over his pants."

Jack again, "Pull him out by his arms. Sammy, why'd you bring a first-timer?"

"He's my kid brother," from a third person.

"Okay, okay. Lay him out on the road. That's good," Jack said. Then louder: "David, Eddie, you guys there?"

"Yeah," David said.

"Come here," Jack directed.

They walked toward the lights framing the mound on the road. David had stopped sweating. His lips were so dry they puckered. To hold down the nausea he took deep breaths of cold air.

"Watch it!" Jack's voice cut through the dark. "You almost stepped on the body. David, get back. Eddie, come here."

Jack pushed on David's chest, and then pulled Eddie forward by his elbow.

"Put your lights on Rabelli's face so Eddie here can get a good look," Jack said.

Eddie stumbled into the pool of light. Rabelli's face was a mask: black shadows filled his eyes, mouth, and neck; his forehead and chin were moon-white.

Jack said, "That would have been you, Eddie. Remember who you owe."

Skin tightened at the edges of Eddie's eyes. Eddie kicked out at Rabelli's cheek; the heel of his shoe broke Rabelli's nose.

David ran to the side of the road and threw up. He kept seeing the hard leather heel sink into Rabelli's splintered nose, blood spurting on the burgundy patent shoe, a sliver of bone jutting up next to the thin sole.

Jack screamed at Eddie: "You're crazy! Don't ever do that! You hear me? He's dead. It's over."

Another voice: "You've messed up your pimp shoes."

Then a different one, laughing: "He's dressed like the colored singers on his show."

And Jack again: "Knock it off. Pull the car out. Someone heard. Cops'll be here soon. Eddie and David, get in your car."

Jack walked with them. "Which one of you is in better shape to drive?"

Eddie said he was.

"Go to the New Amsterdam at 101st and Second. There's a room in the names of Tom and Tony Mix."

Eddie asked, "Who's the movie fan?"

"Shut up and listen!" Jack told him.

Jack went on, telling them who to ask for. He said not to leave the room until late Sunday afternoon, and then to drive directly back to Philly.

Chapter Sixteen
The Drive to New York

Outside the car, Friday night traffic moved in its quiet rhythm toward New York: theater-goers, late diners, truck drivers making deliveries into the city. Inside the Packard, rock 'n' roll screamed out of the speaker.

Eddie had his left hand on the steering wheel. His right, with a lit cigarette upright between his second and third fingers, turned the radio louder. Saxophones throbbed inside the car. David punched the off button. Lyrics continued to swirl out of Eddie, "'Great God A'Mighty!' That's what Little Richard would say. 'Shout!' He's a shouter. 'Slippin' and a slidin'. That's me. I was slippin' and a slidin'. Rabelli couldn't kill me. Bastard tried. Rabelli kept a 'knockin,' but he can't get in. Come back tommora night, and try again.' But then we were ready. You get me, DAVID. WE WERE 'READY, READY TEDDY TO ROCK 'N' ROLL.' Did you see how I messed up that bastard's ugly face? 'WHO-EE.'"

It had been like this since Eddie had driven away from Rabelli's mutilated body. At first David thought he was speaking in tongues. "Eddie, calm down. You're doing seventy. Come on. Stop speeding or let me drive."

Eddie accelerated to eighty, and fixing his eyes on David, broke into

> *"Some that call me Mo*
> *Some that call me Joe,*
> *Some that call me Speed-o,*
> *But my real name is Mister Earl."*

"Eddie, pull over," he said. "If we're picked up we're dead men. I'm serious. We'll be at the bottom of the ocean in cement overshoes."

Eddie started giggling. "'Cement overshoes.' Is that a legal term?"

David grabbed the wheel and wrenched it to the right into a gas station exit. The car wobbled. David stretched his leg until it reached the brake.

"Easy, little cousin," Eddie threatened. "Okay. Let me drive and we'll switch at the gas pump."

The attendant approached slowly and stopped a foot from Eddie's open window. David leaned over and told him to fill the tank. Nervous that the kid might be a fan of *Varsity Dance*, he walked around the car, got in, and pushed Eddie over to the passenger side. Eddie was still laughing. "'Bottom of the ocean'—David you are a hot ticket.

"Come with me
Oh my love
To the sea,
The sea of love . . ."

Eddie's chin rested on his chest. Eyes closed, lips moving. The squeegee swept Eddie's side of the window, moving from the center to the chrome, bubbles of water magically removed. Drool slid down the corners of Eddie's mouth. David was thinking that if he lowered the window on the passenger door, the kid could squeegee Eddie's face. Would that cleanse him of the wear and tear of too much liquor, too rich food, and sex with a sixteen-year-old? Stuffing himself, Eddie starved, an infant that shriveled as it nursed. David wanted to comfort him. David wanted to comfort himself.

"Five fifty." The attendant stood next to David's open window. In the gas station's yellow light, his face looked jaundiced, his acne pustular.

David handed him a ten. The kid gave him back two quarters and counted out the singles and said, "You better get your car fixed. State police will pull you over with a busted headlight."

"Can you do something quickly?" he asked.

"No mechanic here now. Bring it back in the morning."

Twenty minutes to the Holland Tunnel. David drove in the middle lane, hoping to be invisible. A hundred yards ahead, a state trooper had pulled over a Mercury coupe, apricot bottom, cream roof. David's stomach knotted. He slowed down to allow an eighteen-wheeler to pull up on his right, blocking the trooper's seeing the Packard. Suddenly the cab of the long truck cut to the left, lashing its long body as it swerved in front of them. Slamming on the brakes, he flinched at the squeal. Eddie pitched forward, startled. David veered into the right lane, and avoided crashing into the trailer. A siren screamed. In the mirror the red light bled on top of the Chrysler 300 as it shot at them, growing immense in seconds.

"Oh shit." David could barely hear his own voice.

"What's happening?" Eddie asked.

"Shh!" he said as though the trooper could hear them talk.

The Chrysler sprinted past. It had to be doing over ninety. The tightness in David's gut hurt.

The trooper's Chrysler cut in front of the eighteen-wheeler, out of their field of vision. Why didn't they hear the scream of pneumatic brakes? There were sparks and crunching as if a giant had stepped on an enormous beer can. Rising into the sky, the Chrysler floated in mid-air, it's underside a turtle's belly, tires as useless as flippers. The cruiser landed on its roof, windows exploding into glimmering sand.

"What the—? David, don't stop!"

He looked to the right, but Eddie's head blocked the crash scene. Eddie was yelling at him, "What the hell are you doing? Pull back on the road."

David asked, "How do we know the cop's okay?"

Eddie lowered his window, and leaned his head out looking behind them. "We're not doctors, David. Keep going."

He heard the keening of an ambulance and drove off the breakdown lane.

The rain started before they entered the tunnel, one of those storms David thought of as Southern, belonging in Savannah, not outside New York. Water slopped against the windshield, sheeting over as soon as the wipers cleared their half-circle.

Traffic carried the wet into the tunnel. Yellow light washed down the tiled walls like cooking oil, disappearing into the watery black surface of the New York bound lanes.

"David, get out of here!" Eddie's face was sickly, his eyes big as tennis balls.

"That's what we're doing," he said.

"No, I mean now. I can't stand it! We're trapped."

"Trapped?" David repeated, not understanding what he meant.

"We're under water. I can feel the river." Eddie had raised both his arms and was pressing against the roof of the car. The tips of his fingers were white against the gray felt.

"Eddie, close your eyes. We're almost out of here."

"No," he insisted.

"Look," David told him. "There's no one ahead of us. We'll be out in a few minutes. We're okay. The tunnel is fine."

"No. It's not." As he spoke, a thread of saliva danced off his lip. "There's too much water. It's leaking. God damn it, can't you see? It's cracking! The tunnel's breaking up. Hit the gas. We're going to drown!"

He wanted to smash Eddie in the mouth; anything to shut him up. David had a silent monologue running inside his head, one Eddie did not hear: *Can't he see I'm doing everything possible? It isn't as though any of this is my fault. Eddie is the one banging a sixteen-year-old, using Varsity Dance to pimp his high school whores.*

"David, why are we creeping along! This Packard can do over a hundred. Hit it. Oh, God, faster."

"Eddie, we're there. Look, you can see the rain."

The rain fell in a silver curtain. The other side was Manhattan.

Water ran off the front of David's hat brim and onto the worn maroon carpet. He took it off and slapped it against his coat. Rain had soaked through, turning the gray to black. The man behind the reception desk held his hand out. David stared at the scar at the base of his thumb. "Give me the keys," he said. "We'll have the car fixed before you leave."

"Shouldn't we sign a register or something?" David asked.

The man at the desk looked up, startled.

"No," he said. "Here's your key. Take the elevator to the third floor, Room 302. Anything you want cleaned, there's a bag in the closet. Hang it outside your door. Tell me what you want to eat and drink and I'll have it sent up. Jack thought it would be better if you stay in your room the next few days."

Eddie was soaking in the tub, one hand wrapped around a glass filled with ice and bourbon; the other dangled over the side. His diamond pinky ring twinkled like one of the Christmas lights in the shabby stores that bordered the hotel.

"David, I need more ice."

"Get out and put some clothes on," he said. "You're wrinkled like a prune."

"I need to relax," Eddie complained.

"Don't," he said. "You'll drown."

Eddie ignored the sarcasm, and continued his litany of woes. "When I'm not in here, I start shivering. You saw me. Changed into dry clothes and couldn't stop my teeth from chattering. Look at you. Stuffing your face with Danish, and you're shaking like a leaf."

The lemon icing on the pastry tasted like yellow glue. David took a fork and toyed with it, pushing the prongs into the topping and lifting the whole pastry. The sugar had hardened. It cracked as he bit off a piece. The more he ate the more he craved the intense flavorless sweetness. It eased the trembling. He drank black coffee to wash the icing off his tongue, and then stuck the fork into the next pastry, this one with a cheese filling.

"We're prisoners," Eddie said.

"What?" he asked.

"When they brought us the booze and stuff, I heard the lock click."

David looked at the door. "You sure?"

"Try it yourself."

The knob turned, but nothing budged. A moment later he heard the snick of a bolt and the door opened. David looked up at a face with one brown eye and a patch.

"Anything you need?" their guard asked.

Eddie's voice echoed out of the bathroom, "Another bottle of bourbon. Get Jack Daniels this time. And ice! How long are we going to be here?"

The pirate in the doorway was silent. David turned around and reminded Eddie until Sunday.

Eddie yelled, "Save yourself a trip and get two bottles."

The man in the doorway spoke softly to David, "You never saw a man killed?"

David moved his head from side to side.

"I've seen guys like you," he said. "Shakes. Pictures in their heads. You've got to get through the next day. That's all. Your buddy's got the right idea. What do you drink?"

"Chivas," David said.

David was having one of those dreams that come when he was climbing out of sleep. He was standing naked. Mary Beth, in a bright pink dress, was kneeling in front of him. His hand stroked her hair, lifted a comb out of it, and it spilled forward brushing against his belly, his erection growing in her mouth and fingers. A door opened and Naomi walked in trailing a baseball bat across the floor. He slid out of scarlet lips, raised Mary Beth's head to warn her, and it was Eddie's face he was holding. Eddie was staring up, bloodied, his nose broken, wearing the clothes Rabelli died in.

David woke up, startled. His forehead pounded; behind his eyes a weight pressed harder and harder. He closed his eyes to ease the pain.

Somebody was snoring loudly. David jumped out of bed—unsteady on his feet. Leaning against the wall, he slid one foot forward, then the other, and finally made it to the bathroom. David turned on the light switch. With the door open light fell across Eddie's sleeping features. He squeezed his eyes shut and rolled over with his face turned away from where David stood.

The dream evaporated, but not the dread. David knew if he went back to sleep Eddie and Naomi would be waiting.

After closing the bathroom door he ran the shower as hot as he could take it. Stepping in, David felt the water unravel the surface knots. Water alone would not remove the coating of filth. He picked up the razor lying on the soap ledge.

The one-day growth on his face was black wire. After shaving down, his skin still prickled. David ran the razor up, against the grain, and felt the blade catch and pull. It felt good, like wrenching a weed and seeing the roots attached. He rubbed fingertips across his neck and cheeks. The stubble was sheared off at the skin. He knew it would start growing back when he dried his face. David had to stop that from happening. He dragged the razor from side to side, first in one direction and then the other. Slowly, so it would catch. Over and over again, under his jaw-line and across his neck. He had to keep doing it or everyone would see the dark shadow rising under his skin.

David needed to walk on the street, go to the office, lie down next to Naomi, and be invisible again. He poured shampoo on his head, felt the oily Jell-O dissolve and bubble.

He finished soaping and moved his body under the showerhead until every surface, every recess, felt the warmth of running water. David prayed he was cleansed. After turning the shower off, he stepped out.

Moist fog filled the bathroom. Cracking the door, he heard Eddie's snoring, interrupted by gasps and lip smacking, then back to snores. Eddie sounded like a lawn mower when you pull on the rope to get the engine to turn over. David hungered for such sounds, familiar, reassuring, boring.

The cooler bedroom air made the fog on the mirror bead and run. He wiped it down with a washcloth, seeing a reflection briefly, as the glass steamed over again. The face David had glimpsed was a cover from one of those comic books the kids love: a ghoulish head pouring sweat. He closed the bathroom door and stepped back into the shower.

An hour later Eddie was sitting at the table, now covered with empty whiskey bottles and crumbs. David walked out of the bedroom and Eddie said, "Christ Almighty. Look at you. You're ready for breakfast at the Stage Deli."

"Eddie, shower and shave. You'll feel better."

"Why?" he asked. "It's only Saturday. I'm not going to make it. I've got to get out of here, Jack or no Jack."

Eddie took a deep breath, hiked his trousers up, and marched to the door. His loud banging was followed by silence. Finally, it opened. David didn't recognize the man. He was shorter than Eddie, just over five feet.

"Yeah," the man challenged.

Eddie looked down at the guard's shoes and asked, "Flip-tops from Thom McCann's?" Eddie looked up with a grin. "One of my sponsors."

"Is that what you want to talk about?" the short man asked.

"Ah, no," Eddie said. "Look, I don't think I can stay cooped up another day."

"Can't help you there. Jack says you stay, you stay."

"Can I talk to Jack?" Eddie asked.

"No."

Even though it was December, their jailer was wearing only a white T-shirt and a pair of jeans. His left sleeve was rolled up over a pack of cigarettes. David was certain he wasn't twenty yet.

"Let's try it another way," Eddie said.

"Ain't no other way."

"You're supposed to get us anything we need, right?" Eddie argued.

"Maybe."

"No maybe about it," Eddie asserted. "I need pussy. If I can't leave and get laid, you need to bring it to me. You know, more than one way to skin a cat."

"What the hell you talking about?" the kid asked. "What cat?"

Eddie shook his head and said, "Never mind. How about a whore? No old hag with VD. I need a clean hooker that looks good enough to take home to mother. The younger the better."

A toothpick appeared in the guard's mouth. He crossed his impressively muscled forearms and rocked back on his heels. Twitching the toothpick, he said, "I'll see what can be done. Meantime, shower. You got B.O. bad."

The door shut in Eddie's face.

When Jack brought her, the prostitute walked up to Eddie. Staring at his face, she said, "You look familiar. Are you famous or something?"

Jack interrupted, "Honey, I want you to make this joker happy. Think about that and nothing else. Be better for everyone. Understand?"

She held a hand in front of her face and stepped away from Jack. David thought she'd been hit before for saying the wrong thing.

"No problem," she said, taking her coat off and throwing it over a kitchen chair.

She was shifting her weight from one black patent Mary Jane to the other, studying Eddie and David. Betty Lou was the name she gave them, and it went with today's costume: a short-sleeved white angora sweater and a light gray felt skirt with a pink poodle on one side. When she stood too near the window, the sunlight brought out flaws in her makeup, cracked into fine lines like old leather. Eddie wasn't looking that close.

"Jack, I'll give these guys the time of their lives," Betty Lou assured him, "but I got rules."

Eddie laughed and said, "A hooker with rules. I'm getting hard already."

Counting on her fingers, she recited: "Be nice to me. You'll have a better time. I won't be a sandwich. I'll do both of you, but one at a time. If you like watching, that's okay, just sit where I don't see what you're doing."

Jack headed out the door saying, "You work out the details. Betty Lou's been paid through tonight."

It was finally Sunday. The prostitute had left. Eddie was pacing around the table where sections of the *Times* were covered with wax paper and mustard. He had on pants and socks, nothing else. His heavy belly hid the belt. The room stank from cigarettes.

"What time is it?"

It seemed like the tenth time Eddie had asked in the last five minutes. "Still two," David answered.

"David, stop with the Scotch tape already."

He would never get it off his navy blazer. "That damn angora is everywhere," he said. "What am I going to tell Naomi?"

"Tell her it's from a baby cat; you know, pussy hair." Eddie forced a grin.

"Be serious," he said. He threw the angora-covered tape into the wastepaper basket and began making a fresh loop.

"When do we leave here?"

"Four, Eddie. We leave at four."

"Will you stop already with picking at your jacket?" Eddie tried to slap the Scotch tape out of David's hand.

"Why do you need to have a whore dress as someone on your show?"

Eddie stopped circling the table and raised his voice. "What?"

"If you just had a call girl, you know, tastefully done up in a dress, I wouldn't be sitting here picking this crap off my blazer."

Scotch tape was wrapped around David's palm like a boxer's tape. He slid it off and threw it in Eddie's direction.

"You're pissed at me?" Eddie snarled. "What's your problem?"

David didn't feel it coming, the bitterness in his voice. Or the fear he felt at the words he hadn't anticipated. "You. You're my problem. From the time we were kids." David thought he was finished, but he couldn't stop. "I never should have gone to Havana."

The fear iced his gut. He stared at Eddie. David shook his head like a dog drying off. He was relieved Eddie had heard only the words and not his memories. Or his longing.

Eddie said, "I didn't tell you to play Boy Scout, camped out in the bathroom while I got my rocks off. Betty Lou wasn't bad. I mean she wasn't 'Sweet Little Sixteen' or nothing. No Sophia. But she knew what she was doing."

Frown lines dug into Eddie's forehead as it came back to him. "What the hell went on with you two? I was half asleep and heard you screaming at her. Some crap about 'It isn't right.' You telling me you never cheated on Naomi? David, Jews don't have saints. Don't try to be the first one, St. David."

"Shut up!" he snapped.

"What's the time?" Eddie asked again.

"Look at your watch!"

He walked around the table, stopped when he got to Eddie, and walked back to the other side.

"You're really testy," Eddie said. "Locked in this fleabag, no wonder. Come on David, look at the bright side. With Rabelli out of the way, we're golden. *Varsity Dance* goes national in a few weeks. Pyramid will go through the roof. There'll be so much legal work, you and Naomi can live off what you make."

David felt the heat in his face. "What's that crack mean?"

"Nothing," Eddie apologized. "It was stupid. I—oh forget it."

"Is that what everyone *thinks*? That I married Naomi for her money!"

"I said I'm sorry," Eddie whined. "Calm down. Naomi's lucky to have you. That's what people say."

He turned his back on Eddie.

"Jesus, you're going to give me the silent treatment? Come on, David, talk to me. I hate it when you go inside yourself. Is the drive to Philly going to be like this?" Eddie put his hands on David's shoulders and turned him around.

"Maybe it's the sex," Eddie said, watching his face for agreement.

"Maybe what's the sex?" David challenged.

"You're getting in a rage," he said.

Eddie started to move an arm around him, hesitated and let it drop to his side.

"What—?" he shouted, trying to drown out Eddie's voice. David needed to stop this conversation, to get away.

"Like the flight back from Havana," Eddie said.

"You're crazy!" David screamed. "What do you mean 'the sex'?"

David feared Eddie was going to say it; his stomach spasmed.

"I don't know," Eddie said, creases on his forehead. "Does it upset you if you're around, and I'm getting laid?"

Eddie's arms circled David, pulled him close. He smelled Eddie's mix of heavily splashed Canoe and the endless sweat from his glistening fat.

"This is really nuts," David said. "Don't—Don't do that. Put on a shirt. Don't go around half naked." He pushed Eddie back hard with both hands, and then just missed hitting him. "Keep your hands off me, damn it," David yelled.

"What's going on?" Eddie said. "I give you a hug to calm you down, and you take a swing at me? I don't get it. Where are you going?"

"To take a shower," David told him. His back was toward Eddie, the words tossed over his shoulder. "We have over an hour to kill. We need to be apart. It's the only other room."

He stepped into the bathroom and locked the door.

Chapter Seventeen
Return from New York

Everyone had tried to warn me.

Mommy had called at noon. "Naomi, what time are you expecting David?"

"I don't know," I had said. "I haven't heard from him."

"Well, best be ready," Mommy had told me. "You know, look fresh and pretty."

Those were Mommy's code words for sober, showered, and out of the clothes I had slept in.

At two, Liz had phoned. "Did you eat today?"

"I can't remember," I had said.

"Put da phone down. Go to da icebox and look on da second shelf. Plate wrapped in foil. Nice drumstick. Den come back and tell me. I'll wait."

When I got back to the phone, Liz said, "Promise me you eat. Promise?"

"Yes. I swear I'll eat the chicken leg," I said. It was funny. If anyone else talked to me this way, I'd chew their head off. With Liz it made me feel good.

David and Eddie pulled into the driveway at five-thirty. I watched from the window next to the front door. I couldn't get myself to come out and talk to both of them. Besides, I was still in my nightgown and robe. Eddie drove off in David's car without coming in.

I turned on the outside light and opened the door. Probably I should have given David a hug and told him how much I had missed him. I couldn't make the effort.

"You should have called," I said, "told me when to expect you," letting him know it was his responsibility to give me time to wash and dress. As an afterthought, I added, "Have you had supper?" David's face looked thinner in the two days he had been away.

"It was crazy up to the last minute," he said. "I didn't want to delay getting home."

As David spoke he looked at his shoes. When had he picked up Bloomie's habit?

"You never said what it was about," I said. "What kind of business would you need Eddie along for?" Why couldn't I make him feel welcome? I thought about trying, but my irritation kept getting in the way.

David was lost in picking at invisible lint. When he stopped examining his jacket, he stared at the suitcase he had put down.

I cleared my throat. "Pyramid," he replied. He paused, looked up and said, "I'm not hungry, but I'd love a drink. Chivas, no ice. Make it a tall one."

"David, are you okay?"

"What—" He spread his fingers palm down and studied them.

"David, look at me." His head had settled on his chest. I walked over and framed his face in my hands. I lifted it toward me. His eyes, those lovely hazel-green eyes, were wet. "David, what's wrong?"

His lower lip quivered and he began to cry. What was it? He was like a child. Tears wet his cheeks; mucus bubbled out of his nose. Fear twisted inside me. I hugged him. He buried his sobbing in my body, the sound muffled. I pulled him closer, cooing wordless sounds.

I heard my mother's voice coming out of my mouth. Was she scared when I wept, trying to reassure herself that the bone jutting from my leg could be pushed back as though I had not fallen out of the tree?

Who would make it better for me? I needed someone to comfort me. Why didn't David lift the dread I woke with?

"David, wash your face," I said. "I'll get us both a drink. Go on, I'll be right back."

David finished off his scotch in gulps, and said he had not slept much in New York. "That's why I carried on like that. Physical exhaustion. I'll be fine in the morning."

He went upstairs. I followed a half hour later. I sat in the old rocking chair and watched David sleep. He wasn't at peace. His legs were seldom still; sometimes he rolled over. His lips moved, and the words, if that's what they were, never rose to a level I could make them out.

The chair had been Mommy's. She had told me she had rocked in that chair as she nursed me. Someday, she had said, I would nurse *her* grandchildren as I rocked. I had asked if her grandchildren were my children.

"Whatever are you thinking, Naomi? You are my only child. Sometimes you say the strangest things." And she had looked at me, shaking her head.

The plainness of that chair stood out in our bedroom like a visit from a poor relative. Mommy's failed prediction was another reminder that our family was ending with me, the last station on the Luntz line. Strangely, the chair was the only piece of furniture I liked in our bedroom. On the floor next to the chair I put the ice bucket, the half-empty bottle of gin, and my glass.

I woke up in the rocking chair, the morning sun in my face. A headache cut above my eyes. The bottle was empty. So was the bed.

From the day David came back from New York he never slept through the night. I would wake and reach out for him in the dark and find he was gone. I stretched my arm under the covers seeking his warmth. The sheets were cool on his side of the bed. I crawled to his pillows and breathed in, but he had not even left his scent, that smell of heat and flesh brushed by light sweat that I had loved from the first. His clothes were different now: Egyptian cottons and silky wools had replaced starched scratchy dress shirts and coarse woolen suits. But the fragrance that was David had never changed. That was what made him elegant. When I had been lost in movie magazines at fifteen I would smell William Powell in my daydreams, but I had known there were many women who had done that; some had actually been next to him. David's smell was just for me. I couldn't bear that he had gone and not left me his scent.

I went downstairs and found him in the den. A blaze of light fell across his bathrobe, making the maroon silk smolder. I remembered watching the saleswoman at De Pinna lay tissue paper under each fold and then look up at me with a conspirator's smile. Running perfectly manicured nails across the robe, she had said, "You could wear it with nothing else on. As a gift. I've done that for my husband."

I felt the same hunger for David as I had when I first met him at the Kuhns almost twenty-two years ago. My cousin Ronald had taken me to a non-Christmas party for Jewish guys at Princeton. David had roomed with Ronald.

I had loved David's eyes. At first I had thought they were emerald green and had imagined having a daughter with those eyes. It must have been the lighting in the corner of the room. Later, when I had looked again, his eyes had been hazel. But that first time I had seen a woman's eyes in a man's face.

David and I had gone outside and into the back of the Packard Daddy had lent Ronald. We had hugged each other, trying to draw closer. Bundled up in thick cloth, we had squirmed like puppies, delighted and clumsy. I had unbuttoned my coat and tried to shrug out of it, but the sleeves had pinned my arms. David had reached behind me and slid one arm out at a time. He had unbuttoned the back of my dress and I had pulled his head down until his lips were against the base of my throat where there was a shallow dip, an angel's thumbprint. He had touched it with the tip of his tongue. We were both sighing heavily. David had reached behind and unfastened my brassiere.

I had felt something tightening inside. "No," I had said. "Please don't." I had kissed the top of David's hand, crying.

"Naomi, I am so sorry."

"No. Please. I want to be with you," I had told him. "I just can't— Please understand."

David had kissed me on the forehead; I had touched his mouth.

Walking back to the party, I had buried my face against his neck. Under his aftershave, under the oil holding his part in place, I had smelled David—a thin residue of sweat and something that's hard to describe—like heat on summer grass. I had loved it from that first night.

I looked down now at the older David, asleep, his head resting on papers from the office. With my hands under his arms I tried to lift him into a sitting position. "David, come back to bed. You won't get any rest down here. Come on. You'll knot up your neck."

He wrapped his arms around my hips. I wasn't sure he was awake.

Two weeks later at dinner I asked David why his year-end bonus had been so large. He said that Pyramid was pleased with his work, and their billings were growing. "Did it have anything to do with the New York trip?" I asked.

"Why New York?"

"I don't know," I said. "Was there anything different about that trip?"

David's tone was testy. "Why are you harping on that one trip? I'm always working on Pyramid matters. What's so special about New York?"

"Stop yelling," I fired back. "I was just asking."

The longer David kept New York a locked door, the more we argued. He was now on the attack. "You must have had a reason. You didn't pick New York out of thin air."

"You've seemed different since that trip," I said. "And it was the only time Eddie was involved."

"It's Eddie, isn't it?" David pounced. "You've never liked him. He's not polished enough for you. Well, he makes money for all of us—me, the firm, your father. Everyone."

It always ended like this, but I couldn't stop picking at the scab. For now, though, I needed to have it stop. "Please, David, I don't want to argue. I want us to be happy. It's been so long since we've liked to spend time together. I'm so proud of how well you're doing."

"I just bet you are," he snapped.

"What does that mean?" I asked.

My hand was shaking, and I spilled some of my drink on the floor. I knelt down and rubbed the wetness with my nightgown sleeve.

"Stop it, Naomi!" he said. "You're making it worse. Why are you still in a nightgown? Did you ever get dressed today?"

David watched me walk up the stairs to our bedroom. He didn't try to stop me.

The following day, soaking in a tub of bubble bath, I decided to use my Joy perfume, instead of Chanel, to mask the liquor. I hadn't had a drink since three that afternoon and had brushed my teeth and gargled several times. I was still scared he would know about the drinking earlier in the day. I was in a silk blouse and flannel skirt when David came home.

When we sat down for dinner, a small box tied with a blue ribbon sat next to my plate. I looked at David. "Go ahead and open it," he said.

Inside were drop earrings, with a diamond and emerald in each. "Oh David, they're beautiful."

"The salesman at Milner's said they matched the bracelet your folks gave you for your fortieth."

Why was he doing this? I was always at him. I should have been the one with a peace offering. "David, can we afford these? They must have cost a fortune."

"I'm sorry for how I've been acting," he said. "I wanted to see you smile." David walked behind me and squeezed my shoulders. I lifted one of his hands and kissed it.

I thought we would make love that night, but after dinner David said he had something he needed to finish for a meeting the next morning. I went upstairs and changed into a long emerald-green nightgown and put on the earrings. I imagined David coming through the door, tired and distracted. I would stand up, the light playing on the French silk. He would see the outline of my body and would see me as I was at eighteen, my breasts lifting, hips slimmer, and I would be pleased with his arousal.

It was now eleven and David was still downstairs. He was thinking of me as too heavy, an embarrassment when I drank. He was hiding in his office. The weight of my sadness bloated me.

I shuffled into the bathroom and opened the medicine cabinet where I kept a Listerine bottle filled with gin mixed with food coloring. One swallow. That was all I would take. It was all right. Without it, I would start crying. If David came in and saw that, everything would fall apart. I couldn't bear that.

I felt better after the first sip. I closed the medicine cabinet door. In the mirror the face I saw was teary, puffy. I needed another bit of my special mouthwash, just one more swig and I knew the sadness swelling my face would flow away.

I stayed in the bathroom waiting for my face to change, for my eyes to dry. When I opened the cabinet door again, the mouthwash bottle was empty. I thought I had filled it up this afternoon. Maybe I had done it yesterday. Well, I couldn't go downstairs to the liquor cabinet tonight. David might catch me.

Walking back to bed, I slipped and fell on my hip. It didn't hurt. Not now. I was more careful. I got into bed and pulled up the blanket. Something was wrong. Were there slippers on my feet? I thought about lifting up the sheets to see, but I was too tired.

I wasn't the only one needing a little hair of the dog. Every time I saw Eddie he was drunk. It wasn't that we saw him that often socially. But he had this way of appearing at odd hours. Drawn to David like that trick in science class: the teacher had a piece of paper and had put metal shavings on top; then he had moved a magnet under the paper where you couldn't see it, but you knew where it was by following the shavings, always controlled by that invisible force. That was Eddie and David.

I was thinking this was unclear, the booze talking. But I knew I was right. I needed to get this right. For myself. To know I wasn't crazy.

Evidence. I needed evidence against my lawyer husband. I laughed out loud. Good line, Naomi!

The car on the lawn. Perfect. I knew I wasn't insane. Mind still worked.

It had been in the middle of the week. It had also been in the middle of the night. I'm always in the middle. In the middle between David and Eddie. In the middle between Daddy and Mommy. It made sense that Eddie had driven his car onto our front lawn in the middle of the night in the middle of the week. I had drawn back the curtain and watched as I had watched Daddy stare at the moon. Was that a dream? Daddy and the moon? Eddie on the lawn? I saw Eddie and the car and David. I had seen them.

I have to remember. Okay, I've got it again. David had gone out and opened the car door, and the top half of Eddie had fallen out like a drawbridge lowering from a castle. David had pulled the rest of Eddie out of the car and onto the lawn. The grass had been a mess in the morning. Deep tire ruts. David hadn't cared. Now if I were the one who had driven up on the lawn, David would carry on. But his precious Eddie could do anything and David forgave him. Now that's true love!

Anyway, David had put one of Eddie's arms over his shoulder and lifted him up. Eddie's legs had been loose as spaghetti. Bet he had been wearing God-awful shoes. Suede and lizard. Eddie dressed like a *schvartza*.

David had carried Eddie toward the house and out of my sight. I had left the bedroom quietly and listened. The front door had closed and then I'd heard the metal sound as the bolt had been inserted. The little metal wedge into the square hole. See, David could put a square peg in a round hole! No, that's wrong. Both peg and hole were square. Must stop veering off. People will think I'm loony. I'll have to go back and talk to Dr. Flynn. Safer to talk to myself.

David's inhaling had been harsh. Served him right! I had listened to his labored breathing. David had panted all the way to the den; then opened that door. David opened doors for Eddie and closed them on me. The den door had shut. David and Eddie were in their inner sanctum.

Chapter Eighteen
Sophia at the Cemetery

God it was cold, Sophia thought. The ground was the color of dust balls. Where it was frozen it had formed spider webs. She stomped to keep her toes warm. The ice snapped shooting cracks through the tangled webs. She knew this must be what Hell looked like frozen over.

If Uncle Julie were anywhere, he would be roasting in Hell, his skin bubbling and splitting, Sophia thought to herself.

She remembered when the telephone call had come, and her mother had shut down. She stopped eating. When Rose forced herself to take a mouthful, she threw it up. Her hand was ice. Talking to her was the worst. Her eyes saw things Sophia didn't; the voices in her head drowned Sophia out. It wasn't clear Rose knew they were at the cemetery.

The men wore blue police coats; the women and priests shivered in black.

Sophia remembered Julie in his open casket last night. She had heard that dead bodies were drained of blood and then some liquid was pumped in. Gave the skin a bluish tint so they had to use makeup.

The sun was hidden. Overhead it was as doughy as Julie's face against the casket's white satin lining.

Here at the cemetery they were all floating on the icy ground, drifting further and further away from warmth and life. The priest kept repeating that salvation was at hand. Sophia didn't think that was the case for Julie.

When it was over, there was a family line: Aunt Tina, Angie, twins Johnnie and Maria, Paolo, Rose, and Sophia. Paolo hated his name; said it sounded like he was born in the old country. He got everyone to call him Zip, which didn't sound at all Italian. Everyone called him Zip; everyone but the family.

Neighbors, cops, cops' wives, they all came down the line, hugging Aunt Tina, trying to muffle her sobbing. Women wrapped themselves around Angie and Maria; men shook hands with Johnnie and Paolo.

Everyone held Rose up and passed her to the next person in line, afraid if they didn't she would drop to her knees and freeze to the ground. They all walked past Sophia. Most turned their heads away. Some looked through her, the person who shouldn't be there, the embarrassment.

A few gave her the evil eye. Mrs. D'Onofrio lifted up the patch and Sophia felt the curse spurt out of that clouded eye. Sophia knew Mrs. D'Onofrio had planted worms of death inside her. Sophia felt them squirming.

Only the young priest embraced her, and that made it even worse.

Aunt Tina and her cousins left first, in a Caddie from the funeral home. Tina had asked Rose to come with them, but when her mother asked about Sophia, Aunt Tina said there wasn't room.

Sophia and her mother were walking with Rose's closest friend, Angelina, whose family had dropped back a few feet. Sophia was sure their conversation had to do with her. They both kept their voices low, but Sophia made out what was said. Every so often Angelina looked at her. Sophia was trying to figure out whether it was to stop her from hearing or to make sure she did.

"Angelina, something bad's going on. About Sophia."

The two women held on to each other. Rose faced her when she spoke; Angelina stared forward and said, "The talk is that Eddie Greene and his cousin know something about Julie's murder."

Rose hesitated. Sophia wondered whether her mother was thinking about her and Eddie. When Rose replied, she was nervous. "Have the police questioned them?"

"Yeah, but they're not saying anything," Angelina said. "Lawyers protect them, powerful people call the D.A. Cops can't get those two alone and get the truth out of them."

"What does any of this have to do with Sophia?" her mother asked.

Walking fast, Sophia got next to Angelina. She tried to stare her into silence. It didn't work. Angelina's eyes turned to stones. She moved her head toward Rose and said, "Ask her. Ask her how she got her face beat up."

"She said she got into a fight with a girl who thought she was stealing her boyfriend."

"Ask her again," Angelina said.

Angelina's husband, Marco, drove us home. Angelina, Rose, and Sophia were in the back seat; Marco and the two girls in front. When Angelina had told Rose to ask Sophia again, conversation had died. The skin on Rose's face had become tight, pulled pale over her cheek bones and around her eyes, eyes that had lost their warm brown and were now a flat black. As a kid Sophia had thought it was magic, black magic, when this happened. Though it seemed that her small body shrank, as Rose drew inside herself she became denser, heavier, more powerful. It happened rarely. Rose was usually timid. But the tense face, the white spots on her nostrils, were signs the violence in her was about to break. Would it claw Angelina or Sophia? Everyone in the car felt it. Everyone held their breath, wanting to let it out, scared of setting her off, smelling gas building up in a kitchen and panicked some fool would not notice and start to move a thumbnail across a match head.

When the car stopped and they were about to get out, Angelina did not hug Rose the way she always did. Instead she put one hand under Rose's and patted it on top with her other.

Inside the house, Sophia kept her coat on. Rose stepped between the door and Sophia.

"What did Eddie Greene have to do with Julie's death?" she asked.

"Nothing."

"You've asked him?" she said.

"Why would I ask him?" Sophia tried to walk around her and reached for the doorknob. Rose's hand grabbed her above the wrist, nails breaking the skin. Sophia stared at her grip, spots of blood freckling her skin. Rose's fingers tightened.

"Damn!" Sophia pleaded. "Come on! That really hurts!"

"Sophia, look at me." Rose's eyes were dull black glass. "Sophia," she demanded, "did Eddie Greene take your virginity?"

"You're scaring me. Stop it."

"Did Julie know?" Rose asked.

"How do I know? Go ask him."

Rose's other hand closed into a fist and smashed Sophia's already split lip. She spat a gob of frothy strawberry that landed on her mother's coat. Rose's eyes never left Sophia's.

"I don't want to hear it from a stranger," Rose said.

"Hear what?"

"If I knew I wouldn't ask," she said. "Tell me about you and Eddie Greene and Julie."

"You going to beat it out of me?" Sophia tasted her temper at the back of her throat like a coating of chalk. "There's a lot of Uncle Julie in you. You know that? Okay, you want to hear it? Let go of my hand." Sophia looked at her forearm. As the white faded, a purple outline of fingers surfaced.

"Sophia," her mother prodded.

As Sophia told Rose about Julie hitting her and shooting at Eddie, Rose looked like she was being beaten. "You caused Julie's death."

"You got it backwards," Sophia said. "Julie was the one who tried to kill Eddie. Julie was the one did this to me," she said, pointing to her face, "before you added to it."

Rose covered her face with her hands and whimpered like a dog hit by a car. Sophia reached out to her. Rose pushed her away hard and she banged against the door.

"This is God's judgment!"

Sophia couldn't believe what her mother was saying. "It has nothing to do with God or you or Eddie or me! There's a line a mile long wanted to kill Julie!"

Rose was squatting, her coat spread out on the floor like a pool of ink. Sophia moved slowly, afraid to touch her. She needed to do something. Rose's voice had softened to a low moan, and it scared Sophia more than her wailing at the cemetery. There was no more fight in her; she had given herself over to death.

"Sophia, God has used you to punish me."

"This is crazy!"

"No, it's clear," her mother whispered. "I slept once with Julie. Before you were born. I never knew whether he was your father." She raised herself up and slumped into her bedroom.

Sophia knew she had to get out of there. Rose's door was shut. She was inside the dark. If Sophia went in there, she would be trapped inside her madness. If she tried to save her, both would drown. For a crazy instant, Sophia saw their house in flames and a silhouette dancing inside the fire. It was a woman. She couldn't see her face, just black and red and tangled hair like snakes.

Pulling open the front door Sophia stretched her head out. She drank in the cool air and felt the slime wash away in her stomach.

"Sophia, you okay?" It was ten-year-old Maria from next door.

"You're all sweaty," she said. "You coming down with something? I'm not supposed to be near anyone with the flu."

"I'm fine," Sophia told her. "Just needed to get outside." She walked two blocks to the drug store and went into the phone booth.

"WPHL-TV, tops in Philly. How may I help you? . . . I'm sorry you'll have to speak louder. Who is this?"

"Sandy, it's me. Sophia."

"Why are you whispering? This is a bad connection—Honey, why don't you hang up and call back?"

Sophia wanted to pinch her to get her attention.

"No. No. Sandy I can't talk louder. Look, all I want to know is whether Eddie's there now."

"Yeah, but he's busy," she said.

"Tell him I called and not to leave until I get there."

"Sure, but no guarantees. I'm not his mother."

"You okay, Sophia?"

Sammy, the security guard, looked a hundred years old but was in his fifties. There was a pouch of scar tissue covering most of his left eye, and his nose had been broken so many times his breathing sounded like a bulldog.

"Sure Sammy. Never better. Is Eddie still here?"

"If he left, it wasn't past me. I woulda' checked it off on my sheet. Say, why are you all dressed up?"

"Funeral," she said and walked past him.

Eddie was in his dressing room nursing a glass of Mister Jack. "I thought you were tied up with your uncle's funeral," he said. Eddie was annoyed, like Sophia should have his permission to see him. She didn't need him pushing her away, too.

"There's only so much of that I can take," she said. "When we got home, Mom went off the deep end."

Eddie finished off the bourbon in his glass and rattled the ice around. Then he said, "What do you mean? Wait. The show starts in twenty minutes. Let's have dinner after. We can talk then."

"I don't want to talk about her." Sophia heard the pissiness in her voice. "I need you to answer one question."

Eddie had turned away from her, toward a mirror. "Okay, quick. What is it?"

"The cops think you know who killed Julie, you and your cousin," she said. "Do you?"

He was combing the back of his hair sideways from each direction and then down the center with a single tooth to get the line perfect on his d.a.

"That's nuts! Who said that?"

Sophia grabbed his shoulder. Eddie swung around until he faced her.

"Mom's best friend said that's the word on the street," she said. "Most everyone at the funeral were cops and their wives. They made a point of looking through me as if I wasn't there. Do you know how that feels?"

Eddie tried to turn his back on her again, but she held tight to his shoulder.

"Look, we can't talk this through now," he said. His tongue kept flicking out to wet his lips.

"Eddie. Look me in the eye and say yes or no," she told him.

"I can't do that!" Tears washed down his face.

"Why are you screaming at me?" she asked.

He pointed a finger at her. "It's all your fault. Throwing yourself at me! I can't live like this. You hear me? I can't. I'm a family man. Get away from me." Eddie's face kept changing back and forth, dark with anger or bawling like a baby.

"So you did have Julie killed?" Sophia knew the answer.

"Shut up! SHUT UP!"

He took a wild swing at her, but was so drunk it missed by a mile. For a split second she saw nothing. Next thing Sophia knew Sammy had her arms pinned to her side, pulling her back. Eddie's face was bleeding. She screamed, "You bastard! You lousy bastard!"

Eddie had a handkerchief to his face. He lowered it. "Listen and listen good. I'm closing Blueberry Hill. You are never, *never*, to come back here. Sammy, if she shows up, throw her the hell out. Look at you! A witch in black!"

"Mr. Greene, there's no need to call Sophia names," Sammy warned.

"You drunken bum, you want to be fired?"

Sammy's arms tensed.

"Sammy, it's okay," she said. Sophia turned around and left Eddie's world.

Out on the street, she took off her shoes and started the walk home. She wanted to feel the cold cement. Everything was spinning out of control. Sophia kept pushing away what her mother was talking about. Julie could have been her father? At the back of her mouth she tasted something like car grease. Did other people have black slime inside them?

And Eddie? She should've scratched his eyes out! She had tempted *him*? Bullshit! The bastard was an octopus. His hands were all over the girls before the cameras were on, copping feels like they were his private cookie jar. And now he was Mr. Family Man?

She could hear the nuns, if they ever got wind of this, cackling like chickens and pointing their bony fingers at her.

A priest and an old woman walked toward her and broke off their conversation to stare. Sophia turned and looked at her reflection in one of the studio's windows: mascara ran in sooty lines down her face. She thought Eddie was right; she did look like a witch.

"What are you two staring at?" she challenged.

"You look as though you've been crying," the priest said. "Is everything okay?"

"Everything's fine, Father."

"Do you want us to call your parents?" he asked. "We'll wait here 'til your dad picks you up."

She was thinking both of her fathers were dead, if her mother could be believed. The old woman dug into her pocketbook, and her hand came out holding a tissue. "Here dear, wipe your eyes. You don't want to be in public looking like that awful woman on TV, Vampira."

Sophia thanked them and continued walking. It was nice to be around people who were not crazy and furious, but their butter-frosting sweetness was getting to her.

She was so tired. Her coat weighed a ton. She needed to run. But where? She couldn't face her mother. Just thinking about Rose had her crazy. Once at school this really fat girl—must have been two hundred pounds—called her a slut. Sophia bloodied her nose. It wasn't that the girl hit her back. She just sat on Sophia, pinned her hands so Sophia couldn't get at her face again. She couldn't move. Felt buried under her. By the time the nuns pulled the fat girl off, Sophia was nutty inside.

She couldn't stop thinking about Julie and her mother. Did she have his rage in her blood? She needed to get it out of her, like how guys flushed dirty oil out of an engine. What could Sophia use to drain Julie's madness out of her? The heel of her shoe? She sat down on the street and pulled up the sleeve of her coat. Sophia lay her left hand against the curb, soft side up. It hurt like hell when the heel hit. No blood spurted. She raised the shoe in her right hand again, and a cruiser came around the corner. It slammed on the brakes as she brought the shoe down a second time.

"Hey! Hey you! What're you doing? Cut it out."

The cop riding shotgun climbed out. He was in his forties, probably a six-footer. From where she sat he looked eight feet tall.

"You don't want to be doing that."

How did he know what she wanted to do?

"Pull your skirt down and give me your hand," he said. "I'll help you up."

Sophia looked down and saw that her coat was open, and her skirt bunched high on her thighs. She thought here was a guy more than twice her age found her attacking herself like some mad saint in the desert, and he needed her to cover up before he could focus on her problem? Sophia knew he wasn't going to be any help.

"What's your name?" the cop asked. "Look, I'm trying to be of some good. I'm not going to hurt you. I need to know a few things. You can talk, right? You're not mute or something? Okay, okay, stop walking away."

The cop had his hand on her shoulder. She stared at it until he took it off.

"I just came from my uncle's funeral," Sophia told him. "I needed to be by myself."

"So what's with hitting yourself with a shoe?" he asked.

She put on her intelligent look; anything to get rid of this guy. "You're right," she said, "makes no sense."

He pointed to the car door he had left open and said, "Can we drive you home?"

"I live a block away," she explained. "If you pull up with me it'll just upset everybody. Make a bad day worse. Really, I'm okay." She gave him her best big girl smile.

"Why don't you drive back in a few minutes?" Sophia told him. "I'll be home by then. You'll see for yourself that I'm not still on the street." The cop driving the car beeped the horn. She walked around the corner thinking he would give in to his partner.

Another block and she would turn left, and then into her house. Fearful images filled her mind. Would window shades be up, faces on the watch for her? The men would be sent away. This was women's work. It needed a strength men didn't have. At each window would be a face wrapped in a black shawl. There would be no lipstick, no makeup at all. The faces would be the same as their mothers' and their grandmothers' and further back, back to faces on hills in Italy long ago.

Once she turned onto the street a window would open, a mouth would become an "O" and a voice would say "murderer," then another window and another voice. The sound would become thick as a wall. It would stop her at the first step leading to her door. She would try to move back, and the wall would be behind her. Sophia would be trapped inside four invisible walls, unable to reach her mother, unable to leave the street. She would try to talk and no sound would come out. She would be able to see, but not to speak. She would not be strong enough to look away. What had made them faces—the eyes, the noses—would fade, leaving white circles framed in black shawls and the unbreakable wall of sound.

At the corner Sophia turned right to Teresa's. She would call home from there to hear her mother's voice, to make sure she was alive.

Chapter Nineteen
Naomi Home Alone

I thought about Sophia in the weeks after New York. Her voice was so young. The telephone call for Eddie had started everything. Well, everything that weekend. I tried to make up a story that began with the telephone call and explained it all. I couldn't. I tried to imagine what she looked like. Sophia Loren? When Mommy called to ask if we would come to dinner Friday night, I asked, "What is it about Sophia Loren that makes men gaga?"

"Why on earth are you asking?" she said.

"Do you think it's her face?"

"Well, her face is interesting," Mommy said. "But you know men, Naomi."

My grandmother had thought fathers were irrational about their daughters. Mommy had her rules about men as well. I was certain I had nothing to guide me.

"I'm never sure," I said.

"About what?" she asked.

"About men. How they think."

"Well, about Sophia Loren I'm sure it's her breasts," she said. "Men can think about breasts morning, noon, and night. It's a wonder they get anything done."

I laughed.

So I started watching *Varsity Dance* on TV to find the girl with Sophia Loren breasts. But they all wore white blouses buttoned all the way up and cut on the full side. I considered going to the studio and asking around for Sophia. I could just see Eddie spotting me and coming over. He'd make some embarrassing remark and call David.

"Naomi, why are you so interested in Sophia?" David would say. "What's this all about?"

That Friday at dinner my cousin Ronald, David's college roommate who had introduced us, was there with his ten-year-old daughter, Beth.

Last year he and Tess had divorced. Aunt Ida had said to Ronald, over and over, "What did you expect marrying a *shiksa*? I told you to marry a nice Jewish girl. Did you listen?"

Beth had her Katy Keene cutout book open and was putting a strapless dress on her. It hugged the cartoon drawing, emphasizing breasts and hips, and ended in a fishtail. Aunt Ida stared for a moment. "Beth dear, nice girls don't wear dresses like that."

"Mom, stop," Ronald said.

"She needs a mother," Ida lectured, "to raise her right."

Beth looked up at Ida with the same frown Tess had worn for years. "I've got a mother."

"Oh, you heard me," Ida said. "When you play you're in another world."

Ida, Ronald, and Beth were pigeons fighting over a crust of bread.

That's when I got my idea. I would think of a Sophia Loren outfit, maybe the drenched cloth clinging to her in *Boy on a Dolphin,* and imagine it replacing the parochial school outfits I saw on *Varsity Dance.*

I watched who Eddie paid attention to on the show. He would want to hover around Sophia. Make her feel important. Serve his purposes. A bumblebee and its flower. Eddie dressed like a bumblebee some days, all yellow and black. Or maybe that was one of his colored singers in a yellow suit. Where on earth did they find those suits? Well, I had no way of knowing.

The den was where I conducted my Sophia investigation. First, I pulled the puffy leather chair close to the TV, the chair whose cushion was a mold of my bottom. Then I unfolded the TV table with its spindly legs and set up my glass, ice bucket, vodka, cigarettes, and ashtray. We upper-income drinkers had added vodka to our repertoire of booze— clear as water, though it did leave more of a smell on your breath than gin. I usually spilled liquor on the carpet because the table was so wobbly, but I could fold it up and hide its cigarette burns. Next, I drew down the shades and closed the door so that the only light came from the television. The room was now my private movie theater where the only reality was on the screen and my thoughts were hidden in the dark.

I watched for half an hour. The only bosomy girl Eddie buzzed around was a tall blonde with a small nose, large teeth, and the suggestion of large breasts under her blouse. She had one walleye. I was pretty sure she was not Sophia. Eddie held a microphone that he moved back and forth as he and the blonde took turns speaking. He called her Claire.

The project had become boring. I was halfway through an afternoon drink and thinking about Elizabeth, my college roommate.

Why had she come to mind? Elizabeth and Sophia—both sluts. "Sluts" was too strong. God knows Elizabeth had her demons. I thought she'd be okay after marrying Smedley—satisfy all those family obligations. Thought I'd be okay when I married David. Did Elizabeth have an Eddie or a Sophia in her life?

Elizabeth had committed suicide. Was I thinking of taking my life? Why do people think it's suicide that takes your life. Backwards. Your life's already been taken, and when you understand that, then you kill yourself. Who had called and told me about Elizabeth? Doesn't matter. Hadn't been in the papers. David had said that showed the extent of Smedley's influence—to have kept the cause of death buried. Bury a secret, bury a body. Elizabeth's body. So sad.

I couldn't sit in the dark watching *Varsity Dance* any longer. I went upstairs and took to Mommy's old rocking chair. I must have fallen asleep, because the clock now read 4:30. I needed to think about dinner. Thursday was Liz's day off.

I would never get out of this damned rocking chair. I was certainly damned when I sat in it. My depression laid on me, thousands of pounds of anger that had died straddling me. The depression lived in that chair, rocked by my mother. In her eyes, no matter what she said, was the hope that one day she would look at me and find me pregnant. Every time we were together that wish accused me, and my anger grew.

I stood up and went downstairs to the kitchen.

Liz had prepared Thursday's dinner and left it in the refrigerator wrapped in aluminum foil. I knew she meant well, but I took it as another judgment. A real woman cooked dinner for her husband. When she was my age Mommy had cooked for Daddy.

When I was a teenager Mommy and I had made Toll House cookies together, the recipe from the box. A dishtowel wrapped around her hand, she had lifted the baking tray out of the oven. The cookies had puffed up, chocolate peering from under a thin brown crust, protruding like frog's eyes. Using a spatula, she had carefully lifted each one onto a wire rack. Cookie dough and Toll House bits had bubbled and settled as they cooled. Mommy said I had stared at them, my innards quivering, a dog waiting for permission to pounce on a bone. The first bite had been ecstasy, the still warm chocolate melting, its intense sweetness flowing over my tongue. Little in life equaled that moment. By the second cookie I had been dizzy, drunk with sugar.

"Naomi, that's enough," Mommy had said. "We don't want to make our weight problem any worse, do we?"

Saliva spurted inside my mouth. Lifting the lid on the cookie jar, I found it empty. Had David told Liz to stop baking cookies? The fatter I grew, the skinnier David became. *Jack Sprat would eat no fat. His wife would eat no lean.* I checked the freezer; there was no ice cream. Hunger burned a hole in my stomach.

I stumbled out to the living room. There was a lock on the liquor cabinet. When had that happened?

On the climb up the stairs, darkness fell. It was brief, and when it cleared I saw my hand was clutching the banister. Relieved I had not fallen, I pulled my wagon of flesh to the top and into the bedroom.

The game of hiding liquor had risen to championship levels, but I was the top seeded. David and Liz had found the bottle in my lingerie drawer, but not the nips I put inside the sachets. Threw them off the scent. I laughed out loud at my joke.

I pulled the lingerie drawer too hard and it fell on the floor. Silk in colors of cream, honeydew, and cantaloupe flowed onto the floor. On hands and knees I squeezed each sachet; they were all soft and empty. Had they figured it out? Had I drunk the last one? Sweat ran down the middle of my back and I shivered. One drink. One nip. I would be focused again. The dread would lift. Pocketbooks!

In the closet I pulled the crocodile handbag out of its cloth cover. Scaly reptile the color of warmed honey. I was trembling inside. My fingers groped through the buttery suede lining. Nothing. Shoes. Matching shoes. The pocketbook was a clue in the treasure hunt. My hand wormed into the toes. Yes! A bottle the length of my finger with the tiny British soldier in the red jacket. I twisted the metal cap and gulped. Waiting.

I stood up and walked over to the chair. Now that I was calm I could figure out what I would make for David's supper. Something light. Since New York he did not eat much. A heavy meal left him in pain. He had been a red meat and potatoes man. Mommy had Estelle make a marbled rib roast the last time we were there. When Daddy had put a thick slice on his plate, blood running, David had jumped up and excused himself. I had followed him. He had been outside in the cold without a coat, his face pale.

"Naomi!"

Why was David shaking me?

"Naomi, you fell asleep on the floor."

"David, can we go out for dinner?"

"Let's do this," he said. "While you freshen up and set the table, I'll go out and get us a pizza."

He didn't have to say anything more. David was embarrassed to have others see me.

Chapter Twenty
The Police Question Naomi

David had been jumpy from the moment he came back from New York, but it grew worse when the police notified the firm they wanted to question both of us. Bloomie had made a call, and we were interviewed at the firm. When the detective fussed about this, Bloomie told him it concerned David's trip to New York on firm business.

Bloomie tried to have David and I interviewed together. The detective, I think his name was Synge, spelled like the Irish playwright on his card, that's why I remember it—anyway, he became very angry. It ended up with Detective Synge interrogating us separately, though Bloomie was present. Synge also wanted to examine me before David. Bloomie wanted it the other way around and called the District Attorney. I went first.

David stood up to leave.

"David, if you have your pocket diary with you," Bloomie said, "we can set up a date that's convenient for everyone."

"Why don't we do it today?" the detective demanded.

"That's fine by me." Bloomie said. "I've cleared an hour for Mrs. Greenberg's interview. I see no reason why you can't finish both of them in that time."

Color rose on Synge's cheeks, and he jumped up from the chair. I thought he was going to punch Bloomie, but he "settled his feathers" as Liz would say, and they finally agreed to meet with David in a week. I was nervous that the detective was in a foul humor and would take it out on me.

Detective Synge asked me whether I knew a Julius Rabelli. I told him I had read the name in the paper. Then he asked if I had seen a Buick near our house the night David and Eddie left for New York. I told him the only car I could recognize was a Packard. Bloomie thought I was making a joke and laughed, but it was really the truth.

The detective spent a lot of time asking the same question over and over again. It was whether I had watched David and Eddie drive off, and had another car followed them. I told him I had said goodbye in the house and never went outside.

"I went back to reading my book," I told him.

"What book was that, Mrs. Greenberg?" he asked.

Bloomie said I couldn't be expected to remember that.

"It's okay, Nelson, I do remember. *Death in Venice*."

"Is that a murder mystery, Mrs. Greenberg? Like the killing of Lieutenant Rabelli?"

"Oh no, detective. It's about an older man enraptured by the beauty of an adolescent boy."

Detective Synge's mouth fell open, as though I said I was reading one of those magazines for homosexuals.

"Isn't that a strange book for a married woman to be reading?" the detective asked.

"No," I told him. "It's a beautiful story."

Synge looked over at Bloomie, who volunteered, "Detective, *Death in Venice* is by Thomas Mann. I believe he's a Nobel laureate."

"A what?" Synge asked.

"He won a Nobel prize in literature," Bloomie explained.

Detective Synge shook his head back and forth. "The world gets stranger all the time."

I thought he was finished, but then he looked right at me as though Bloomie had left, and said, "Mrs. Greenberg, we've gotten sidetracked. Maybe on purpose. You're a lot sharper than you let on. Let's get back to my question. Did you see your husband drive away, either because you were outside or through a window?"

The detective was angry, and I got upset. I hate it when people raise their voice to me like I'm to blame for something. Bloomie bristled and told Synge that I had answered that question several times and to either move on or the interview was over. Their shouting made me cry. Bloomie had his secretary take me to the ladies' lounge to splash some water on my face, after whispering to me "to regain my composure."

Anyway, if that's what Synge put me through, and I knew nothing, he would be much tougher on David. I said that to David later to show I understood. I really said it very nicely, comforting him, you know. But he flew off the handle, so I dropped it.

I had read about that policeman, Rabelli, being found shot to death in Bucks County. The *Bulletin* said the killing was "gangland style."

After Synge asked me about Rabelli, I wanted to ask someone, David or Bloomie, to explain why the police were asking David and me about it. But I knew David would grow angry and Bloomie would pat me on the head like I was a ten-year-old.

It was not clear to me what the police thought we knew.

Chapter Twenty-One
The Police Question David

The day after Naomi was questioned by the police, Bloomie walked into David's office. "Here," he said, "are some receipts I want you to become familiar with."

David unwound the string sealing the large brown envelope and pulled out papers. The one on top was an itemized bill from the Plaza for a suite for the weekend he and Eddie were in New York. It was made out to David Greenberg c/o Schmidt, Harris. It included charges for breakfasts and liquor. On separate sheets were bills for dinner at Mercurio's and at Lutece.

"There's more," Bloomie said, pointing to the envelope.

David pulled out two lavish menus and opened the one from Mercurio. There was a red check and a blue check next to hand-scripted appetizers, entrees, and desserts. David looked up.

"Chumsky gave me this package last night," Bloomie said. "When you're questioned, if Synge pushes for details, I'll have my secretary bring in the receipts. If he asks, pause and then tell him one of the dishes. Don't remember everything. No one ever does. You had the red-checked items, Eddie, the blue. Keep the menu locked in your desk. That's just for you. If they question Eddie, I'll get them back from you."

"Wait! Wait," David said. "What were we supposed to be doing in New York?"

"Meeting with mid-level executives at CBS to finalize details for the first national broadcast," Bloomie answered. He looked older, skin as gray as mushrooms grown in the dark.

"What if the police check?" David asked. "This guy Synge seems sharp. You said so yourself. This is the killing of one of their own." He stopped, swallowed to relieve the dryness in his mouth, and then said, "Synge will go up to New York. With snapshots of Eddie and me. He'll go to CBS and the restaurants, checking."

Bloomie nodded. "Chumsky's counting on that. While you and Eddie were at the New Amsterdam, two guys of your general build and features were at CBS and the Plaza and ate what's checked off on the menus."

"What? Are you sure this will work?" he asked.

"Lower your voice," Bloomie said. "I don't know all the details, but it's brilliant. For this kind of thing, Chumsky's a genius. I asked him would anyone remember a quiet lawyer and a forty-four-year-old flashy dresser. You know what Chumsky did?"

David shook his head. He saw Bloomie was pleased that he was beginning to understand all that Chumsky brought to the table.

"He looked at me with those dead fish eyes of his," Bloomie said, "and I thought he wasn't going to answer." Bloomie widened his eyes, made his mouth into a small "O" and then closed it like a dying fish on a dock. He laughed. David forced a smile.

"Then he said," Bloomie continued, "'these two are unemployed actors. They were given photos of David and Eddie. They were told to tip well.'"

Bloomie did a fair imitation of Chumsky in phrasing as well as inflection. He changed back to his own voice. "At CBS the actors had some general info I had conveyed to Jack, and were told not to agree to anything. In a jam, they had an unlisted number to call without being given my name."

Bloomie picked up the brown envelope, and pulled out two more sheets.

"David, look over these time sheets I made up for you to give you an idea what was discussed at CBS."

Bloomie went back to his Chumsky mimicry: "I'm not saying if the police questioned everyone within a day or two it would work, but by the time they go to these places weeks will have passed and the witnesses will say 'That's them' or 'I can't be sure, but it looks like them.'"

Bloomie patted my shoulder. "We made certain that the guys at CBS had not met you before. David, you're going to be fine. You've got real heavyweights in your corner."

Synge, Bloomie, and David had been in the small conference room for twenty minutes, and David had not said a word. When the detective had arrived, Bloomie's secretary had also been there.

"What's the big idea?" Synge had asked.

"This way we'll have a record and won't have to rely on memory," Bloomie had said. "Possibly conflicting memories."

"Let's get this straight," Synge had threatened. "I'm conducting this investigation. Not you, Mr. Bloomenthal. I'll take the notes. And you can be damned sure they'll be accurate!"

"Now, now detective, there's no need to use that tone of voice. I'm sure your notes will be just as accurate as Mrs. Wilson's," Bloomie had said, holding his hand out toward their best stenographer as though introducing her to a jury.

"Look, I have an idea," Bloomie had said, as though it had just occurred to him. He had walked over to the credenza beneath the wall of books, slid back the door, and lifted out a tape recorder, which ordinarily was kept in a secretary's desk. "We can set this up, and let Mrs. Wilson go. We'll make a transcript and provide you with a copy. In fact, we'll even loan you the tape itself so you can satisfy yourself as to the accuracy of the transcription. Can't be fairer than that."

Bloomie and Synge had looked like they had stepped out of Disney's cartoon of *Alice in Wonderland*: Bloomie the Cheshire cat, Synge the beet-faced Queen.

"You keep playing games and we'll just take Mr. Greenberg here in front of a Grand Jury," Synge had said. "No defense lawyer. Just Mr. Greenberg and the D.A."

"As you know, detective," Bloomie sparred, "the District Attorney has no basis to believe that either Mr. Greenberg or his wife have any information regarding the death of Lieutenant Rabelli. They have been made available to you because of the high personal regard we have for the District Attorney."

After a call to the D.A., it had been agreed to make a tape recording.

The table in the conference room was ten feet long and four-and-a-half feet wide. Bloomie and David were on one side, Synge on the other. Each camp had been provided with paper tablets. The recorder sat in the middle, with the on-off button nearest Bloomie. Mrs. Wilson had left a coffee service on top of the credenza. David was more than a little worried that the scalding coffee could provide Synge with a weapon if Bloomie's baiting escalated.

After David was sworn in and identified, Detective Synge began, "Mr. Greenberg, are you related to Eddie Greene?"

Synge was dressed identically to David: charcoal gray suit, white shirt, striped maroon tie. It struck David as strange. He wondered whether Synge was trying to get into his head by being his double. Bloomie tapped his shoe against David's to snap him out of his reverie.

"Eddie's my cousin," David said. "First cousin."

"Did he come to your office on the afternoon of Friday, December 20, 1957?"

David picked up the tip of his tie and then looked over at Synge's.

"Detective," he said, "how did you know I would wear this tie today?"

Synge looked at Bloomie, who turned to David and said, "Do you want a moment before we proceed?"

David wondered whether Bloomie was thinking it had been a mistake to insist on a recording of his interrogation.

"I'm okay," David said. "Yes, Eddie came into the office that afternoon. His face was bloody. He said Lieutenant Rabelli had shot him an hour earlier." David wanted to get this over with. Bloomie had told him not to volunteer anything, but that would mean the questioning would drag on for hours.

"What did Mr. Greene say about the shooting?" Synge asked.

"He said Lieutenant Rabelli was crazy. That everyone knew that. He had threatened Eddie not to have Negro boys dance with white girls on the show."

Bloomie had coached David to wait for an opening and tell this story. It would make it sound as though that was why Rabelli shot at Eddie, not because of Sophia.

He went on. "Rabelli came on the show and tried to beat the boy to death. Sounds like Rabelli should have been jailed himself. Why would the police allow a man like that to remain on the force? That's what Eddie said."

Synge leaned over to push the off button. His face was close to theirs.

"Mr. Bloomenthal, I've heard you can be slippery as an eel. You've done a hell of a job rehearsing your colleague."

You had to look at the edge of Bloomie's eyes to see the anger. He didn't raise his voice. "Detective, it sounds like the Department had a mess on its hands with Lieutenant Rabelli. He was out of control. A monster who headed up Vice. I heard he beat up defendants. Even beat up someone in the D.A.'s office."

Synge pulled the knot down on his tie. He was so angry he hadn't noticed Bloomie restart the tape recorder.

"If you think you can cover up what your witnesses, and maybe you, know about this killing," Synge yelled, "think again."

"Detective," Bloomie said, "this interview is over. It's clear you want to intimidate Mr. Greenberg, and possibly this firm. You have no interest in hearing what Mr. Greene said when he arrived at this office. Speak to the District Attorney. See if he wants to have a Grand Jury investigation. See if he wants to have testimony about Lieutenant Rabelli's violence. Ask him if he wants to call Assistant Sullivan, Mrs. Kelly, and you before the Grand jury to testify about the Lieutenant's being a wild animal. Maybe the Department doesn't want it known that it turned a blind eye to this madman. Or who in the Department had a motive to kill Lieutenant Rabelli."

Synge had bitten his bottom lip, and a drop of blood surfaced as he opened his mouth. "This interview is over when I say it's over!" Synge shouted.

"Detective, you may ask Mr. Greenberg if he saw Lieutenant Rabelli anytime on Friday, December 20th. You can ask him if he saw the Lieutenant the week before that, or for that matter, at any time. You can ask him if he has any knowledge as to how Lieutenant Rabelli died. But you cannot harass Mr. Greenberg."

Bloomie walked over to the credenza and poured himself a cup of coffee. With his back to Synge, he asked, "Detective, would you care for a cup of coffee?"

Synge walked stiff-legged to the door. As he opened it, Bloomie said, "I'll have a copy of today's tape delivered to the District Attorney by five."

Chapter Twenty-Two
Naomi Watches *Varsity Dance* and Calls David's Office

It was a week since David and I had been questioned. Bloomie called today and told me he had spoken to the District Attorney, and we would not be contacted further by the police.

One thing was clear: I was not the only one who wanted to know about the trip to New York.

Damn Eddie! What was it about him that hypnotized David?

I looked at my watch. It was a few minutes past five. *Varsity Dance* would still be going. I turned on the TV and settled back in the rocking chair. There was Eddie, microphone in hand. Like a little boy holding his penis. I laughed at my off-color joke.

When Eddie spoke his words were slurred. Rocking back and forth he almost fell, but reached out and put his hand on the shoulder of a boy near him. Eddie was talking to a short girl in a ponytail, "Rosalie, how would you rate 'That'll Be the Day?'"

Deep creases cut into Rosalie's forehead. "I'll give the words a six, and a nine for danceability." A broad grin broke out on ponytail's face. "I just love Buddy Holly."

So lyrics must not be that important. I was learning the rules of this adolescent world where Eddie was king.

When the record began to play, the camera moved off Eddie and onto the dancers. Some pairs were both girls. In my day we only danced with boys. I tried to see if there was something different about the ones dancing with other girls. I couldn't put my finger on anything in particular. They probably danced with each other if a boy didn't ask them.

Even wearing uniforms from Catholic schools, the girls' sensuality came through. The pleats on their skirts emphasized the flatness of their bellies. I felt sure they all had perky breasts and firm rear ends.

My body had never been like that, but it had not been the bowl of Jell-O I lived in now. I patted my belly and looked down at my chest. Gravity and age had made it necessary to find bras with more "uplift." Funny word. As though breasts were spiritual. I reached over and pinched the loose flesh hanging from my arm.

What kind of business was Eddie doing in Jersey? What business would a man in his forties have with a teenager? Monkey business! I laughed again. Actually, a giggle. I wondered whether Shirley Temple's laugh still came out as a giggle. She would be younger than me. What would Shirley and I find at Eddie's place? Our husbands up to no good? Their hands up someone's skirt, someone who had forgotten to put on panties?

A taste of salt was on the tip of my tongue. I felt the wet on my cheek. Why was I crying? The clock read twenty minutes after five. Was David still at the office? No point in going downstairs and being reminded of my failings as a cook if he was still at work. Maybe he'd suggest we go out to dinner. He often did. Sometimes David's offer would make me feel worse, like Liz's leaving a prepared meal with a note spelling out how to heat it up. Tonight I'd just reply to David, "That's sweet of you. Where would you like to go?"

I went over to the phone and dialed. I was rehearsing my acceptance, really feeling a little better. I was still sad, but I was sure I wouldn't start crying a few sentences into the conversation. The receptionist answered and put me through to Catherine Marie.

"Mr. Greenberg's not here, Mrs. Greenberg."

"Oh. I need to know when he'll be home. To plan dinner. Did he say where he's going?"

"No. Let me look in his book," she said. "Hmmm. it just has five to seven blocked out. Nothing else."

Was David having an affair?

"Would it be too much to ask—?"

"Mrs. Greenberg, are you okay? It sounds like you're crying. Is anyone home with you?"

"There's no one," I said.

"No one with you?" Catherine Marie asked.

"No one."

Mommy asked me if I were alone. Every time she called. I wasn't in a wheelchair. I didn't need a nurse.

"Would you like me to come over?" Catherine Marie said. "I can grab a cab and be there in twenty minutes."

"I'm perfectly *capable*. Do you hear me?" I told her.

"I'm sorry. I didn't mean to upset you."

"I'm not upset," I explained to her. "Why would you say that?"

"Mrs. Greenberg, let me check with Mr. Bloomenthal," she said. "Perhaps he knows where I can reach Mr. Greenberg and have him call you."

"No, no. Absolutely not! Don't tell anyone I called. Do you hear me? I won't have it! You are not to tell anyone." I stomped my foot on the rug.

"Please, Mrs. Greenberg—"

I hung up.

I had to get out of the house before they all started calling. Bloomie. Mommy. Daddy. They all knew where David was. Everyone knew but me. It wasn't right! They were covering for David. Protecting him. Thought they could fool me. Well, they didn't. Naomi was a lot smarter than they gave her credit for. David must be in Jersey with Eddie and Sophia and God knows who else. That's why he wouldn't put it in his book. But they all knew. Bastards! Every one of them.

I opened the closet where David kept his clothes. His jackets were filled with notes. When I sent them to the cleaners I checked his pockets. All kinds of paper scraps. Bank deposit receipts. Reminder lists. Most of the time I didn't read them. Just left them on David's bureau.

What had he worn when he went off to see Eddie in the middle of the night? I kept on asking if he wanted it cleaned. David said no. Well, it wasn't a suit. Here it was. I knew it by touch. Buttery. Cashmere. I pulled out the blue jacket and laid it on the bed. The inside pocket had a torn ticket from the Academy of Music. And a folded piece of yellow paper. At the top, faint and underlined, "Blueberry Hill."

The phone was ringing. If I answered it I was caught. Let it ring. Hoped it was David and that he was worried. Let him feel guilty. He should feel guilty. All of them should. I looked in the full-length mirror. I was wearing a salt and pepper skirt and matching twin sweater set. And pearls. I ran a comb through my hair. That was better. Freshened my lipstick. Damn, I hadn't meant to put that much on! Kleenex would fix that.

Ok, Naomi, downstairs and hold on to the banister. That-a-girl.

I put on my charcoal coat, patted the pockets. Gloves were there. I went through the kitchen door into the garage. I pushed the button and listened to the garage door creak open a section at a time.

Last week I started the car and forgot to open the garage door. David flew out yelling about carbon monoxide and killing myself. I wished he wouldn't yell at me. I just forgot. Not today. David wasn't that lucky. I would get to Blueberry Hill and catch him with his pants down. I giggled. I was as funny as Bob Hope.

Chapter Twenty-Three
Naomi at Blueberry Hill

I opened the driver's door and walked in front of the headlights. My silhouette slanted as high as the gate and disappeared in the darkness on the other side. There was a sign, blotted by my monstrous shadow. Moving to the side, I made out FOR SALE, with a Philadelphia telephone number. Moving closer, I reached out and pulled back and forth on both gate sections. Neither gave.

"Is anyone here?' I asked. My little girl voice was swallowed in the silence.

They thought they were so smart. David, Eddie, and Sophia inside that huge house, with all the lights off. They had been called and warned. Seeing headlights as the Packard came up the far side of the hill, they knew who was coming. "It's Naomi. Hit the lights. The gate will stop her. She'll leave."

Probably laughing at me. Standing in the dark. Rubbing against each other. Feeling safe. Excited too. Damn them!

I returned to the car and backed it up to the top of the hill. Daddy always said a Packard was built like a tank. I looked over to the passenger's seat. I didn't see anyone, but I knew Daddy was there. He wouldn't let David and Eddie treat his Princess this way.

I pressed my foot down on the gas. The engine throbbed. It was not just the noise. There were vibrations I felt through my skirt, against the back of my thighs, down there between my legs. The Packard strained. I giggled. I *was* driving by the seat of my pants.

I jammed it into Drive. The tires spun and caught. The Packard lurched forward. Stones pinged against the car. The speedometer was at thirty, forty, the weight of the Packard, the angle of the descent, working. Rising from the seat, I stood on the gas pedal. The last speed I saw was fifty-five. I didn't look down again.

The gate popped. My teeth bit into my lip. The front windshield spotted red. Hurled back, I slid down the seat and the pain erupted. Bone and flesh screamed.

The engine stopped. I heard the hiss of steam. I hurt so much. I didn't know if I could move. Why didn't David come out of the house to help? I leaned on the door; my left shoulder jumped with pain.

I had to get out of the car. I pushed against the door and heard my high-pitched screams. The door swung out. Shifting my weight, I got my legs out. And still no one came from the house. What were the three of them doing?

I stood next to the car, leaning against the open door, and felt the heat of the dying Packard. In the dim light from the car's overhead bulb, I looked at my right hand. It clutched my crocodile handbag. With everything else that was going on, this was the most startling. What was it doing here? Mommy had said a thousand times, "A lady never leaves the house without her pocketbook." I stretched my fingers out and down the smooth part of the skin. Then I curled my thumb across the other side against raised scales the shape and size of mahjong tiles.

My right hand was unhurt. I felt queasy. A vinegary acid filled my mouth. I bent over and threw up. Darkness blinked like a traffic light. I explored my lips with my tongue. They were chalky and bitter. Stung where my teeth had cut through. Laying the purse on the car seat, I pried the snap open with my good hand and lowered my fingers to find a handkerchief. I wiped the sour wetness off my lips where it didn't hurt. Icicles stabbed through my head. From shoulder to fingertips my left arm dangled. Fear clotted in my stomach as I watched it hang. I knew I had to get into the house. They had to have a phone there. It would force David to see me. He'd have to help.

My thighs were sore, but my legs held. I took test steps and everything worked. I moved to the front of the Packard, and there was no light. When the headlights had worked, I had seen a driveway like a long U leading up to and turning in front of the house. Now in the dark, I was scared of falling down on my broken arm, of anything touching my head. I looked into the sky. A thin curve of moon was growing. How could the moon be out this early? When I reached Blueberry Hill it was quarter after six. I found a cigarette lighter. In the flame, my watch read eight o'clock. Had I blacked out in the crash?

The moon became full and turned the driveway silvery white. I crunched toward the house, ankles off-balance in the shifting oyster shells.

The front door was locked. They were not making it easy for me. I saw a door knocker. At first I thought it was a lion's head. The moonlight brightened and I saw it was a woman's privates. What I had thought was mane was pubic hair. What was this place?

I put my purse under my chin and knocked hard. The sound cracked out in the quiet. Bet it gave them quite a start.

I walked to the end of the house and turned at the corner. It was hard to see. Moonlight splattered against the side of the house. I touched it and felt glass running higher than I could reach. Had to be either windows or French doors. I looked around for a branch or a rock, but the ground was bare. Holding on to the strap, I swung the pocketbook against the glass. It bounced off with a soft thud. Were they laughing at me? I felt tired and started to cry. Sliding a finger down, I popped the flap open. It took some juggling, letting go and catching, but finally I wedged my hand into the purse. My fist was wrapped in crocodile. I stood at an angle to the high glass and put my substantial hip into the swing.

The glass broke, some in blades, most in pebbles. I felt the impact all over; my head and broken arm howling with pain. I punched back and forth, knocking down glass slivers, some slashing my coat. I felt my cheek sting.

I stepped through, Alice slipping down the rabbit hole into a darker and more dangerous Wonderland, a world of men and whores. In the room there was less moonlight to guide me. I wedged the purse under my chin, groped with my right hand across the unbroken glass until I touched what felt like a solid wall. With my head bent, trailing one arm, and reaching out with the other I pictured myself, an old blind woman setting out on a journey.

My fingers touched a row of light switches and I flipped them down one at a time. Section after section of the room lit up, the darkness ebbing back. I was in a very long room. Sheets covered scattered furniture like sleeping ghosts. Best not wake the spirits of seasons past. David and Eddie knew that. I knew that. I had no idea what Sophia knew, though girls her age thought they knew everything. The walls were very high, and must have once had paintings hung across the top because there were large squares that were paler than the rest of the walls.

The chill in the room came through my coat, through my sweaters, through my skin, and settled on the floor of my stomach. Cold scissored my innards, a crab grinding with its pincers. I saw the hard-shelled scavenger eating ribbons of flesh fluttering in my body's currents. Cold, so cold.

I slapped the purse across my cheek and shocked myself awake. The three of them were watching, ghoulishly enjoying my slipping away.

"Damn you!" My voice echoed in the great room.

I needed a phone. I looked at the base of the walls. No black cords snaked across the floor. The phones must be beyond the doors opening off this barn of a room.

I walked over to the closest door, pushing myself harder as the numbness grew in my legs and arms. It opened. Leaning against the doorframe, I flicked a switch. A soft light came on, one that would flatter beer bellies and bald heads. Ceiling and walls were mirrors. The patrons could watch stag films in which they were the stars, and the girls did all the work.

I slid down a glass wall until I found myself staring at a low bed across from me. Blood-red satin sheets and an undulating form that made no sense. There were too many parts, extra legs and arms and heads. In the center was the back of a head with long gleaming hair. At the rear was an upright torso of a man, the front of a centaur. It was joined to the raised rear end of the female. The centaur's head was Eddie's.

"Eddie! Stop whatever you're doing and help me!" I shouted. "Do you hear me?"

The centaur was lost in the illusion of the boy-man he once had been. In front of the woman's bobbing head was another upper body, lying on its back. From the hips down it was hidden under the girl. Concealed in shadow, it groaned in David's voice.

"David? Oh God, I am freezing inside. Look at me! My lips must be blue. Don't let me die."

David sat upright, and reached over the girl to Eddie. He ran his fingers through hair curled tight as snails, and traced the outline of Eddie's cheekbone. It was a lover's touch. I lifted my purse and threw it at the three-headed monstrosity. It should have been killed at birth, had its umbilical cord wrapped around their throats and cut off the air to the three sets of lungs.

The room turned black. Red spots flared. One by one the flames blew out. I saw nothing. I heard nothing.

Chapter Twenty-Four
Naomi's Recuperation

The pain in my face was dull. It was better when I kept my eyes shut and stayed hidden in the dark. I wiggled the toes on my left foot, relieved that I could. I moved my left foot to the right until I felt the other leg. No cast. Not like my left arm.

"Naomi."

It was David. I wasn't up to a conversation. Not yet. I did not want to talk or open my eyes. He'd have to go along with that. I took a deep breath and reached up to my forehead. Softly, very softly. I still winced.

"Naomi, you are in a hospital."

"Shush. Please wait your turn, David."

That was one of the problems with men. They couldn't wait. What was worse was their lack of respect for patience in a woman. They looked down on it. Called it plodding. Or indecisive. Mind you, if they did it, it was cautious, thoughtful. Valued traits.

"Naomi?"

"Okay, okay already," I said. "Hold your horses."

Why did he have to be in the room when I woke up? I needed a little time to myself, to get things in order, to think through what had happened. If I said I didn't remember, and there really were parts I didn't, they'd all say I blacked out from drinking and whisk me off to dry out. I'd be with crazy drunks. They'd hurt me. I'd seen them on the street. Flailing around at things they saw. Things that were not there. Mustn't tell David about seeing him and Eddie and that girl. What did David know? Had they found me inside that whorehouse?

"What did you say? I couldn't make it out. Are you ready to talk?" David asked.

No, I wasn't. "David, my head really hurts. Be a dear. Go and see if the nurse could give me something stronger than aspirin."

There was the sound of David's chair as he stood up and the quiet tread of his shoes on the floor. How much time did that give me? A few minutes, anyway. Where was I? Oh yes, how did the accident happen? Maybe I hit the gas by mistake when I tried to stop at the gate? That could happen to anyone. I believed my story. That was how I crashed into the gate. Then I needed to break into the house to call for help. Nothing else around. Okay, the story was reasonable. I'd stick with it.

"Naomi, they can't give you anything else without a doctor looking at you. They're trying to reach him."

"David, what hospital is this?"

"U. Penn," he said. "The ambulance brought you to New Jersey Regional, where they set the cast. That was early Friday morning." David's tone was weary.

"How long have I been here?" I heard the fear in my voice.

"Three days," he answered.

"What?"

"Yes," David said. "When they said they were not sure about the extent of your head injuries, we moved you here. Are you up to talking?"

"Not really."

"The police wanted to know why you were there," he said. "I didn't know what to tell them."

There it was again, the implied accusation: Naomi was David's burden. Damn hypocrite!

"Did they ask why you, Eddie, and Sophia were there?"

"What are you talking about?" he asked. "You were the only one there. Why did you go there? How did you find it?"

"David, tell me why the knocker on the front door is a woman's . . . you know—her—?" David said nothing. "Cat got your tongue?" I said. "Young cat?"

What would happen if I said "pussy"? Would David be shocked? Had to watch what I said. Mustn't give them a reason to put me away.

I opened an eye. The light stung. There was nothing to see that was worth the added pain.

"Naomi, let's not get into a fight." David's voice was quiet, cleansed of anger. "I'm just trying to help."

"I know you mean well," I said. "What I really need is to get out of here. That would be a big help."

"I'll try. Your folks have been asking to see you. Also Woodberry. I'm sure the report on your trust fund can wait until you feel up to it."

"I'd like to see him," I said. "I always feel better afterwards. It's not just about the money."

I had first met Mr. Woodberry in 1935 when I was eighteen. "Princess, come into the living room. There's someone I'd like you to meet." Daddy and the stranger had stood up as I came in.

"Princess, say hello to Mr. Woodberry," Daddy had said.

Woodberry was six feet tall, the same height as Daddy, but much thinner. He had said, "It's a pleasure to finally meet you, Miss Luntz. Your father and I have worked together for many years now. Really, it's more than a business relationship. As I like to say, we've extended the right hand of friendship to each other."

As he said this, Mr. Woodberry had extended his right hand. His large bony hand had felt powerful, though he had held mine as if it were an eggshell. His face had been narrow, with a long thin nose over a sliver of mouth; large ears laid flat against his skull. But his hair was what I had remembered after that first meeting. It had been black, with a few silver flecks. In an attempt to control it a barber had cut it shorter than was the fashion and had given up using hair oil to achieve the flat glossy style that was then in vogue. Over Woodberry's forehead a clump had shot up in a cowlick, a miniature twister. It had made his face look like a character from Dick Tracy.

Over the last twenty-two years, Mr. Woodberry's hair had added a little gray, but that was the only change in his appearance or in his turn of the century courtesy.

I woke up and saw Mr. Woodberry standing at the foot of the bed. He was wearing a shiny blue serge suit, a dress shirt with a starched collar, and a thin bow tie so worn I couldn't tell what color it had once been.

"Well, Mr. Woodberry, I can't extend the right hand of friendship today."

"Miss Luntz, any hand you extend is the hand of friendship." Woodberry might sound corny, but it worked on me every time.

"You're very sweet," I said.

Woodberry had told Daddy that he had a divorced daughter and a teenaged grandson and had not spoken to either one for ten years. He had no other family. Maybe that's why he always called me by my maiden name.

"They tell me you'll be going home tomorrow," he said.

"I can't wait. I hate this place. They're always watching me and writing down stuff," I told him.

"Can't be pleasant," he sympathized.

I had lost track for a moment of what he was telling me. "I'm sorry, Mr. Woodberry. Would you say that again?"

"I'm the one who should be apologizing. Here you are in a hospital bed and I'm blathering on about investments. We'll take this up when you're feeling better."

"I'm listening," I said. "Is there a deadline?"

"Yes, yes there is," he said. "If you're sure you're up to it."

"I know I don't have your investment skills and I don't follow you as well as Daddy, but I really enjoy our conversations. And it means a great deal to me that you always discuss what you are thinking." I squeezed Woodberry's hand.

"Two years ago we put some of your trust money in the hands of a young man from Omaha," Woodberry said.

"Oh, yes. He was recommended to you by the professor from Columbia."

Woodberry beamed. I had a decent memory for a daily drinker. "Very good." Mr. Woodberry went on, "He has done well, extremely well, with your money. And your father's, I might add. He has formed an investment fund, and is seeking additional capital. I think we should place a million dollars with him. That's ten percent of your assets. I know that's a lot, but I am very taken with Mr. Buffet. He is considerably younger than your father or me."

"Are you going to stop? I would miss you terribly." If Woodberry were handing me over it would be another judgment that Naomi was not worth the effort.

"Nothing like that. And I fully intend to have the pleasure of your company for many years to come. But no one has impressed me as much. I think he will do very well by you and your family. Developing a relationship now gives us the opportunity to see if I'm right. Since the actuarial tables predict he will outlive me, it gives us an opportunity to make a smooth transition."

"No one could ever replace you," I told him.

Mr. Woodberry shifted from foot to foot and kept clearing his throat.

"I'll be around longer than you can put up with me," he said.

He turned around, removed a handkerchief from his suit pants and honked. I felt my eyes filling as well. We may have been a maudlin pair, but it was the best I had felt in weeks.

The next day David drove me home from the hospital. The table was set, and Liz had prepared swordfish.

There were no wineglasses out.

"Liz, let's have some white wine. It's a celebration: my coming home."

David coughed and said, "Naomi, it's not chilled."

"Then make me a gimlet, David. On the rocks."

"There's no liquor in the house," he announced.

"What?" I said.

"I had Liz go on a hunt. On my instructions she cleaned out all the wine, gin, vodka, all alcohol in this house. Everywhere. Down here. In your mouthwash. Don't blame Liz. It was my idea."

David's voice grew louder as he handed down my punishment: *Naomi is hereby sentenced to be dry for the rest of her time here on Earth.* I looked over at Liz. She was staring at the floor.

"David, you have no idea what you're doing," I said.

He looked me in the eye, probably imitating some "throw-away-the keys" judge. "Naomi, we've got to deal with your drinking!"

David's anger nourished his self-righteousness.

"What are *you* going to deal with so I don't drink?"

"What are you talking about?" he asked.

"Never mind," I said. "Look, David, did you consult a doctor before coming up with this Draconian cure for my little problem?"

"Draconian?" David's skin was pale and tight, the anger twitching at both ends of his mouth.

"Draconian," I repeated, hitting the table with my fist. "Are you dumbstruck that I know the word? Or is your problem that it's the right word? That your real interest is in punishing me, and you couldn't care less if it is of any help in solving my drinking problem? Have I told you how sanctimonious you can be?"

"Naomi, I know you're angry at me." A white spot grew on David's cheek.

"Come on David," I begged, "let me have one little drink." I held up my thumb and forefinger an inch apart.

He nodded to Liz. When she came back from the kitchen, she held a glass for each of us.

I lifted my wineglass. "Thank you," I said. "Here's a toast to being home."

David's glass was a tumbler filled with scotch and ice, which he raised three times and emptied. He stood up and went to the kitchen. When he returned, he was empty-handed. I thought about commenting, but decided I'd do better letting him grease his own squeaky wheel.

"Liz, the fish is perfect," I told her. "You can't believe what they try to pass off as food at the hospital."

"Thank you," she said. For the first time since we sat down to eat, Liz's face relaxed into a smile.

"Don't you agree, David?"

"Excellent, Liz," he said. "You've outdone yourself."

David had eaten very little and was moving the swordfish around in his plate with a fork. He stood up and again went into the kitchen. It was several minutes until he returned. He bumped into the table before he got to his chair. I looked over at Liz, who avoided my stare and disappeared into the kitchen. She reappeared with the chardonnay and filled my glass, whispering about the goose and the gander.

"David, what's wrong?" I asked. He looked up and I saw a little boy who had come down from his nap and found no cake or presents on his birthday. I went over to him and cradled his head, stroking his hair. "It's okay," I told him. "Really it is. Please don't worry about me. I swear I won't drive unless I'm sober. Nothing bad is going to happen to me."

"I know, hon."

"What has you so sad?" I asked.

"It's just so unfair," he said.

I put my hand under his chin and lifted his face so I could read it.

"What is?" I asked.

"After all he's done for them, they're turning on him."

I felt the heat in my face. Why was I invisible to David?

"Does this have to do with Eddie?"

David heard something in my voice, something that he could sense through the fog of scotch. "It's unbearable at the office."

I kept quiet hoping David would continue, and not retreat into silence. "Bloomie screamed at me about taking the time to pick you up today," he said. "Jay's demands never end. *Varsity Dance* has gone national. It's a golden goose."

David cupped his hands so that I might see this invisible backbreaking treasure. "Last month the firm billed Pyramid over $100,000. It's made all of them richer—Jay, Bloomie, Chumsky, your father."

David knew that Daddy had transferred some Pyramid shares to me. He must have left me off the list to show how sensitive he was.

"I'm sorry," I said. "I had no idea you were under so much pressure. I should have picked a better time to crack up."

David's mouth and eyes opened as though I had slapped him. "No one's angry at you. I'm certainly not. I swear, Naomi, this has nothing to do with you. What none of them appreciate is what Eddie has done for them."

So it was about Eddie. All of this drinking and wallowing. I was a distraction for David. Son of a bitch!

"Now they're all on Eddie," David continued, "a pack of dogs. They're going to fire him. Throw him out. Bring in a Mr. Clean, a Pat Boone."

Holding his face in my hands I locked in David's attention. "There's something missing," I said. "No one throws out—what did you call him?—a 'golden goose.'"

David's eyes darted back and forth over my shoulder, scurrying away from me. I pressed firmly on both sides of his forehead.

"They all blame Eddie," he said. "Stories."

"What stories?" I asked. There was sympathy in my voice. This was what I'd been hoping for. Eddie had shot himself in the foot. If I couldn't break his spell on David, maybe Eddie would do it for me.

"Stories about his drinking," David whispered. "That he's had sex with girls from the show."

"High school girls?" I said, forcing my tone to be shocked, not gloating.

"Yeah," David confessed.

I studied David's lips to make sure I did not miss what he was saying. "Sophia?" I asked.

"That's the rumor."

"Have you had sex with Sophia?"

"No. Of course not! How can you think that?" David's eyes resumed their frantic bouncing, a rubber ball dropped down stairs.

"David, whatever you've done I need to know."

"What, what do you need to know?" his lips quivered. "I've never had sex with any girls from *Varsity Dance*. Never."

I thought about asking what went on at Blueberry Hill that night. I started crying instead.

"Are you okay?" he asked. "What's wrong?"

My body went slack and I slumped down in the chair next to David. "I'm fine," I assured him, "just a reaction to this last week. So damn good to be out of the hospital." I patted his arm and tried to smile.

"Look, David, Liz is here with me," I said. "Why don't you have some coffee, take a shower, and head back to the office. Hanging around here will only make it worse. Really. Liz and I will be fine."

By the time Liz had returned from the liquor store, Mommy called and I had Liz tell her I was napping. Slouched against the kitchen doorway, I said, "Liz, sit down and talk with me. Have a drink. Supposed to be bad to drink alone." She was taking beef out of the refrigerator. Without looking up, Liz said, "No. Wouldn't be right. I got to cook dinner. Why don't you come and sit in de kitchen? Let me make a fresh pot of coffee."

I sat down and watched Liz prepare the brisket. Her hands patted the meat as she seasoned it.

"I never appreciated how competent you are," I said. "Professional."

"I do like cookin'," she said.

"Liz, was Eddie here while I was in the hospital?"

She paused. "Sometime."

"Did he stay overnight?"

Her face sagged, but she looked at me. "I couldn't say."

"I wish David thought about me the way he thinks of Eddie."

Chuckling, Liz said, "Don't talk crazy! Mr. Greenberg's not one of them." She let her hands hang limp at the wrist, and took a few mincing steps, swaying her hips. I giggled.

"It's good to hear dat laugh," she said. "You had me worried you forgot how to."

"I didn't in the hospital. The nurses and the doctors were angry." I jabbed my finger in the air. "Do this. Do that. Don't you dare get out of bed!"

Liz made a clucking sound, shaking her head from side to side. I did enjoy an appreciative audience. "They resented having to take care of me," I said, "like I was to blame." I looked away. I had trouble convincing myself I was not responsible for the accident. Really wasn't an accident. But Liz would not correct my version. She watched me with a full face of sorrow. Encouraged, I said, "No one felt a bit of sympathy. And lunch today with David. I'm just another piece of baggage he's got to carry."

I hit the table with my fist. Liz looked up, walked over to the stove, opened the blue can, and measured out the ground coffee in a small scoop.

"Mister Greenberg's under a lot of pressure," Liz said. "Told his boss to back off so he could fetch you from the hospital."

Why was she siding with David?

"Oh, Liz," I snapped, "he only thinks of Eddie. Feels so sorry for Eddie. *Poor put-upon Eddie.* Damn Eddie! Plays around with high school girls. Drinks like a fish. Watch, he'll land on his feet like a cat. A big fat tomcat! What'd I say that's so funny?"

Liz had to swallow her laugh before she could talk. "Mister Eddie sho is a tomcat."

I closed both my hands into fists, but didn't pound on the table for fear of knocking my glass over. Liz wouldn't stop cooking to go out and get another bottle.

"See, you're doing it too," I sniffed, "feeling sorry for Eddie. It's so unfair, the way he gets away with everything."

Putting my hands flat on the table, I pushed myself up.

"Where you goin'?" Liz asked.

"Let me have some coffee. I have a letter to write."

> *Editor*
> *Philadelphia Transcript*
>
> *A well-known host on a teenage dance show watched by millions is nothing more than a drunken pimp for those girls, particularly the one who calls herself Sophia. Why don't you dig out the truth about what went on at "Blueberry Hill" in Jersey?*
> *Medea*
> *cc: Philadelphia Bulletin*
> *   Commissioner of Police*

I liked my pen name. Angry and powerful.

"What you typin'?" Liz asked. "It must be funny the way you gigglin'."

I skimmed the *Transcript* at breakfast and the *Bulletin* before supper. Liz said I was a hawk looking for field mice. I laughed and said I was after bigger prey, a fat rat. She looked at me and nodded. That was the last time Liz commented on my newfound appetite for news.

The first story appeared a week after my letter, though Eddie created this problem without the assistance of Medea. It was a small piece buried near the obituaries. I laughed at my little joke. The powers that be were still protecting him, or more likely trying to avoid having *Varsity Dance* tarred with the same brush.

EDDIE GREENE INDICTED ON DRIVING CHARGE

Eddie Greene, host of the popular television show *Varsity Dance,* was charged yesterday with running a traffic light at the corner of Cottman Street and Bustleton Avenue. The arresting officer, patrolman Buonocotti, reported that at 9:00 a.m., when the incident occurred, this is one of the busiest intersections in Mayfair, part of Philadelphia's great Northeast. A delivery truck for Stein Your Florist ran into a parked car in its unsuccessful effort to avoid being struck by the Cadillac convertible driven by Mr. Greene. When officer Buonocotti arrived at the scene Mr. Greene was shouting at the Stein's driver in a "loud, slurred voice" according to the police report.

A spokesman for *Varsity Dance* said that Eddie Greene is "on vacation" at the present time. Telephone calls to Mr. Greene have not been returned.

The *Transcript* story was my first taste of blood.

It was two days after the story about Eddie's "driving under the influence of alcohol." From four o'clock on I had no liquor. I put on a long pleated skirt and a freshly ironed white blouse. Liz brewed coffee, and I had two cups.

David came into the kitchen through the garage door. I watched from the dining room. He was stooped over, briefcase in tow, and lifted his head like a dog sniffing something on the stove. "Coffee smells good, Liz," David said. Unable to sustain the moment, he bent over again, went off to his office and returned shortly.

I went up and kissed him on the mouth. Surprised, he looked at me and asked, "What's the occasion? You're all dressed up."

I couldn't tell David I was celebrating Eddie's beginning the tumbrel ride to the guillotine. "Nothing special," I said. "I know you're fond of this skirt."

I pinched the skirt with both hands and swirled it from side to side, flirting with my husband. David looked over to the table and noticed the newspaper folded next to my plate. He walked over and saw that it was open to a follow-up story on Eddie.

"Isn't this a shame?" he said.

Hiding my pleasure, I tried to mirror David's gloom. "I read that Eddie's been let go," I said. "Is that true?"

"Yes. It's awful. I get calls from him and he's crying. Says there must be something I can do." David was wringing his hands.

"Is there?" I said.

God, I hoped not.

"I swear I've called everyone I can think of. Naomi, would you speak to your father?" David's eyes were wet. "Bet Eddie could sell cars," David said with faked enthusiasm. "Just until he gets back on his feet. He tells me the bank has begun foreclosure."

I shook my head. David knew Daddy would never do that.

"Think we could put them up?" he asked. "They have no one to help them—no one."

"I don't think we can, David. His boys are little savages, and Thelma—"

"Exactly," he said, "they just add to his misery. What if we just have Eddie stay with us?"

"Damn it, David!"

His eyes widened, unable to figure out the source of my anger. Liz was standing in the kitchen doorway. I said to her, "Mr. Greenberg will have his dinner in his office. He's going there now. I'll eat here."

Five days later the *Transcript* broke the story on Blueberry Hill.

Grand Jury Investigates Teenage Vice Ring

The United States Attorney for New Jersey has convened a Grand Jury to look into allegations that adolescent girls were transported from Philadelphia to a mansion in Blueberry Hill where orgies were conducted. Well-heeled businessmen are claimed to have paid lavishly to attend sex-for-pay parties. An anonymous tip was received by this newspaper, the *Bulletin,* and the Philadelphia Police Commissioner. Since the girls were claimed to have been transported across state lines, the information was passed along to the Federal Bureau of Investigation. Their tireless efforts led to U.S. Attorney John Bancroft beginning to present witnesses to a Grand Jury yesterday. Bancroft told this reporter that he was "shocked" by the testimony heard so far. Since the F.B.I. and U.S. Attorney's office have clamped down on revealing anything further, it is not known whether the witnesses driven to the Federal Courthouse in Camden in F.B.I. vehicles with darkened windows are the prosperous clients or the underage hookers. The names of the Grand Jurors are also being withheld.

I circled the story in red and left it in front of David's plate.

"What's this?" The newspaper was trembling in David's hand.

"Have you been questioned about Blueberry Hill?" I asked.

"What?" David's voice cracked.

I pressed on. "The night you were there—after the Christmas party—did anyone see you?"

"I was there to see Eddie," David answered in a tone that implied he had now explained everything.

"When you came home, you wanted me to act like a whore, so I wondered what went on," I said.

David looked up from the paper. "Naomi, this is crazy talk. Keep your voice down. Liz will hear." Sweat blossomed on his upper lip.

"David, I need to know how much trouble you're in. This is not just between you, Eddie, and me. It's in the news."

"There's nothing about me in the papers," he said loudly." Eddie's name isn't here."

"Was Sophia at Blueberry Hill the night you were there?" I asked.

David's Adam's apple surfaced as he swallowed. "How would I know?" he said.

"David, she called here looking for Eddie the night you went to New York."

He stood up and looked down at me. "Why do you keep bringing New York up?" He turned his back on me.

"David, where are you going?"

"Where I won't get the third degree," he said as he walked out. A minute later I heard the door to his office slam.

A week passed with no follow-up story. Had Pyramid fixed the case? Would Eddie wiggle out of this? That morning the *Transcript* had a new story. I was still in my bathrobe. Beads of coffee slid down the lapel, muddying the pink satin braiding. I patted it dry.

"You look like da cat wid a bowl of cream," Liz said. "What you find in da paper?"

"Come here and I'll show you."

"I hain't got time to stop. You tell me while ah'm cleanin' up."

Maybe Liz couldn't read. Or maybe she wanted to hear my voice. Help her figure out what had me going. Mommy said that colored folks could see right into white people's heads, but not the other way around. I'm not sure I believed her, though.

"Eddie had another accident," I told her. The *Transcript* was folded in thirds so that the story on Eddie was the only one visible. I waved it in the air as I told Liz, "The little girl in the car he hit is in the hospital. He kept on going and plowed into two parked cars."

Liz clucked her tongue against the roof of her mouth. "They best take his license away 'fore he kills hisself or someon' else."

"A bastard like that hurts others and walks away unscratched," I said. "How does he get away with it?" I slapped the paper down, shattering the cup and spinning the saucer into the air.

"Was he drunk?" Liz asked. She picked up a dishtowel and wiped the spilled coffee.

"No," I told her, "but the paper says Eddie had just learned he was indicted for having sex with an under-age girl."

The words felt satisfying. Eddie's luck was running out.

It had taken two months until Eddie's criminal trial was held. In the meantime, Pyramid had settled with the injured girl's family. David never told me for how much. The jury had not agreed on Eddie's guilt in his relations with Sophia. Maybe they thought she looked like a grown woman.

"I just can't believe it!" I shouted.

David had his hands out toward me, patting the air. "Easy. Take it easy! You just missed knocking the Steuben off the table. Put the paper down. That's better. Are you sober?"

I looked at the table. The vase seemed fine to me. Not even wobbling.

"Go to Hell, David. Don't you dare patronize me!"

He had his hangdog look, asking God what he had done to be punished with such a wife. "Okay," he said, "I'm sorry. Can you tell me what's causing this outburst?"

I really wanted to bloody his nose. "Of course I can tell you, if you use a different tone of voice."

"I'm sorry, hon." David heaved a great sigh. "Please, let's just talk. What has you carrying on like this?"

Why was I the only one who was upset? "Your damned cousin," I said. "He has more lives than a cat. You probably know already. You talk to him every day, don't you? Take his calls, not mine."

The tension left David's face. We had been through this so often. Once it was clear that my fury was directed at Eddie, David told himself I was being irrational.

"Is this about the hung jury?" he asked.

"They should have hung Eddie is who they should have hung," I said.

"Why are you so angry at him?" David asked. "He never did anything to you. And look at him now. The bank gave him a week to pack and move out. I don't understand. You always have a big heart, except when it comes to Eddie. Naomi, where are you going? Please don't walk out while I'm talking to you. I never do that to you."

I picked up the Steuben and hurled it at the fireplace.

Chapter Twenty-Five
Dinner at Sol and Ruth's

Catherine Marie cleared her throat softly and said, "Mr. Greenberg."

David looked up. She was worn out like a hand-me-down dress. After her younger sister had died, Catherine Marie had married her brother-in-law out of a sense of responsibility to the six kids. David didn't think there was any romance and wondered if they shared a bed.

"Anne called to remind you that Mr. Bloomenthal needs to look over the new syndication agreement for *Varsity Dance* before his meeting with Mr. Karp. She asked whether I was finished with the last revisions."

Catherine Marie was looking at him with a desperate hope that he had a rabbit to pull out of his hat. She had been waiting all day.

She walked up to the desk and pointed. "Is that the agreement?"

Technically it was. Except on top of it was the letter from Eddie. A lot had happened in the three months since the District Attorney had decided not to retry the case. Pyramid had fired Eddie, and he had taken a job in a different state. Not that it mattered.

"Do you want me to take it to Nelson Schwartz?" she asked. "He's been working closely with you. You would have final authority over any suggested changes."

David handed the document to her. Catherine Marie's eyes were shimmering. As soon as she stepped out of his office, she would run to the ladies lounge and cry. Though they never had the conversation, they both knew his days at the firm were numbered.

As the door closed, he went back to the week-old letter, Eddie's last letter.

> *I think Kansas City will work out. I host a radio show. KCR is not a big operation, so I do the news, have a call-in talk show, as well as being a D.J.—you know, chief cook and bottle washer. I feel like I'm back at the bottom of the*

ladder. But it pays the bills. I try to go to A.A. meetings when I can. Hopefully I'll stick to it. Thirty days without a drink. If you call the station, ask for Ed White. I had to change my name. KCR insisted. Can't blame them.

He put the letter down and called home.

"Greenberg residence."

"Hi, Liz, can I speak with Naomi?"

"No sah," she said, "Miz Naomi took her pills an hour ago and is sleepin' like a baby."

"Liz, can you stay?" David asked. "I don't think Naomi should be alone."

"You not comin' home?"

"No, I'll be home," he told her. "It's just, well, I seem to get her upset. You're the only one she's calm around. I have things—some work I have to do. It would be a big favor." He paused, but she didn't let him off the hook.

"Liz, you can do it, can't you?" David wondered what would he would do if Liz refused. "It would mean a lot. I mean to Naomi. For her to find you there when she gets up. I'll be home by six. We're having dinner at her parents'."

He moved papers and pens to the side, leaving Eddie's letter in the center.

"Mister Greenberg, it's not my place to say, but what she needs is a nurse. Dat's what Doctah said. Either a nurse or they goin' to put her in a hospital. She gets awful sad in hospital."

"I can't do anything tonight," he said. "Damn it, why can't people just help *me*?" he pleaded. "I can't do everything."

Eddie's letter was crumpled in his fist.

"Ah knows," Liz said. David heard her disappointment in him. "Ah'll stay late tonight, but I can't be doin' this every night. You get someone for her. She deserves dat."

"And what do I deserve?" he demanded.

Liz's silence was angry. Why not? Her loyalty was to Naomi. She saw him through Naomi's eyes.

"Okay, I stay tonight. When you gonna be here again?"

"In a few hours." David felt the clamping in his jaw relax. He had not been aware of being tense. "I told you. I'll be there by six."

He slammed the receiver down.

David believed it wasn't his fault. Naomi was the one who was the embarrassment. Even Sol had lost patience. Not that he hadn't contributed. Forty years of "Princess" and "Daddy" would drive anyone around the bend.

Dinner was just the four of them. Since the auto accident at Blueberry Hill, Sol and Ruth didn't have other people over when they were there.

Ruth answered the door. "Naomi honey, let's freshen you up a bit."

Naomi's face stiffened. "For God's sake, Mommy, let Daddy take my coat."

"Of course. Please don't get upset," Ruth said.

"Well, what's the problem?" Naomi asked.

Everyone but Naomi could see it. There were stains on her light yellow dress. Probably spilled food. A greasy slab of red spilled over her lips and colored her front teeth. David had thought about saying something at home, but Naomi would have snarled, "What have I done wrong now?" Maybe David had wanted Sol and Ruth to see what he lived with. Liz had left when he got home, and there was no one else to clean up the messy child.

When the two women came out of the powder room there were large wet circles across the top of Naomi's dress, as though she were lactating for the phantom child David couldn't father. Now all of her teeth were off-white. There was a dusting of talcum powder on the un-plucked hair above her upper lip.

"You girls were in there a long time," Sol observed while he made a show of looking at his watch.

"Mommy had a lot of repair work to do. That's what you really mean, isn't it, Daddy?"

Sol's face drooped. With age had come jowls. What did he see when he looked at them? A woman whose money kept her off the streets; a son-in-law whose seed was dead and who was about to be thrown out of a job?

The table was set for four: Sol at the head, Ruth to his left, Naomi and David across from her. Everything gleamed. A heavy white damask tablecloth reflected the light from the chandelier. The dishes were white, rimmed in an ornate gold pattern. Naomi had once told David that the china and crystal were pre-war Rosenthal. For some reason it stuck in his mind. Being in this room felt like stepping back in time. He knew that the Luntzes could replace everything. Something in this house had died years ago. David felt like he was in that movie about the faded movie star, the one with Gloria Swanson.

"I'd like a gimlet," Naomi announced.

When Sol handed it to her, she took a sip and scowled at him. "This is all lime juice," she said. "It tastes awful."

Naomi stood up and headed for the liquor trolley.

"Princess, it's supposed to be half Rose's," Sol said.

"Oh, Daddy."

She poured her drink into a larger glass and filled it to the top with vodka. Holding it with both hands, she walked carefully back to the table.

"See, I didn't spill a drop. Old Naomi can hold her liquor." She burst into her trademark giggle. "Come on, it's a joke," she said.

Sol and Ruth were staring at the shrimp cocktails Estelle had placed in front of them. Sol speared one, turned it over to cover it with horseradish-flecked catsup, and raised it to his mouth. The three of them watched half the shrimp disappear over Sol's lower lip.

"Daddy, we never had shrimp when Bubbie lived with us." They heard the sadness in Naomi. Sol rushed to fill the silence.

"We went out for shrimp," Sol said. "Bubbie wanted the house kept kosher."

"I miss Bubbie," Naomi said and it sounded like a code for all the disappointments in her life.

"I miss her too, Princess," Sol said. David noticed Ruth dab at her eyes.

"She loved me," Naomi said. "No questions. No dirty looks." The accusation hung over all of them.

"Please don't cry, Princess," Sol said. "We love you. Mommy and me. David, of course."

David knew he was the intruder from Sol's point of view.

Ruth stood up.

"Mommy, sit down, damn it," Naomi snapped.

David got up.

"You sit down, too," she ordered. Naomi's forehead tightened into furrows.

"I'm glad Eddie is dead!" she said.

David felt the heat in his face, the tightness around his nose. He wanted to reach out and slap Naomi hard, to see the mark of his hand on her face. Most of all he needed to silence her, to move the spotlight from her anger to his. "Hadn't he suffered enough? He'd lost everything."

Sol and Ruth stared at them. When Sol spoke, David had to strain to make out the words, "Princess, please."

Naomi got a hard edge to her high-pitched voice, "You don't understand. You never have."

Estelle stood in the archway with an empty tray in her hand; she turned and went back to the kitchen.

"Look Princess, you've been through a lot," Sol said. "Auto accident, whatever else drives you to drink so much. Things will get better. They always do." He smiled at Naomi, but she did not respond. Sol tried again. "I've been under some stress myself. What with Eddie and the show. His thing for young girls. The *Transcript* runs a story every now and then. Putting the needle in."

Sol pointed a finger past Naomi at David. "What was wrong with him?" he said, but David knew Sol didn't expect an answer. "When something like this happened, Bubbie would say a man like Eddie—he's not good for the Jews."

He felt Sol was blaming him. With Eddie being his cousin, it was as if he'd done it. David thought all of them were cats playing with a dead bird.

He startled himself, shouting, "Eddie gave his life for you!"

Ruth raised her voice, "David, don't talk crazy. You've got to be strong. For yourself. For Naomi. Like Sol is for all of us."

"I apologize, Ruth," he said. "I don't want to hurt you. Ever."

"David only wants to hurt me," Naomi said, stabbing her fork prongs into the table. "Right, David? Naomi's okay to hurt. Don't feel sorry for Naomi. Only for Eddie. Daddy, you know when it started?"

Sol's eyes were blinking. He rubbed them, but they didn't stop. "When what started, Princess?" Sol said.

"When you and Morris Chumsky hatched up the plan to send David off to sow his oats with Eddie in Havana. So Naomi's precious virginity would be intact at the wedding. For you. Not for me."

Naomi's voice carried throughout the house. David saw a corner of Estelle's skirt. By tomorrow all the colored help would have the story; by the end of the week every Jewish family would know.

"David was different when he returned," she said. Ruth lifted a fork and put it between her knife and spoon.

"Naomi, what are you talking about?" Sol asked. He reached up and dug his fingers into the measles' scars he had gouged in childhood.

Everything was happening in slow motion. Naomi's little girl voice hung the words on a clothesline, one by one, so Sol and Ruth could see them. Not just hear her accusations, but watch them flapping on the line, snapping at David's eyes. He couldn't hear his own responses. David's voice was drowned out by Naomi's. "Eddie destroyed our marriage," Naomi said and turned to him. "I couldn't compete. The two of you in your office in the middle of the night. Door locked. Our bed—*our* bed— empty. Damn both of you!"

"Naomi, stop it," David said. "Eddie was drunk. I put him in the office to sleep it off."

Naomi faced her father. "Why was my virginity so precious to you?"

"Naomi, don't talk to your father like that!" Ruth half-rose from her chair and swung an open hand through the air. Naomi was too far away for the slap to reach her. Naomi glared at Ruth, and turned back to him.

"Close your mouth, David. You look the fool. Does it shock you that Mommy can get angry? You must think that women are stupid cows, that we see nothing and feel nothing. And if we go off the deep end it's hysteria. Right? Well, I didn't imagine your trip to Blueberry Hill in the middle of the night. I didn't fantasize your behaving like a bastard when you came back. Treating me like a whore. Naomi, do this, do that. Or that call from Sophia before New York. Or your drinking and crying and staying awake all night ever since."

Sol's face was gray as meat gone bad. Ruth slammed an open hand on the table. "Stop! Stop. I don't know what you're talking about. But look at your father. Do you want to give him a heart attack? Sol, drink some water. Loosen your tie. David, take her out of here. Right now!"

"No, Mother. No more fairy tales. Daddy, look at me. I'm sorry you're upset. I've been upset for twenty years. You made up this fairy tale. I was the Princess. You were the King. I was a doll, not a person."

Sol was waving a hand in front of his face, trying to protect himself from the buzz of Naomi's swarming words.

"For God's sake Naomi, stop," Ruth shouted. "Look what you're doing to your father!"

"You've all got to listen. We can't live in make-believe anymore." Naomi's voice was a command.

Sol stood up, his hands on the table. "Make-believe? Is it make-believe for a father to want only the best for his daughter? What did you want from me, Naomi?"

"I wanted you to see *me*!" Naomi's voice lowered. "Me, not some Princess *mishigoss*. Love me because I'm smart, not because I'm some story in your head; no brains, just a hymen."

Ruth picked up her wine glass and threw it, missing Naomi but trailing a blood red stain across the tablecloth. The four of them stared at the red slash.

Naomi stood up. None of them could take their eyes off her. "Daddy, look at me. I want to see your face. Make sure you hear. Princesses end up mad, locked in towers. I thought David would rescue me. I was wrong."

In the closet David found Naomi's coat and returned to the dining room. Ruth took Sol's napkin, laid it across the stain, smoothed it out, and then put her hand across it. Sol lowered his head.

"I left this home and never found another," Naomi whispered.

David wasn't sure Sol or Ruth had heard.

Chapter Twenty-Six
David's Disappearance

David's office at home had changed as he had changed, buried in paper as depression filled every nook and cranny of his mind. Six months to the day before he disappeared, he started going to it after dinner, entering our bedroom only to take a shirt out of the drawer, a suit from the closet. Sometimes he went to work directly from the office. Since he no longer hugged me or lay next to me in bed, I was spared the worst of his unbathed stench. The closest we came was opposite ends of the dining room table, an eight foot buffer zone. There were times he came into the house and immediately went into his office. I only knew of his presence by checking whether his car was in the garage. He locked his office door when he left.

The morning after the dinner at Mommy and Daddy's, the night when I spilled the beans and Mommy spilled the wine, I woke with a fierce determination to get inside David's office. I called a locksmith and said we had lost the key. I knew he didn't believe me, but he opened the door and made a duplicate key.

As soon as he left, Liz and I went in.

"Oh Lawd!" she said. Liz pulled her hand out of mine and hid it in her apron.

She walked to the window and pulled up the shade. The wall above David's desk was layered with magazine photos. Eddie's eyes stared out, embracing the camera. The most recent photograph was from *Life*. Eddie looked like Orson Welles in *Touch of Evil*, eyes coiled under swollen lids. When that issue of *Life* had come out, it was all I heard about for a week. Eddie had gone to the photo shoot alone. He must have been plastered. Jay Karp had been hysterical. Said *Life* was out to destroy Pyramid. Bloomie had screamed that Eddie was David's responsibility. Even Daddy had been angry.

Liz called me over to the desk, pointing to a pile of newspapers, the *Transcript, Bulletin, Times*. All were open to Eddie's obituaries from last week. The morning they had appeared David had called Eddie's wife to find out when the funeral would be held. Thelma had told him 11 a.m. He had asked why she hadn't called so he could have bought plane tickets. Thelma's voice had screamed out of the phone that she hadn't wanted him there and hung up. David had looked up at me and said, "It's the time difference. Five o'clock in the morning in Kansas City. Must have woken her. People only call that early with bad news."

"David," I had reminded him, "she already knew Eddie was dead."

"People don't always hold on to something that terrible," he had said. "Maybe she had forgotten and I brought it all back."

That conversation with David should have been a warning.

I picked up the December 14, 1958 *Transcript.*

EDDIE GREENE, TELEVISION PERSONALITY

Eddie Greene, a pioneer in television entertainment, died in an automobile accident yesterday on the outskirts of Kansas City. He was the original host of *Varsity Dance*, the popular teenage dance show that began broadcasting from Philadelphia in 1957 and is now viewed nationally by millions of people.

Mr. Greene, born Edward Greenberg in 1913 in Philadelphia, enjoyed great success in radio. In 1956 on his show *Teen Hit Parade* he introduced his youthful following to what was then called Rock-a-Billy music with Carl Perkins' rendition of "Blue Suede Shoes." Mr. Greene is credited with introducing Negro vocalists, such as Fats Domino, to white audiences. He moved to television with *Varsity Dance* the following year.

Jay Karp, the President of Pyramid Communications which produces *Varsity Dance*, said, "We have lost a giant of the industry."

Three months ago allegations of improper conduct with adolescent girls who appeared on *Varsity Dance* and incidents of driving under the influence of alcohol led to his leaving Philadelphia and obtaining work at a Kansas City radio station.

I asked Liz to get a large box for cleaning up. There were candy wrappers, empty whiskey bottles, and the like, and I was nervous as to what else we might find. I did the sorting and handed Liz what I chose to throw out. I hoped to find clippings with details of the accident, but David had not kept those.

Eddie's car had been found at 1 a.m. against a tree, steam pouring out of the radiator. He had died instantly, his chest crushed against the steering wheel. One of the teenage girls in the car had her head in his lap facing him. Kansas City's medical examiner thought she had also been killed immediately when her neck broke. I was sure the autopsy had found part of Eddie's penis lodged in her mouth. The other girl had been in a coma for a day before she died. Hand-rolled marijuana cigarettes had been found in the backseat. I looked forward to reading the stories in the supermarket tabloids.

Liz could keep a conversation going when I was in the bleakest of moods, but not that morning. It took me hours to pick through the office. In the months David had spent alone in that room his sadness had overflowed into creating an altar to Eddie. Liz opened a window. Even though it was bitter cold, we needed to clear out the suffocating smell if we were to get the job done. At the end, I left Liz to vacuum the liquor-stained rug and I went upstairs to shower. In the scalding water I stared at my feet to see what swirled off. There were only soap bubbles in the drain. Grief has no color.

That night we were to have dinner with Bloomie and his wife at the Warwick. I was certain everyone had heard the story of the aborted dinner at Mommy and Daddy's. I called David at the office and Catherine Marie said he was in a meeting. It was a lie; no one met with David anymore. I told her I had a severe migraine and she agreed to let Bloomie and David know that dinner was off.

The next morning. I think a lot about that morning. I had not heard David come in. That meant he had arrived in the middle of the night. I never fell asleep before one, and was wide awake by four. I threw off the covers and went downstairs. David's office was closed; a border of light outlined the bottom of the door. I had been worried since yesterday about David's reaction to finding his office cleaned up, his privacy violated.

I went down to the kitchen to make coffee, thinking about how David and I lived separately in the same house.

Swimming in silence, I rose from the breakfast stool and went up the stairs without breaking the surface. In the bedroom I pulled a thick sweater over my head, and the next thing I remembered I found myself outside the house. Icy pinpricks stabbed my forehead. The sunlight was painful. Raising a hand to shade my eyes, I saw my breath. I returned to the front door. Had I left it open or was someone else in our house? I was startled that it was unlocked.

In the center of his desk, David's wedding ring sat on Eddie's obituaries. Nothing else. He had been too filled with rage to leave a note.

Daddy and Bloomie discretely called hospitals, but no one fitting David's description had been admitted. Jay Karp used his contacts with the police, but David's body was not in the morgue. The only official report I filed was of a stolen vehicle, David's Packard.

My guilt clung to me like a howling infant. To fall asleep I drank until I passed out. I woke up at noon in the dark bedroom my head screaming with pain, too scared to turn on the lights. I think Liz was in the house around the clock. I'm not certain, but I believe I was never alone.

Helping me into my robe, Liz said, "Let's git you downstairs. I made some fresh coffee." She opened a bedroom window, and then with an arm around my back moved me through the door to the stairs.

"Miz Naomi, don't be leanin' on me," she said. "You too heavy for me to hold. Lift your feet. No slidin'."

I don't remember going downstairs or drinking coffee or talking to Liz. She told me later I spent the next three days drinking until I passed out.

On Thursday, Mommy woke me, leaving the door open behind her. "I have Dr. Flynn on the phone."

"Who?" I said. My mouth was so dry I had trouble forming words.

"Dr. Flynn," Mommy said. "I didn't know who else to call."

She walked the phone around the bed trailing the long cord. Mommy lifted the handset and wormed it between the pillow and my ear.

"Naomi," the voice said, "this is Dr. Flynn. Can you hear me?"

"Why are you calling in the middle of the night?" I asked. "Did someone die?"

"Your mother called and told me what's been going on. Ordinarily I wouldn't do this, but she sounded very upset. The question is, would you like to see me? Would it help you? I really shouldn't be doing this. It breaks all the rules. But your mother was insistent."

Then he was silent for a moment. "I apologize," he said. "Please forgive me. This is an intrusion."

"When can you see me?" I said.

I hadn't seen Liz enter. She opened a closet door and reached in for a dress.

"David's disappeared," I said. "I broke into his office. Now he's gone."

Liz laid the dress at the foot of the bed, and walked over to my chest of drawers.

"Naomi, give me a moment to check my appointment book. I think you need to come in today. Here," he said. I pictured his finger moving down the hour-lines. "I can see you at five. Call a cab to bring you. Will you do that?"

"I'll try," I said, and handed the phone to Mommy.

I never made it to Dr. Flynn's. The call came two hours later. Liz answered and then handed me the phone. "Is this Mrs. Greenberg?" a man asked.

"Yes, who is this?"

"My name is Harry. Harry Schultz. I run the Acme Parking Garage. On Monday a man parked his car here. He was sitting in it when we opened. A Packard."

I heard myself moan. Mr. Schultz kept on talking, "Today, I got the weekly police list of stolen cars. It says the Packard belongs to your husband."

The voice waited and then said, "Do you want to pick it up?"

Time passed. I was confused and didn't know what to tell him.

"Would you rather have me call the police and have them do it?" he asked.

My breath had left me. When I replied, I couldn't hear myself.

"Mrs. Greenberg," he said, "please speak louder."

I handed the phone to Liz and said, "Tell him we'll be down as soon as we can get a cab."

The Acme garage was the old Luntz movie theater. By 1955 the upkeep was more than the money it brought in and Daddy sold it. Because it was near the Academy of Music, the buyer turned it into a parking garage. I hadn't seen it for years. As the cab pulled over, I looked out the window. The marquee that used to have "SHIRLEY TEMPLE—THE LITTLE COLONEL" in large red letters, now read "All Day Parking $3.00." Where "LUNTZ" had run from top to bottom in seven-foot letters, it now had "ACME." Since "ACME" was only four letters, at the top was a grayish white recessed letter box like the scar tissue where a tomcat had lost an eye in a fight.

I handed my purse to Liz, climbed out of the cab, and held on to the door to keep my balance.

"Miz Greenberg, you want him to wait?" Liz asked.

"No," I said.

After she paid the cabbie, Liz came around and squeezed my hand. Tear tracks were drying on her cheeks. Both of us took deep breaths and walked under the marquee. The car entrance had sliding gates across it. On one side was the old movie ticket booth where a young girl sat chewing a wad of gum.

"Got your ticket?" she asked.

Liz squeezed my hand again, a mother prompting her child.

"I'm Mrs. Greenberg," I said. "Mrs. David Greenberg." I stopped, but there was no response in the doll face. "My husband's car is here," I said, thinking it was now clear. She had resumed chewing, a far-away look in her eyes.

A heavy-set man in his fifties stepped into the booth behind her.

"Mrs. Greenberg, I'm Harry Schultz," he said. "Your father sold me this building." He had red apple cheeks and a thick neck. His tie-less white dress shirt was crisp. "Sally, push the button," he told her. There was a buzz and a door next to the booth popped open.

Liz and I stepped through. It took me a minute to adjust to the dim light and shadows. We were in an open space as large as a baseball field. It had been the grand lobby and auditorium of the old Luntz. All the seats and carpets were gone, leaving a dirty silver cement surface dotted with oil puddles. The original sconce fixtures on the sides of the walls shed enough light to distinguish the make and color of the two dozen parked cars. It looked larger than I remembered when it had endless rows of maroon plush seats squirming with families. Where the stage had stood under the movie screen, a driving ramp now led to the street behind the theater.

Daddy had been so proud of the three-story high walls and ceiling, its plasterwork an Arabesque fantasy, part Gothic cathedral, part great mosque, filled with intricate geometric patterns, stylized flowers and a few nymphets. He had refused to permit the bare-breasted goddesses that adorned other movie palaces. In Daddy's shrine to Shirley Temple, girls never reached puberty. Much of the lower portion of the plasterwork had been destroyed in the conversion to an indoor garage, but the vaulted ceiling, grimed with car fumes and poorly lit, was intact.

Mr. Schultz took one of my arms and led me around a limousine. A now visible Packard was on the other side with a license plate ending in "99," David's. I knew I would never see him again. An unseen fist sledge-hammered into my chest. My legs melted and my body flowed to the floor. Mr. Schultz threw an arm around my waist and tightened his grip on my elbow. My weight dragged us both down.

"Are you okay?" he asked.

I flapped my hands, but didn't try to stand up.

"Don't move," he said. "Take some deep breaths. Your face is very red."

I felt hot. The pounding of my heart terrified me. Liz's face was ashen.

"I did this," I said. "I cornered him at Mommy and Daddy's. Then I took away his last refuge. There was no place he could go. He had to run."

Mr. Schultz turned his head toward Liz.

"I'll stay here," she said. "If you could call us a cab, then call Mr. Luntz to git the car."

He looked relieved. As soon as Liz sat on the floor and cradled my head, I started making that awful sound that still wakes me at times. Years later Liz told me it was the sound women made at graveside to let the pain out. It was the last I remembered until I woke up in the rear of the car driving through the night to the private mental hospital in Massachusetts. I saw Liz's face in the light of oncoming traffic. She put a pill in my mouth and held a cup of water to my lips. I remember her wiping the wetness as most of it drooled out. I felt safe for a moment. Then David stepped into my thoughts. I whimpered as I fell into a drugged sleep.

Chapter Twenty-Seven
The Actor's Story

There were five men in the small room. On one side of the table sat a forty-five-year-old unemployed actor in prison-issued shirt and pants. After a week in a New York jail, his reddish blond hair dye had almost vanished. The remaining patches floated on the un-dyed mousy gray. Next to him was a fifty-year-old man in a three-piece chalk stripe suit set off by a maroon tie with white dots. He looked like a mannequin from Paul Stuart, his favorite men's store.

Sitting across from them was a police detective still wearing his fedora, an Assistant District Attorney, and the police sketch artist.

"Mr. Mortimer," the prosecutor said to the prisoner, "you are facing murder charges. You should have criminal counsel. I have no doubt that Mr. Rhodes has your best interests at heart, since you say he is a very good friend. But he has never tried a criminal case in his twenty-five years of corporate practice. If this goes to trial, the court may insist on your obtaining another lawyer. The nature of the crime, the brutal death of a woman during violent sex, is difficult for the most seasoned defense counsel."

"The purpose of this meeting," Rhodes said, "is to avoid a trial. Mr. Mortimer knows that he is to keep silent unless I tell him otherwise. He is in possession of valuable information relevant to a major crime figure. If we can come to a suitable plea agreement, he will disclose that information and be a witness at trial, if he is needed in the future. He is fearful that most of the criminal defense bar might be compromised in their allegiances."

Detective Reilly lifted his hat, scratched his forehead, and returned the fedora to the permanent crease marks it had made on his thick hair. "Tell us who you're talking about," Reilly said, "so we'll know if there's any point to continuing this conversation."

"Morris Chumsky," Rhodes said. He was silent for a moment, watching Reilly and the Assistant D.A.; then he said, "It is helpful to remember that the death occurred in the context of consensual 'rough' sex, nothing more. We will plea to a count of involuntary manslaughter, no jail time, and Mr. Mortimer's being placed in the witness protection program."

The detective laughed. "He's crazy, right, Katz?" and he nodded at the prosecutor.

The prosecutor said, "I think Detective Reilly is correct. I would have to hear your story, and pass it on to the D.A. to see if there was any interest. What you're asking is out of the question. Mr. Mortimer savagely beat the victim to death. Her face was jelly and bone fragments. If you have something valuable, maybe we'd agree not to seek the death penalty. But at this point there's nothing to talk about."

"Then why did you agree to this meeting and to our request for a police artist to be present?" Rhodes asked. He folded his hands across his vest certain he had scored a point, even if it wasn't measured in the usual dollar value to a business client.

The prosecutor said, "I'll need an offer of proof. You know how that's done?"

Mortimer looked over at Rhodes, who hadn't reacted to the taunt. "Of course. I did my homework," Rhodes said. "Here's my hypothetical. It goes without saying that this is not an admission by Mr. Mortimer, and can't be used in court."

Rhodes leaned forward and spoke directly to the Assistant D.A., who had taken out a pen and written the date and time at the top of a yellow legal tablet.

"Mr. Katz, I have been told you have an excellent mind and a near photographic memory," Rhodes said. "Until we have an agreement in writing I must insist that you take no notes."

The prosecutor put the pen down.

"For the sake of discussion," Rhodes began, "let's say that an actor like Mr. Mortimer was approached by a man who said he was in the employ of Morris Chumsky."

"What was this man's name?" the detective interrupted.

"In our story," Rhodes said, "he did not give a name. But an actor, like Mr. Mortimer, has a well-trained memory for faces. That may be why we requested a police artist."

"So describe him," the detective said.

Assistant D.A. Katz held his hand up and said, "I'd like to hear the story through once, and then we can get a sketch."

Detective Reilly nodded.

Rhodes resumed, "This man said he had an acting job for Mr. Mortimer and another actor, James Perse, who has since died. Mr. Mortimer was given photographs of two men and asked if he and Perse could make themselves up to pass as the men in the pictures. We still have the photos and will provide them if this works out."

The prosecutor pointed at Rhodes and raised his voice. "Withholding evidence in a criminal investigation is a felony."

Rhodes leaned back on the wooden chair, dangerously balanced on the two rear legs. "We will withhold nothing, assuming the photographs have not been lost."

Reilly jumped up and ran around the table, swinging his arms to knock Rhodes over.

"Stop it!" the prosecutor yelled. "Not that Detective Reilly didn't have good reason, but I'd like to get through this once and see where we are."

Rhodes leaned over, smirking, and whispered low enough that only Mortimer heard, "We've got 'em," and then resumed his narrative, "Our hypothetical actors were given a schedule running from Friday night December 20th through Sunday afternoon, December 22nd," Rhodes said.

The prosecutor reached for his pen and asked, "What year?"

Rhodes stared at the pen until it was put down, and then replied, "Last year, 1958. Seven months ago. We also have that paper. It's typed, not hand-written. It specifies a hotel to stay at, the names to use, restaurants to eat at, etcetera."

"What names were they to use?" the detective asked.

"David Greenberg and Eddie Greene," Rhodes said. "I've done a little research on my own. Eddie Greene was the D.J. on that TV show, *Varsity Dance*, until he got in trouble. I believe he died in a car crash. They were to have the hotel bills made out to Schmidt, Harris, Cardozo & Green in Philadelphia."

"What's that?" the detective said.

Both Rhodes and the prosecutor said "law firm."

"Do you have the hotel and restaurant receipts?" the prosecutor asked.

"No," Mortimer volunteered, and Rhodes put a finger to his own mouth.

"No," Rhodes repeated, "our hypothetical Mr. Mortimer had to turn over all of those to the man who hired him."

"Did you contact Schmidt, Harris, or David Greenberg?" the prosecutor asked.

"No," Rhodes said. "I'm not the police and I didn't want to mess up your investigation."

Detective Reilly let out his breath and said, "Good."

The prosecutor opened his hands to show Rhodes and Mortimer they were empty. "I don't see what you think you have to offer us. A man, whom we have no way of identifying, says he is speaking for Morris Chumsky, and gives you a list of where to stay and where to eat. Not only can't we prove he was sent by Chumsky, but there's no crime being committed. You'd better get yourself a crackerjack criminal attorney today, so we don't waste our time any further."

"I agree," the detective said. "But since we have hauled Jim Janofsky down here"—nodding toward the man with the sketchpad—"let's finish up. Mr. Mortimer give him your description of the man you say you met with and let's see what we have."

"*I'll* give it to Mr. Janofsky," Rhodes announced, and then took out a typed page from his suit pocket. "This man was about Mr. Mortimer's height. That would be five feet eleven inches. His head was square, coming down to a pointed chin. Large head. Hair was black with white flecks."

The police artist was moving his charcoal quickly back and forth, sketching in hair. Mortimer whispered into Rhodes ear.

"The hair's too long," Rhodes said. "It was a buzz cut."

Using his thumb, the artist cut back the hair, leaving a gray mist on top.

"The most striking feature was a scar running from the top of his head to the left eye," Rhodes said.

Looking up, the police artist said, "This will go a whole lot faster if Mr. Mortimer tells me what to sketch in, so I don't have to guess at it and get it wrong."

"Mr. Mortimer can't do that," Rhodes fumed nervously. "I won't permit it!"

"Counselor," the detective laughed, "this is all Mickey Mouse. We could've gotten through all of this a damn sight quicker if we had a real shyster here instead of a banker."

Rhodes stood up and pounded on the table. Spittle sprayed out of his mouth as he tried to translate his embarrassment into a crushing response.

The prosecutor rose and pointed to the door. "Out! Get out now! I'll handle this." As the detective moved away, a smirk appeared on his face out of Rhodes' and Mortimer's sight.

The prosecutor continued, "I apologize. Legal niceties are lost on Detective Reilly. I have a suggestion. I'll leave also, along with Mr. Janofsky. When we come back we won't know which one of you drew the scar line on the sketch."

In the hallway, the prosecutor said to the detective, "Looks like you were right. The guy who set this up was Chumsky's right hand guy. If Mortimer I.D.'s the photo, the D.A. said to send the whole package to Philly, and they can decide whether there's something here. Right now, it's a mystery what Chumsky was up to."

Back in the room, the scar had been drawn in. The prosecutor took a photograph from a file and handed it to Mortimer. "Is this the man who gave you the photos and the script for that weekend?"

"Yes," Mortimer said, as Rhodes stepped on his toe.

Rhodes asked, "Who is he?"

"Here's his rap sheet," the prosecutor said, handing him a sheet of paper.

> JACOB SHTOWSKI a/k/a/ JACK SHIT
> b. Belorussia (town unknown) 1927–1928 (exact date unknown)
> Believed to enter U.S. through Newark, New Jersey in late 1930's

Juvenile facility—felony rape during commitment of armed robbery—1943

Charged with labor racketeering and murder—double homicide—1949; charges dropped when one eyewitness murdered and another reneged on testimony at trial.

Believed to be a member of crime organization headed by Morris Chumsky, Philadelphia, Pennsylvania.

Chapter Twenty-Eight
Meeting in District Attorney's Office, Philadelphia

"Since you asked for this meeting Detective Synge, why don't you start?"

District Attorney Boyle's full head of white hair was set off by a deep tan from regular attendance at Phillies games on a season ticket provided free by Pyramid.

"The stuff from New York is the break we've been waiting for in the Rabelli murder," Synge said. He had stood up as he started to talk. Now he stepped forward and then back, rubbing his right fisted hand with his left.

Ned Tate remained sitting, licking his lips with his tongue and avoiding Boyle's stare.

"I don't see it that way," the D.A. said, "but I could be missing something. Lay it out for me, Terry."

"Eddie Greene was the bait," Synge said. "We know the Lieutenant tried to kill him earlier that Friday." He lifted his right thumb and recited, "We got the doorman at Greene's apartment on that."

"I agree," the D.A. said and Tate nodded.

"Greene and his cousin, the lawyer, leave the lawyer's house telling Mrs. Greenberg they're going to New York." Synge raised his forefinger. "She's told us that."

"The first hole we got to fill," the D.A. said, "is that no one saw Rabelli follow them. I looked over the transcript again. She may be a little flighty, but she stuck to her story that she didn't go outside or look through the window."

"I'd like to question her again," Synge said. "I thought she knew more than she let on. I don't buy that Gracie Allen act."

"Well she's just back from a fancy mental hospital in Massachusetts," the D.A. replied. "Nobody's going to see her for a while."

"How the hell do you know all that?" Synge challenged.

The D.A. frowned. "I just do. Let's get back to not having any proof that Rabelli followed Greene and his cousin that night."

"That doesn't mean it didn't happen," Synge insisted.

"Come on, Terry!" the D.A. raised his voice. "Judges throw out cases on 'could have happened.' The next hole is that no one saw the Lieutenant shot. Christ, it was way out in farm country late at night."

"We got the actor I. D.-ing Jack Shit, who tells the actor he's setting up the weekend scene at Chumsky's request," Synge said, raising a second finger.

"Come on, Terry, you've been in court and seen Judges kick that out as hearsay. It's not Chumsky saying it. If we had something more, maybe we'd get it in. Besides, I thought you'd checked, and the earth's swallowed Jack. Without him it's clearly hearsay. Court won't allow the actor to tell the jury what he was told unless Jack's there to testify or take the Fifth. We need someone to tie Chumsky in."

Synge pointed to his stomach. "My gut's telling me Eddie Greene and the lawyer saw the Lieutenant murdered."

"Maybe so, but Greene's dead and the lawyer's missing," the D.A. said. "Frankly, I think you blew it."

"What the hell are you talking about?" Synge demanded.

"Like I said," the D.A. replied, "I read over your interview of David Greenberg. Bloomenthal offered to have you ask Greenberg if he had ever seen Rabelli. If you hadn't had your Irish up, you would have asked him. Instead you got into a shouting match with one of the sharpest attorneys in the city. He suckered you, and you blew it."

Tate stood up and said in a voice the D.A. couldn't hear, "Take it easy, Terry. The brass are looking for an excuse to cut you loose." Tate softly pinched the knotted muscles on Synge's shoulder.

Synge took a deep breath and said, "How about this? I bring Chumsky in and see what I can get?"

The D.A. laughed. "Terry, you've got nothing to use! Nothing! He'll deny he ever told anyone to hire the actors, even if he admits knowing Jack. He'll call the Mayor and say you're harassing him. He'll hang you out to dry."

Synge's face reddened, and he shrugged off Tate's hand. "How come you know what Chumsky's going to say? Did you talk to him? Or was it

Bloomenthal you talked to? Did he tell you to read over the Greenberg interview? Did Mister Bloomenthal tell you to lecture me on hearsay? You're not bright enough to have all of that at your fingertips, are you?"

The D.A. rose and pointed a finger at Synge's face. "You've got ten seconds to apologize!"

"Up yours!" Synge shouted. "The Lieutenant had his faults, but he was a cop, one of us! He deserves better. What's happened to you? You used to be a good guy, before they bought your soul. I'd rather never see a baseball game, and whatever else you're getting, than bury a cop killing."

Synge reached into his pocket and brought out a handful of coins. He threw them at the D.A. "There's your thirty pieces of silver!"

The D.A. came around the corner of the desk swinging his fist as Tate dragged Synge back. "You're through! You hear me! Off the force. Tate, have the Commissioner call me. Today!"

Chapter Twenty-Nine
Synge at Naomi's

Synge dressed that morning with an eye to looking professional. He took a white shirt off the hanger fresh from the cleaner. This was his first day off the force. He had met the day before with the union rep and told him what had gone on with the D.A. The rep thought the firing would stick, but advised him to appeal the decision anyway.

The navy suit hung loose on the left side where his service revolver had been holstered. Before leaving headquarters yesterday he had turned in his shield and handgun. He took off the jacket and found the matching vest in the closet. With both on, the ballooning effect was not as noticeable.

At eleven that morning he drove past the Greenberg house. No cars were parked outside, so hopefully no one was visiting. When he rang the bell, a thin, elderly colored woman answered the door.

"Can ah help you?" she asked.

"I'd like to speak with Mrs. Greenberg."

"She seein' no one." And the woman started to close the door.

He put his polished black wingtip against the door and said, "I think she would like to see me. It's about her husband, David. Some new information has surfaced."

"I just don't know. Miz Naomi's just back." But she stopped trying to close the door.

Synge handed her one of his cards. He still had a few at home that had not been confiscated the day before. On the back was written:

> Mrs. Greenberg,
> An arrest by N.Y. police has lead to new information about the weekend spent in N.Y. by your husband and Eddie Greene. It throws new light on your husband's disappearance.

A few minutes later the woman reappeared. "Miz Naomi said for you to wait in the living room. She be with you soon."

Synge followed her into a large room. He chose to sit in a blue chair separated from the sofa by a small table.

"Can ah get you some coffee?" she asked. "Ah just made a fresh pot."

"That would be nice. I take it black, no sugar."

When she left, Synge sneezed. It smelled musty, and the dust drifting in the sunlight looked like a drizzle of rain. If the colored woman was the only household help, that would account for it.

She reappeared holding a tray with two cups of coffee, both rattling from the tremor in her hands. Walking behind her was a much thinner version of the woman he had interviewed six months ago. Even though it was July, and the room was warm, she had a black shawl draped over her shoulders.

"Thank you for seeing me, Mrs. Greenberg."

"I hope you are more cordial than the last time, Detective." Naomi took the two cups off the tray and placed them safely on the coffee table. "Thank you, Liz," Naomi said. "I'd like to speak with Detective Synge alone. At least for now."

"Ah'm in the kitchen. Just call if you need me."

"I surely will." When Liz had stepped into the hallway, Naomi turned to Synge. "Detective, I don't know whether this was the right thing," she said. "To meet with you."

"I'm here to bring you information, not to interrogate you," Synge said.

"You said that on the back of your card." Naomi looked at Synge directly. "I thought about calling Bloomie or Daddy while you were standing outside. They would have told me to send you away." The shawl slid off Naomi's shoulders. She pulled it up and held it in her hands, buried in the black fabric. Naomi went on, "But I want to hear what you have to say. I can always call after that."

"Fair enough," Synge said. He watched her circle around him and sit down on the sofa. She never came closer than five feet from him.

"Let me tell you what I know," Synge said. "Do you know of a man named Jacob Shtowski who works for Morris Chumsky?"

Naomi shook her head. "No."

"He has short hair and a scar that runs from his hairline to his left eye."

Synge traced a line with his finger down his own forehead.

"Detective, what does this have to do with my husband?" Naomi frowned, and began to stand up.

"Shtowski hired two unemployed New York actors to pretend to be your husband and Eddie Greene," Synge said. "He gave them photos of both men. He told them which hotel to stay at. The hotel bill was signed David Greenberg and was charged to your husband's law firm."

Naomi's eyes grew large; her mouth popped open. "I don't understand any of this," she said. "Why would anyone want to have actors pretend to be David and Eddie? It makes no sense."

"The actors signed into the hotel late on the Friday night that Lieutenant Rabelli was shot," Synge offered.

"Detective, I made a mistake letting you into the house," Naomi said, and this time she did stand up. "I'll ask you to leave."

"I believe that your husband did not disappear because of some reason of his own," Synge said. "I think Shtowski, or someone else working for Chumsky, followed him to the Acme Garage, and after he left, killed him."

"This is the craziest story I've ever heard," Naomi said. She took off the shawl and began to fan herself with both hands.

"Mrs. Greenberg, didn't you wonder why your husband vanished?" Synge asked. "I've checked, and none of the usual reasons existed. He wasn't in debt; he wasn't carrying on with another woman. It made no sense."

Liz appeared in the doorway and said, "Miz Naomi, you want me to call Mr. Luntz?"

Naomi was startled, and then said, "No Liz, I'm fine. I need to talk alone to Detective Synge. Why don't you make some lunch for us?"

When Liz had gone, Naomi looked at Synge. She moved the coffee cups to one side of the table. "Is there a way you can explain what this is all about, Detective? I'm having trouble following it. There are facts you must know that would make this clear."

"Some of this will be speculation on my part," Synge said.

Naomi nodded.

"And I'll be telling you things that are known by only a few people," he said. "I'll have to trust you not to repeat them."

"I can't agree to that until I hear what you have to say," Naomi answered.

"Well, I won't get any further without your help," Synge said, "so here goes." He watched her eyes and mouth to determine whether Naomi was following what he was saying, to see if she believed him.

"Morris Chumsky is a major crime figure," Synge told her. "There are files on him in the Philadelphia Police Department and at the F.B.I."

"I can't believe that," Naomi protested, drawing her arms around herself. "My father has done business with him for years. He was at my wedding. You're making this up."

"Mrs. Greenberg, if you can't accept that there's no point in my going any further." Synge stood up.

"Sit down, Detective. You didn't take the risk of coming to see me just to get in a huff."

Synge was still standing.

"Let me tell you something about me, Detective." Even in the high register of her voice, Synge heard something authoritative. Whatever had caused her to be hospitalized, she was now stronger than she had been at the law firm interview.

"I'm not going to help you or listen to you if you try to boss me around." Naomi favored him with a smile. "You are an intelligent man. David said that. So did Bloomie. If you believe Morris Chumsky is a criminal, tell me your reasons." She raised an eyebrow and said, "Tell me what's in those files, not just that there are such files."

Synge sat down. At first his lips moved without sound.

"Detective, when you've finished talking to yourself, let me in on it."

He laughed. "Well, I've gone this far." Synge exhaled and went on. "Okay, here's a thumbnail sketch. When he was in his thirties, Chumsky made his first fortune running booze down from Canada during Prohibition. That's the only conviction on his record. It doesn't bother the businessmen he does deals with, but it is a felony and it does keep him off bank boards." Synge grinned. "I've heard its one of the few things that pisses him off." Synge blushed. "One of the few things that frustrates him."

Naomi crossed her arms over her chest. "You're going to have to do better than that, Detective, to convince me he's a criminal now."

"Well, I can't show you files, but maybe this will do it." Synge reached into his inside jacket pocket and brought out a folded newspaper story. "This is from a few years ago. Piece from the *New York Times* updating the 1950 Kefauver Committee hearings on organized crime." Synge smoothed out the creased paper on the coffee table. "Kind of a 'where are they now' story." He handed it to Naomi. One of the paragraphs was bracketed in ink:

> At the time of the hearings Meyer Lansky denied any role in the so-called Murder, Inc. enforcement arm of organized crime. He pointed to his modest life-style as proof that he was not a mobster. When it was claimed that the Committee had information that he had secret ownership in casinos in Las Vegas and Havana, Lansky challenged that he'd "like to see it." It's reported that the Committee's source was an informant who was later found slain "gangland" style. Mr. Lansky currently resides in Miami and lists his income as "investments."

"You've lost me again, Detective. What does this have to do with Morris Chumsky?"

"One of the investments listed on Lansky's tax return is Keystone Liquors," Synge replied. Naomi's shoulders slumped. "Morris Chumsky stays with Meyer Lansky every February. It's believed that Lansky hands over a suitcase full of cash. Part of that is to reimburse Chumsky for the check Keystone sends Lansky as a 'return on investment' in Keystone. It's all a fiction. What we call 'money laundering,' making illegal money appear legitimate so that it can be declared on tax returns. The rest of the cash is Chumsky's share of profits in various criminal enterprises."

Naomi flapped a hand in front of her face, brushing aside the detective's words like an invisible fly.

"Are you still with me, Mrs. Greenberg?" Synge asked.

"It doesn't matter, Detective," Naomi said. "You've convinced me that Morris has some business relationship with this Meyer Lansky. What's that have to do with David's disappearance?"

"You need to understand what Chumsky is to follow the rest of what I'm going to tell you," Synge told her.

"Okay, okay. Go on," Naomi said.

"As I said, the dates are the giveaway," he continued. Synge held up a finger. "Friday, earlier in the day, Lieutenant Rabelli tried to kill Eddie Greene. We have a witness to that."

"Why?" Naomi asked.

"Eddie Greene was carrying on with the Lieutenant's sixteen-year-old niece," Synge began.

Naomi's face squeezed into a question mark.

"Carrying on, as in having sexual relations with her on a regular basis," Synge added.

"Detective, what was the niece's name?" Naomi asked.

"Sophia," Synge told her.

"She called here looking for Eddie," Naomi said.

Synge smiled and said, "Go on."

"It was that same Friday night you're talking about," Naomi said, "the night David and Eddie drove to New York."

"Who spoke to Sophia?" Synge asked.

"I did," Naomi said, "but I was—well, I had taken several drinks. I do remember her name. Eddie and David came in while I was on the phone. Eddie spoke to her briefly. Told her they were going to New York."

"Did your husband tell you why they were going to New York?"

"Just business, though it did seem unusual that Eddie would be needed." Naomi smiled at Synge. "Eddie wasn't much of a businessman."

"Did you see a car follow them when they left?" Synge asked.

Naomi's mouth became a straight line.

"Please don't take offense, Mrs. Greenberg," Synge said. "Force of habit to go over details."

"I've been doing a lot of talking," Naomi said. "You're supposed to be telling me about David's disappearance."

"Like I said, some of it is speculation." Synge leaned forward. "This much I do know. Eddie Greene had a place in Jersey where he pimped some of the girls from *Varsity Dance*."

"Blueberry Hill," Naomi said.

"Right," Synge nodded. "Here's where the speculation comes in. If the Lieutenant were to kill Eddie, the whole story would spill out immediately, and that could have ended *Varsity Dance*, which was a major money maker for Pyramid. Morris Chumsky is believed to be the second largest shareholder in Pyramid."

Naomi sat up straight, her body stiffening.

"Detective, I own some Pyramid shares," Naomi said. "So does my father. David told me Lee Steinhardt has a substantial holding. Why are you telling me this if you think we had Lieutenant Rabelli murdered?"

Synge let out a deep breath.

Naomi said, "Don't start talking to yourself again. You've gone this far, finish your story."

"A man like Morris Chumsky must have income that is legitimate and above board so that he can account for all the expenses he has," Synge said. "The house he lives in with his mother, the charities he gives to, the money needed to support his style of living. A threat to his legitimate sources of income opens him up to tax investigations. That's how they got Capone. Lieutenant Rabelli's actions threatened a very large source of lawful income. For Morris Chumsky that is the stuff of nightmares."

"So what does that have to do with David and Eddie going to New York?" Naomi asked. "You've lost me again."

"They were the bait," Synge said. "The Lieutenant followed them; Chumsky's men killed him. I think Eddie and your husband saw the murder. They would have been loose cannons if left on their own. The actors went through appearing to do business that weekend, while David and Eddie were kept out of sight."

Naomi took a Kleenex out of the wrist of her dress, and wiped her eyes. "David was never the same after that weekend." Her voice broke.

"Morris Chumsky never leaves loose ends," Synge said. "Eddie probably died by his own demons in Kansas City. But David was still alive."

Naomi lowered her head and began to sob. Liz moved through the room silent as a ghost. She sat down beside Naomi, reaching into the shawl for her hands.

"You get out right now!" Liz said, glaring at Synge.

Naomi took small sips of the now cold coffee and put the cup down, saying, "Mommy had me drink water to stop crying when I was out of control." Patting Liz's hand, Naomi said, "It's okay. The detective is telling me things I need to know."

Liz shook her head in disagreement.

"Really, Liz, it's very important." Naomi managed a small smile. "He's letting me know that I didn't drive David away. Something else was going on. Something we didn't know about. I need to hear the rest of what he has to say."

Naomi stood up and helped Liz to her feet.

"Lunch is gettin' cold," Liz said, and looked over at Synge. "Miz Naomi needs to eat more than listenin' to you."

"Keep the soup warm," Naomi said. "I promise to have it as soon as we finish. But you can't come in anymore. Promise?"

Liz stared hard at Synge and left.

"Is there anything else you have to tell me, Detective?" Naomi asked. "You must want something from me. Why did you come here today?"

"I wanted to bring Morris Chumsky in for questioning, but the Department and the D.A. wouldn't let me." Synge scowled and went on. "They're in Chumsky's and Pyramid's pocket."

"I'm not a lawyer, but it doesn't sound like you have direct evidence against Morris," Naomi said.

"That's their position. When I pushed, I was let go." Synge admitted.

"I don't see—" Naomi started.

"Here's the thing," Synge began. "I figure that after New York, both Eddie and your husband were scared. Who wouldn't be? Eddie drank himself out of a job. And Blueberry Hill caught up with him. How was your husband different after that weekend?"

"I'm not going to talk about that," Naomi said.

"Answer this for me," Synge challenged. "Did your husband and Eddie exchange letters after Eddie moved to Kansas City?"

"Yes, but I threw all of that out after David disappeared."

"Are you certain?" Synge leaned his body toward her.

"Positive!" Naomi said. "And I won't let you rummage around in my life—our house, because you want to get Morris Chumsky."

"If Eddie wrote to David, it's safe to assume he wrote back," Synge pressed on.

"Just tell me what you want Detective, and stop beating around the bush."

"Okay. I want to go to Kansas City and see if I can find your husband's letters." Synge was talking rapidly, not letting Naomi break in. "Maybe, just maybe, he mentioned what went on that Friday night to the only other person he could confide in. If not, that's the end of it for me, and Chumsky gets away with killing a cop." Synge slapped the table and the coffee jumped out of his cup. "I can't let that be on my conscience. What I want from you is a letter of introduction to Eddie's wife. I caught what you said to your maid. Whatever your reasons, you want to know why your husband disappeared." Synge stopped.

Naomi sat silent. Synge watched her, but said nothing. Minutes passed.

"Okay, Detective, I'll do what you ask," Naomi said. "But you must let me know what you find. If you obtain any of David's letters, they are mine. You will return them to me."

Synge tapped a finger on the table. "Here's my problem, Mrs. Greenberg. If they are relevant to a murder investigation, I can't do that. If not, I have no problem. I'll do this. If I find any, I'll call you from Kansas City and tell you what I have. That's the best I can do."

"Do you have another card, Detective?" Naomi put her hand out.

She took Synge's business card and walked into the kitchen. Naomi was gone for five minutes. When she returned, she handed him a sealed envelope with "Thelma Greene" handwritten on the outside and his card. On the back was written "Naomi G. DE7-4361." She was carrying a deeply scratched crocodile handbag.

"Detective, I don't know if Thelma will be helpful," Naomi told him. "I didn't have a warm or cordial relationship with her. But I explained that you are a well-regarded detective investigating David's disappearance and I would appreciate any assistance she can provide. I wrote that I have retained you privately since your retirement from the Philadelphia Police Department, where you had worked on this matter."

"Thank you," Synge said as he stood up.

"I also enclosed a check for a thousand dollars, to tide her over," Naomi added. "Knowing Eddie, Thelma needs the money." She then opened the purse and took out a handful of fifty dollar bills. "You'll need money for your trip to Kansas City and your fee," Naomi said. "I wouldn't lie about having retained your services."

Chapter Thirty
Kansas City

The woman answered the door. She was five feet two, and Synge guessed she weighed over three hundred pounds. In the heat she wore a sleeveless housedress. Synge thought she had not found one with sleeves she could squeeze her upper arms through.

"Whatever you're selling, I'm not buying."

He was certain she was reacting to his suit. "My name is Terry Synge. I'm an investigator working for Mrs. David Greenberg. I'd like to talk with you. I have a letter of introduction from Mrs. Greenberg." Synge took the letter out of his inside pocket.

"You can just tear it up," she said holding out her pudgy hand, "or give it here and I'll do it myself."

Synge held the letter behind his back where she could not reach it. "I don't think you want to do that," he said. "I believe there's a substantial check inside made out to you."

Thelma's eyes narrowed. She pursed her lips.

"You have anything to prove who you are?" she asked.

"Here's my card," Synge said, offering one that he had printed for the trip. It read:

Terry Patrick Synge
Discrete Inquiries

and listed a Philadelphia telephone number. All of this was in raised gold print. He'd had the printer add the great seal of the Commonwealth of Pennsylvania in navy.

Synge then showed her his driver's license, and added, "Please call Mrs. Greenberg. I believe you have her telephone number. Ask her to describe me."

Thelma rubbed her thumb across his embossed name. "No, I'd just as soon not speak to that stuck-up Jew."

Synge kept his face blank. "Mrs. Greene, is there somewhere we can sit and talk?"

The woman pushed strands of gray-brown hair away from her eyes. It was beyond her control and immediately fell back. "Kitchen table's best I can do," she said.

Dishes were piled in the sink. On the stove a fry pan was next to an unopened can of Spam. When he was a boy his family had eaten a lot of it. The memory of being warm under the blanket next to his brother Brian, licking the greasy residue off his lips, flooded his mouth. For the first time since he had met her, Synge felt sympathy for Thelma Greene.

They both sat down on chairs with metal tubes forming the back and legs. The Pepto Bismol pink vinyl seat and back cushion were split. Synge knew she had bought them at a garage sale. He handed her the letter. She leaned over to a kitchen drawer and took out a carving knife. As she carefully slit open the envelope, Synge looked at her hand. An indentation on her wedding finger marked where the ring had submerged into marshmallow flesh.

Thelma unfolded the letter, took out the check, and threw both envelope and letter into an empty grocery bag. Synge said nothing.

"Okay, what do I have to do to keep the money?" she asked.

"Give me the letters David wrote to Eddie," Synge told her.

"What letters?" She looked away from him.

"Mrs. Greene, I didn't come here for my health."

Thelma arched an eyebrow. "That the best you can do?"

"I've read Eddie's letters to David." Synge had always been good at guessing at facts that should have been there. "The ones he sent since all of you moved here. They mention David's letters. 'Thanks for keeping in touch' or 'You asked how the job's going.' So, let's cut the crap about 'what letters?'"

"How do you know I haven't gotten rid of them?" Thelma asked. A smile played at the corners of her mouth.

"That would be a shame," Synge said flatly. "I'd have to call Mrs. Greenberg to stop payment on that thousand dollar check."

Thelma retrieved the letter from the bag, flattened it with the side of her hand, and read it, her lips moving silently word by word.

"You're full of shit! Naomi don't say nothing about turning letters over to you. She says"— and Thelma looked down at the letter, moved her finger to the end—"she says 'this is to tide you over.'"

"And I'm telling you, if I don't get those letters, that check is worthless!" Synge threatened. "What's your call?"

Thelma heaved herself up from the table.

"Let me take a look."

She shuffled out of the kitchen. Synge listened to the alternating sighs and wheezes as she went up the stairs. He went over to the cabinet and took out a jelly glass. A fly had died in it. Shaking his head, he went over to the sink and ran the water until it was hot, picked up a tattered yellow sponge, tapped some Palmolive liquid on it, and washed it. He stared at it some more, put it down and went to the refrigerator. Finding an unopened Pepsi, he pried off the cap, rubbed the top, and drank from the bottle. He finished it and sat back down. He left the drained bottle and a quarter on the side of the table where Thelma had sat.

She returned in a half hour.

"This is going to take some time," she said. "Eddie was a slob, but if he didn't want me to find something he was cunning as a fox."

"Maybe I could help," Synge offered.

"Maybe you could, but I don't want you to," Thelma said. "Come back tomorrow morning."

Synge noticed that the check was not in sight.

"Give me the check back," he said. "We'll do an exchange when you have the letters."

"No, I'll hold on to it," Thelma challenged. "Naomi said nothing about the money being for the letters. I called while I was upstairs. You made that up. But I asked her to describe you. That part's true."

"What time do the kids leave for school?" Synge asked.

"Eight-thirty," she answered.

"I'll be here by nine," Synge said. His nose twitched at a sharp smell.

"Is something burning?" he asked, looking at the toaster's frayed cord.

"Outside," Thelma said, shaking her head toward the side of the apartment. "Incinerator. I'm always scared the wind will blow stuff against the building and start a fire. Landlord says: 'Be careful. I'll hold you responsible if that happens.'"

When Synge left, he rolled down the windows and sat in the rented Chevy until the air conditioner lowered the temperature in the car. He looked at the window on the first floor apartment. Thelma was smoking a cigarette facing his car. He waved at her. A moment later the blinds closed.

He drove three blocks, made a U-turn and parked under a tree. The Greene's apartment was the last building on the street. It was just empty lots beyond that. Synge had headed in the opposite direction where there were more apartments and a small grocery store. His hunch paid off. Five minutes later Thelma drove by in an old junker belching puffs of oily black smoke. All the car windows were open.

Synge fell in behind her when she was two blocks away. Even with half a dozen cars in between, he had no difficulty following her smoke signals.

Thelma pulled into the parking lot next to the First Bank of Kansas City, and walked in. She came out forty minutes later. Synge checked his watch and said out loud, "Three. Kids should be getting home soon."

He gave her a ten minute start.

At three twenty-five a yellow school bus stopped at the corner. Synge was close enough to read the black letters across the back: DO NOT PASS WHEN LIGHTS ARE FLASHING. Two teenagers walked toward the apartment. The shorter one walked behind, pushed the books out of the other's hand and raced through the front door.

"She'll be distracted yelling at them," Synge said to himself. He got out of the car and walked within a block of their place.

Thelma Greene waddled out of the front door carrying a grocery bag. Something fell out of the top. She put the bag down, picked up a piece of paper, put it back in the bag and noticed him. The speed of Thelma's shuffle surprised Synge. She reached the edge of the building and was out of sight. Synge ran, sweat filling his eyes, dizzy from the sun.

He turned the corner and found her holding the bag high, shaking a snow shower of envelopes into the orange yellow flames of the incinerator. Synge hit her with his hip, tumbling Thelma to the ground. He grabbed at envelopes which turned to ash in his hands, shaking fingers pricked by the fire. Synge retrieved two envelopes that were partially burned. He stomped on them to put out the flames, but the red embers kept expanding, a toothless red mouth chewing on the letters inside. Dropping to his knees, he pressed his palms on each, screaming from the pain.

Gingerly, he extracted the first sheet. There were two lines of typewriting left that were mostly legible even with pinholes from the fire:

> ". . . miss you. VD has new D.J., squeaky . . . looks like
> Pat Boone. Kids and colored singers don't . . . as much
> as you. Naomi's drinking . . ."

The second letter had turned the color of light toast. Synge did not touch it, afraid it would crumble like moth wings into a brown dust. But in the afternoon Kansas sunlight, the dark handwriting was legible:

> ". . . nightmares persist. Rabelli's body on the road.
> Jack's saying: 'Remember who you owe.' Will
> Chumsky have us killed? Don't laugh! Bloomie . . . fire
> me any . . ."

Above and below these two lines, charring had obliterated the words.

Synge took out a pocket notebook and a pen. He didn't hear Thelma behind him. Water poured onto the two sheets, dissolving them into a brown liquid.

As Synge stood up, he flung out a hand to deflect the empty pail Thelma swung at him. He wrenched it away from her and hurled it at the incinerator. A swarm of sparks flew off the top.

Thelma cringed in front of him, her forearms crossed in front of her face. Synge looked down and saw his hands were knotted into fists.

Thelma's voice came from behind her barrier of arms, "Go ahead! Eddie always did, God damn him."

Synge moved forward, his hand aching to hit her.

"Don't, Mister," the shorter boy said.

Synge looked up. Both boys were at the corner of the building, frozen.

The taller one pushed his brother. "Go." And then said to Synge, "You better leave now. Sam's calling the cops."

Synge thought of picking up the galvanized pail and crashing it against Thelma's face. Just once. And then leaving.

Instead he hissed, "You have no idea what you've done."

He heard a distant wail. Police? Fire? Synge walked past the boy pressing his body against the wall.

"It's okay, son. I won't hurt your mother." Synge touched his hair. Urine spread in a circle across the boy's crotch.

Chapter Thirty-One
Chumsky at Home

The man with the scarred knuckles towered over Chumsky. "Anything else I can do?" he asked.

Chumsky's white on white shirt gleamed. He lifted his right arm and looked at his watch, "It's eight, Sammy," Chumsky said. "The housekeeper's gone for the day. Come back in a half hour to help Ma upstairs." The man nodded and left the living room.

Chumsky's mother had on black leather shoes laced up to her ankles. Both were perched on the wheelchair's fold-down metal footrests. When anyone other than Chumsky or one of his men was around, she insisted on being placed in a straight-back chair.

He pulled a chair up next to the old woman. Her black dress had long sleeves and came down to mid-calf. From the hem of the dress to her ankles, her legs were covered in tan cotton hose. One calf was thick, the other bloated. Even with the air-conditioning unit blasting in the window, her face glistened as though she were in the grip of a high fever.

Chumsky's bulldog head leaned on his mother's shoulder. She stroked his hair.

"Oh *boychik*," she sighed, "your mother's not well. All the doctors talk about is cutting off my leg. The diabetes is awful!"

"I know, Ma."

"I'd love to have you sit in my lap, but it hurts so." She held his chin, turning his face toward her. "It's been awhile since we did that." She made a low clucking sound. "Do you miss it, Morrie?"

He nodded.

"We're getting on, you and I," she said. "You're in your sixties, and your mother's no spring chicken. I'll be eighty-eight in September. Will I still have both legs in a month?"

"Ma, don't," he said, picking up her hand and kissing it.

"I had Sammy buy me a gun," she said, and wheeled over to a small table. She pulled open the drawer and took out something wrapped in rags.

"Ma, this is crazy!" he said. "I'll kill Sammy. I knew he wasn't bright, but I never thought—"

"Morrie, don't blame Sammy. I told him it was your idea," she said. "You know, if I needed to protect myself." She had put it in her lap, and begun to un-wrap the oil-soaked rag.

"You don't know how to use a gun," Chumsky insisted. He stood up and began walking toward her, with his hand out. "Come on, give it to me before you shoot yourself," he said.

She smiled at him, and lifted the gun with her finger on the trigger.

"What's so funny?" he asked.

There were gunshots in the house. Chumsky turned toward the door as it was kicked in. A man stood there, a revolver in his hand.

"Who are you?" Chumsky said. A shot was fired from behind Chumsky, and wood splintered on the half-opened door to the right of the stranger.

The man in the doorway pulled the trigger, and a soft sigh came from the old woman.

Chumsky turned and saw his mother slumped in the wheelchair. One brown eye stared sightlessly from behind her glasses; the other lens was shattered, tiny shards stained with red.

A shot boomed behind the man in the doorway and the top of his head exploded into brain tissue, bone chips, and blood.

Fifteen minutes later the police walked in. The stench from the bowel movements released by the corpses made the three officers gag.

Sammy lay across the feet of the man in the doorway. He was dead from abdominal bleeding caused by the two gunshot wounds in his back. The man in front of him was initially unidentifiable, as much of his face had been destroyed.

Across the room, Chumsky howled like a cat in heat. The sound was not human. One hand pressed against his heart, the other held his mother in an embrace.

The policeman in a suit kneeled in front of the pair. "Mr. Chumsky. Mr. Chumsky, can you talk? Can you tell me what happened?"

Chumsky was facing his mother. He did not turn toward the man speaking to him.

The officer took out a flashlight and held the light on Chumsky's eyes. The pupils were enlarged.

Standing up, he told one of the uniformed police, "Find a telephone and call in. Tell them there are three dead, and Mr. Chumsky is in shock. He can't respond. Tell them to send an ambulance."

A few minutes later, the officer returned. "An ambulance is coming. They'll call the hospital to let them know he's on his way. Do you think he sees or hears us?"

"No."

The three men looked at Chumsky and his mother. The outpouring of feces had flattened her body. Remembering the rumors, one of the uniformed officers said, "She looks like an elderly version of one of those blow-up dolls guys get for sex."

The other two did not laugh.

Chapter Thirty-Two
The Next Day at Naomi's

"Do I know you, Detective?" Naomi asked.

It was three in the afternoon. She was dressed in a hyacinth blue skirt and a Liberty print shirt. They were seated across from each other in the same chair and sofa that she and detective Synge had occupied four days earlier. A glass of iced tea was on a coaster in front of Naomi. Tate had declined.

"We've never met," he said. "I had worked on Lieutenant Rabelli's team, along with Detective Synge." He paused, and she was silent. "Did you see the story in today's paper about the killings at Morris Chumsky's home last night?" he asked.

"Yes," Naomi said. "Awful business. Why would anyone shoot her, an old woman, like that?"

"Well, we don't know for sure, but we did find a revolver in her hand, and the lab's checking whether a bullet taken out of the door matches the bullet that was fired from her gun."

Naomi shifted her weight on the sofa. "Lieutenant, you never did explain why you are here."

"I'll get to that," Tate responded. "Like I said, I worked with both Lieutenant Rabelli and Detective Synge. After the Lieutenant was found shot to death on that country road—you know what I'm talking about?"

Naomi sipped her iced tea. Tate held up the coaster and looked at the drawing of an Egyptian pyramid. He put it back, felt side down. "That's an unusual design," he said. "Can't say I've ever seen one like it."

"I think you know exactly what it is, Detective. If this is a police investigation, I'm going to ask you to leave and contact Mr. Bloomenthal if you want to pursue this."

"This is not an investigation," Tate said. "I'm trying to help you."

He let out his breath, and continued, "Might get myself in trouble. Doing this because of Terry Synge."

Naomi raised an eyebrow.

"You need to let me tell it my way, Mrs. Greenberg." She sat back against the cushions. "Terry brooded about the Lieutenant's murder," Tate said. "Thought Chumsky was behind it. I think you know that."

"I have no idea what you're talking about."

Tate heard the lack of conviction in her voice. "I didn't come here to argue," Tate told her. "It'll go quicker if you relax and hear me out."

Naomi nodded.

"Recently we caught a break, and got information that Chumsky's right-hand man had set something up in New York that looked like it was connected to the Rabelli killing, but it wasn't enough to make a case against Chumsky."

Tate noticed that she didn't ask him for any details. "I think," Tate said, "that was the last straw for Synge. He snapped. Carried on that everyone was bought off, and got himself fired. That was five days ago."

Naomi had made her face blank. Tate thought she would be good at poker, if she played. "I was one of the police called to Mr. Chumsky's house last night," Tate told her.

He took note of the deference, or fear, he showed toward Chumsky. He was pretty sure Mrs. Greenberg picked up on it.

"Here's our take on what happened. Synge broke into the house and shot Sammy the Bull." Naomi frowned. "Sammy Bluestein," Tate explained. "Part of Chumsky's criminal operation. Recently he's been used as a bodyguard, as though Chumsky knew Synge might be after him. Or maybe someone like Chumsky always has a bodyguard. Anyway, Synge ran past Sammy and into the den. That's where Mr. Chumsky and his mother were found. We think she fired at Synge and missed. We don't know why she was armed. Synge shot back and killed her."

Tate took out a police photograph and handed it to Naomi. It was in black and white. Naomi thought it was lurid. The angle was from overhead. The old woman was embraced by a white shirtsleeve; one of her eyes stared at the camera. Where there should have been a second eye it was shiny black like licorice.

"Terry had not finished off Sammy, who came up behind and shot him." Tate put his hand on the back of his own head. "Most of his face was missing, so I went through his pockets. I found his wallet. I couldn't believe it was Terry." Tate's voice broke. He took a deep breath, reached into his shirt pocket and took out one of Synge's cards. Leaning forward, he handed it to Naomi.

She looked at it, and said, "You've already told me it was Detective Synge."

"Turn it over," Tate directed. On the back of the card in her handwriting was "Naomi G. DE7-4361."

She looked up. "I slipped that into my pocket," Tate said. "Neither Mr. Chumsky nor the officers with me saw me do it."

He reached over and took the card. Holding it by one corner, he took out a Zippo. When the flame had caught, Tate dropped the card into the ashtray. Neither one said anything as it curled into a gray worm.

"You wouldn't want that in a police file," he said. "Too many questions. And Chumsky would learn about it." Tate stood up. "I'll let myself out."

Naomi stared at the glass ashtray. As she heard the front door close, she said aloud, "I never thanked him."

Epilogue
Naomi at the Dedication of Chumsky Stadium— 1970

The football stadium smelled of paint and newly planted sod. A stage was set up on the twenty yard line, facing two rows of folding wooden chairs holding people associated with Chumsky through business or investments. I was in the first row. To my right were Jay Karp, his wife, and their three porcine children. In fact, the entire first row held the largest shareholders of Pyramid: the Bloomenthal family; Sol, Ruth, and Woodberry, recently named co-head of the Luntz Family Foundation; and the children and grandchildren of Lee Steinhardt. With the recent purchase of Pyramid by Bay & Eastern, they had all become immensely wealthy. A year ago each had received a slip of paper with a dollar amount, placed within a letter explaining that Morris Chumsky had pledged ten million dollars to Kensington University for a new athletic stadium and he thought that the addressees would wish to join him in raising the balance to complete the project. While the letter was drafted by the Vice President of Keystone Liquors, the amount on the enclosed slip was unmistakably in the scrawl that Chumsky's hand produced since his stroke. The Luntz family assessment was $1,000,000.

The dedication ceremony was almost over. Behind the podium, the President of the University was elegantly gray from his marcelled hair to his Huntsman double-breasted suit. "Ladies and gentlemen, I have a surprise for Mr. Chumsky and for you. This dedication is a preview of our first graduation ceremony to be held in this stadium two months from today. At that time Morris Chumsky will be bestowed with an honorary doctorate in the humanities for all of his contributions to this University, culminating in this magnificent facility." I helped Daddy to his feet, as everyone rose and clapped. Woodberry did the same for Mother.

The University's football coach was behind Chumsky's wheelchair, pushing it to center stage. The applause grew and held. Chumsky lifted his right arm and waved it slowly. Earlier, when he had been lifted onto the platform and into the chair, the coach had raised each finger on Chumsky's left hand and locked it onto the wheelchair arm, even the pinky finger that jutted out like a hawk's talon.

A microphone was held next to the mouth of the seated figure by the President. The right side of Chumsky's mouth opened; the left had been frozen since his stroke. Even with amplification, the growled "Thank you" was hard to hear. A silver thread of saliva hung from the colorless lips. Chumsky raised a handkerchief and patted it dry, a signal to wheel him back.

Another round of vigorous clapping, and people began walking to the exit from the field. I was walking next to Woodberry and asked, "I wonder what the applause sounded like to Morris? People being polite and nothing more? I hope so."

Woodberry's forehead burrowed into ridges. He began to bend over to say something, but then stopped. Woodberry looked around. No one was looking in their direction.

As the attendees came out of the darkened stadium tunnels, they broke into small clusters walking to the parked cars. Daddy and mother went to their 1958 Packard. It was the last year Packards had been manufactured. I wondered what Daddy would do if he couldn't keep it running while he was still alive. "I want to chat for a moment with Mr. Woodberry," I said, "if he'll drop me off afterwards."

"Of course," he said.

Standing beside Woodberry's fifteen-year-old Packard, I told him, "Morris had his stroke when his mother was killed in his presence." I paused. "He deserved it!" I added.

Woodberry looked around the parking area. All the cars had left.

I looked up into his face. "He killed David," I said. "Not directly. Not with his own hands—but he ordered it."

Woodberry's eyes widened. He shook his head from side to side. My voice lowered to a conversational tone, but I never looked away. "It never made sense that David just disappeared like that," I told him. "I thought at first he had left because of Eddie. Eddie in disgrace and then dying with those young girls." I spit out the words like spoiled meat. "Eddie always needed young girls. For something dark in him. Something stunted. *Varsity Dance* fed that need."

My face settled. Woodberry reached for the handle on the passenger door, but I put a hand on top of his. He looked at me. "David also had needs," I resumed. "Well, we all do. I thought I couldn't satisfy David's needs; that only Eddie could."

"Naomi, I . . ." Woodbury took a step back, away from me. He looked around again. We were still alone. "I see you are shocked," I said. My voice was calm. "Repulsed. But that's what I believed when David vanished."

I smiled. Woodberry told me years later that he never spoke to anyone of this conversation.

"Detective Synge explained why Chumsky needed to kill David. It all made sense." My head bobbled up and down at the clarity of what Synge had told me and I offered that same comfort to Woodberry. "It had nothing to do with Eddie. Or with me."

Woodberry reached out to hug me. He had never done this. I patted his chest with my hands and stopped the embrace. "Thank you, but I'm not finished. It's important that you understand."

I breathed in, let it out, and plunged forward. "Chumsky is clever. Like a wolf. Detective Synge explained all that. Chumsky's cunning— that's what drove Synge to try to kill him. So Chumsky couldn't get away again. Synge was right."

I studied Woodberry's face and found something there. "Do you think Synge failed? Because he killed Chumsky's mother?" I shook my head again. "Oh no. This was even better. That's why I came today. To see Chumsky."

I took a step forward, squinting to see if Woodberry saw what I did. I explained, "Chumsky is dead within his body. It's a shell. The real Chumsky lives inside that shell. The real Chumsky only sees Synge coming through the door. Shooting his mother. The other detective, whatever his name was" —I flicked my hand at the name I could not pluck out of my memory at this moment—"gave me the card he found on Synge's body. I had written my name and telephone number on it. He took it so Chumsky wouldn't find it. Then he burned it."

My little girl voice rose in the empty parking lot. "I wish Chumsky had found that card! I hope that inside the shell the animal figures out that I had him destroyed!"

Woodberry found his voice. "I don't understand what you're saying, Naomi, but I don't think you ought to talk about it anymore. *To anyone.*"

ACKNOWLEDGEMENTS

First and foremost, credit must go to Eric Beebe, publisher of Post Mortem Press. It is clear that Eric loves his authors.

Thanks to Elizabeth Jenike, PM Press's outstanding copy editor.

Before the book was accepted by Eric, I received wonderful guidance from three people. Tara Masih drew upon thirty years of publishing experience. From querying through the final edit, Tara was involved in every step of bringing this book to a successful submission. Her work was superb.

Prior to Tara I received excellent private edits from best-selling author Jenna Blum and from Stuart Hurwitz. I was also privileged to be in a Master Fiction workshop with Jenna. Jenna first made me believe that the characters had freestanding lives of their own. Stuart imposed structure: delete this; add that.

Tara, Jenna and Stuart are all part of the wonderful Grub Street Writers in Boston, Massachusetts.

Finally, a shout out to Gary McCluskey at PM Press for his masterpiece cover.

Marshall Stein
Boston, MA

Made in the USA
Charleston, SC
26 April 2013